"I thought we ha⸺ said.

"Friends?" Anna's ⸺ould say that agreement was made under duress."

"No," Roark said, frowning. Her obvious disbelief piqued him. "We agreed to be friends."

Anna gazed at him solemnly. With a quicksilver change, a smile flashed across her face. "Then as one friend to another, I do not wish to discuss Julian. I only want to enjoy today."

Roark studied Anna, debating what tack to follow. Suddenly a lone fiddle arose across the other noises. He cast Anna a look of challenge. "Then let us enjoy the day."

He grabbed Anna's hand, ignoring the sensations it caused, and led her toward the fiddle's sound. By the time they had wended their way through the crowd, a space had been cleared and people were already swinging into a country dance.

"This time we *will* dance with each other," Roark said, tugging upon Anna's hand.

"Oh, no. I could not . . ."

"Enjoy the day, remember?" Roark teased.

She laughed and offered him no further resistance, following him into the dancing throng. The pace of the country dance was fast and furious, unrestrained and exuberant. Anna became part of it all. She was laughter, sun, and flashing movement as she twirled from one step to the next.

Roark found himself unable to tear his gaze away from her. Her cheeks wore a high flush, and she glowed from the exertion. An errant tendril of her soft brown hair had slipped free and clung to her temple. Roark clenched his hand tightly. He wished nothing more then to be able to reach out and smooth it back, to touch her. . . .

Books by Cindy Holbrook

A SUITABLE CONNECTION
LADY MEGAN'S MASQUERADE
A DARING DECEPTION
COVINGTON'S FOLLY
A RAKE'S REFORM
LORD SAYER'S GHOST
THE ACTRESS AND THE MARQUIS
THE COUNTRY GENTLEMAN
MY LADY'S SERVANT
THE RELUCTANT BRIDE
THE WEDDING GHOST

Published by Zebra Books

THE
WEDDING
GHOST

Cindy Holbrook

Zebra Books
Kensington Publishing Corp.
http://www.zebrabooks.com

ZEBRA BOOKS are published by

Kensington Publishing Corp.
850 Third Avenue
New York, NY 10022

First Printing: June, 1999
10 9 8 7 6 5 4 3 2 1

Printed in the United States of America

One

"I do hope he likes me," Beth said, twisting her hands in her lap and staring out the carriage window. Her sewing box lay untouched beside her.

"Which *he* do you mean?" Anna asked, as she turned a page of the book in her lap. "The reclusive, ogrelike brother or the . . ." She lowered her voice. "The ghost."

"Anna, please," Beth said. She visibly shivered.

"Hmm, you are right," Anna said, lifting her finger to her chin in consideration. "Meeting either one could be a sticky wicket."

"Do not tease me so," Beth said, a flush rising to her cheeks.

Anna laughed. "Forgive me, dear, but you know I think this all so much stuff and nonsense. That you must meet the duke is understandable. He is head of the family, after all. However, since he is famous for being a recluse who never creeps from his craggy castle, I do think seeking his blessing upon your marriage is shooting in the air. But that you are also expected to hold your wedding in the family chapel in order to see if an ancestral ghost will appear to put a damper upon it is the outside of enough."

Beth giggled. "It does sound odd, but it is very important to Terrence."

"I know," Anna said, frowning. "I truly do like Terrence. Indeed, he is perfect for you in all respects, but this one, that is. It surprises me he can believe in such superstitious twaddle.''

"It isn't twaddle," Beth said. "You know it isn't. The ghost appeared at his brother Roark's wedding five years ago."

"I know," Anna said dryly. "Because Tiffany Templeton was untrue. In my opinion, any living person with half a wit could have divined Tiffany Templeton would never be faithful without the assistance from a ghost. I doubt Tiffany ran from the altar merely because she saw a ghost, but because she realized she was missing out on a large London wedding. That, coupled with the thought that marriage to Roark Seeton just might bury her in the wilds of Devonshire for life."

"Anna," Beth gasped. "I cannot believe you could be so cruel."

"I am sorry," Anna said, flushing. She gazed at her younger sister, whom she had raised since Beth was seven, their parents having been killed while traveling abroad that year. Beth was such a sweet and gentle person. In her dimity muslin frock picked out with delicate purple violets on a creamy background, she looked as graceful and peaceful as a golden afternoon in the English countryside. In fact, *sun kissed* was the term Anna fondly attached to her little sister, both in looks and deed. "Only it infuriates me to think of you being forced to submit to such a tradition," she finished.

"I am not being forced," Beth claimed quietly but firmly.

"You could have had such a large and beautiful wedding in London."

"I do not need a large wedding."

"Good," Anna said. "Because the *ton* will not be traveling to Devonshire—certainly not in June." Faith, even her London servants had balked at the thought of spending the next few months in the wilds of Devonshire in an archaic castle. In truth, she could not blame them. Although she could have demanded their services, she decided to rest upon Terrence's assurance that bringing her own servants would not be necessary.

"I do not care," Beth stated. "You know I've always wanted a June wedding."

"Yes," Anna said dryly. "It is fortunate the Seeton tradition coincides with your wishes." Beth giggled and Anna smiled. "Very well, I own I am splitting hairs. But indeed, it rankles me. You should have a June wedding because you desire it, and not to follow some idiotic dictate set by tradition."

"It is not idiotic," Beth said, her tone weak. "Not really."

Anna rolled her eyes. "Yes, it is. To wed in June and in the family chapel just so that a ghost can give you the once-over and approve your marriage to Terrence *is* idiotic, not to mention rather morbid. The very notion of why the ghost appears can send one into the doldrums."

"Yes," Beth sighed. "The poor man. To have your bride run off with another lover on your appointed wedding day must be frightful. It is no wonder he flung himself from the castle turret and killed himself."

"And now he loiters about to pop in and ruin everyone else's wedding," Anna interrupted. "Definitely a poor sport."

"He only does that if one of the lovers is untrue," Beth said, wide-eyed. "Terrence is positive he won't appear at our wedding, and . . . and so am I. I mean, there is no reason for him to appear. So he won't . . . will he?"

"Of course not," Anna reassured her. "Because there are no such things as ghosts. To give credence to their existence can lead to nothing good. Indeed, look what it has done to Terrence's brother, the Duke."

"That is because his heart was broken by Tiffany Templeton," said Beth.

"Perhaps," Anna admitted. Her own heart felt a sympathetic twinge, but she steeled it. "Yet it was his choice to become a woman-hater and recluse because of her betrayal. Plenty of people have had their hearts broken and not buried themselves."

"Was your heart ever broken?" Beth asked hesitantly.

Anna stared at Beth, then looked down at the book in her hand. "No, dearest. You have to fall in love for your heart to be broken. I simply have never fallen in love."

Both ladies were silent for a moment. Beth leaned forward. "What are you reading?

"Poetry from a Lady of Devonshire," Anna said. She chuckled. "I thought it quite appropriate to the occasion." She closed the book, a wistful sigh escaping her before she caught it. "Now there, I believe, was a lady who loved and loved deeply."

"Perhaps I should read it," Beth said, her brow wrinkling.

Anna laughed. "I don't think you will like it. It is very old verse, with all the 'thees' and 'thous.' "

"Oh," Beth said. "I do find those so very distracting. Yet perhaps I should read more. Do you think Terrence would like that?"

"No, dear. You are perfect just the way you are. You wouldn't want to turn into a bluestocking like me, now, would you?"

"You are not a bluestocking," Beth retorted with sisterly ire. Her gaze skittered to the basket of books nestled beside Anna. The grays, blues, and browns of the leather-bound tomes were almost obscured, so well did they blend with the russet sarcenet shawl Anna had tossed about her shoulders. Her carriage dress was of a sturdy, woven paisley print of teal, brown, and antique gold. "You . . . you just read a lot, that is all."

"Of course," Anna said, chuckling. The carriage turned a bend and slowed its pace. Anna glanced out the window. Her eyes widened. "Oh, my stars!"

"What is it?" Beth asked.

"We have arrived, I believe," Anna said, leaning farther over and gaping. "No wonder there is a ghost. A castle like that simply *must* have one . . . or two or three even."

"What do you mean?" Beth asked, leaning across to peer out. A low moan escaped her. "Oh, no!"

"Oh, yes," Anna murmured.

The vine-ridden slate monstrosity they approached could only have been considered imposing. It sprawled across the entire landscape, its turrets towering above the worn, moss-covered stone walls. Hewn arches of gray chiseled stone loomed overhead as the carriage passed through. Because Anna did indeed read—even the Gothics—she should have felt, by all rights, something ominous, threatening, brooding. She didn't. Instead, she felt immediate warmth toward the crusty old castle. What history it must hold. How many lives it must have sheltered and protected within its walls over the ages.

"Anna," Beth whispered. Her voice was weak.

"What, dear?" Anna asked, still gazing in awe.

"I am frightened."

Anna cast her a quick look. Beth's sherry-colored eyes were round. "Don't be, dearest. There are no such thing as ghosts."

"But Terrence saw it."

"Terrence only believed he saw—" Anna bit her lip. It would have been a useless discussion. She smiled. "Very well, he might have seen one. However, until I see one myself, I shall think it mere poppycock, and so should you."

"I'll try," Beth said obediently.

"Besides," Anna firmly stated, "Terrence did say the ghost only appears at the ill-fated weddings, and yours won't be ill fated. It will be a blessed one."

"Yes. Yes, it will," Beth said, appearing to receive courage. The deepest sigh came from her. "I won't see the ghost."

"No, you won't," Anna said. "So just cast it from your mind. You have nothing to worry about."

"I have nothing to worry about," Beth repeated, smiling. Then her face fell. "But what of Terrence's brother?"

"Well, now, I do believe you will see him," Anna said dryly. "I fear that cannot be avoided."

"I know," Beth sighed.

Anna laughed. "Surely you'd rather see him than the ghost?"

"Oh, yes," Beth spoke very seriously. "But what if he doesn't like me?"

"What of it?" Anna said. She squelched her own foreboding upon that head. She had no fear of a ghost blighting her sister's happiness, but the older brother might be able to do so. She stiffened her spine. *Just let the ogre try!* "It is clear he does not like *any* woman, so what should it matter if he does not like you? You will be in the best of company, as it were."

"Terrence thinks highly of him," Beth whispered.

Anna's eyes narrowed. "Perhaps, but Terrence loves *you.*"

"Yes. Yes, he does," Beth smiled. The coach came to a complete halt. "Oh, dear."

"Remember," Anna said, collecting up her basket of books. "There are no ghosts, and as for the duke, it will not matter. You have nothing to worry about."

"I have nothing to worry about," Beth repeated dutifully, clutching her reticule and sewing box.

The coachman opened the door and the sisters alighted. Standing in the center of a cobblestone courtyard flanked on all sides by three-story walls was daunting. Each sister felt suspiciously like an ant at the bottom of a well. They knew the clear cerulean sky, which had ushered them along their travels, was up there somewhere. They just couldn't tell where from their vantage point.

"I . . . I . . ." Beth gurgled, gazing up the towering stone edifice.

"Nothing to worry about," Anna murmured and reached for Beth's hand.

The castle's massive oak doors, each carved with a crest spanning its height, swung open. Terrence bolted out. A small lady, covered in shawls, drifted out behind him.

"Beth!" Terrence cried, rushing forward with outstretched arms.

"Terrence!" Beth squealed. She ran to him, dropping her things to fly into his arms.

"Yes, how lovely," the small lady said, nodding her head. "Young love."

Beth drew back from her fiancé's arms, a charming flush upon her cheeks. "Oh, forgive me."

"No, no," the little lady assured her. "You are young. You are behaving exactly as you ought."

Terrence laughed. "Beth, this is Aunt Deirdre. Aunt Deirdre, this is my sweet Beth—and her sister, Anna."

Aunt Deirdre turned the lightest blue eyes upon Anna. "Hello, Sister Anna. You must be both pleased and anxious for your dear Beth."

Anna started back slightly. "Well, I . . ."

"You can say it," Aunt Deirdre smiled. "After all, I

raised my two boys. Their mother and father passed
away too, you know."

"I know," Anna said, smiling despite herself.

"But let us not stand here," Aunt Deirdre clucked.
"Do let us go into the house. I am sure you will wish
to freshen up, and then we can have tea. I've been waiting days for it."

"Days?" Anna asked.

"Yes, I informed Cook three days ago to make her
very special scones for us," Aunt Deirdre proclaimed,
beaming.

Terrence laughed. "Aunt, I keep telling you that
Cook can prepare them anytime you wish."

"Oh, no, dear," Aunt Deirdre said, drifting toward
the door. "Then they wouldn't be very special, would
they? They would then be humdrum. Do come along."

Terrence laughed and, bending down, picked up
Beth's reticule and sewing box. "Aunt is right. I've been
waiting for days . . . not for the scones, that is, but for
you to finally arrive."

"Thank you," Beth said, starry-eyed, as they all followed Aunt Deirdre toward the castle. Only when she
was upon the threshold did she halt, her entire body
stiffening. Wariness replaced the stars.

Anna came up and placed a comforting hand on
Beth's shoulder. "Remember . . ."

"I will not see the ghost," Beth chanted. "I have nothing to worry about."

Anna, flanking Beth, stepped inside. Her eyes widened and she gasped loudly.

"What?" Beth queried, nestling in close to Anna's
side for assurance. "What is it?"

"It is magnificent," Anna said.

She studied the huge cavernous hall, which spanned
a distance equal to that of several ballrooms in the
grandest London town homes. Pointed stone arches

soared three stories high. Between each arch hung a massive tapestry picked out in rich colors depicting one of the four seasons. These graced one side of the hall while the other side held four tapestries picturing the events in the history of the dukedom when each of four wings to the great hall were added. Each tapestry hung above an enormous fireplace. Anna felt she could see medieval banquets with entire oxen cooking over the flames in the eight fireplaces, which were presently unlit. Yet even in the daytime, centuries later, large sconces of intricate wrought iron lit the hall. The ceiling between the arches was crossed and crisscrossed by carved oak molding. In each diamond of oak was set a gold-leafed crescent moon matching the three crescent moons rampant on the family crest carved into each stone mantel. Anna had known the Seetons to be wealthy, and she and Beth were quite accustomed to luxury themselves, but it took great wealth to maintain a castle to such a degree.

"Do you like it, dear?" Aunt Deirdre asked, smiling. "I do try to keep it cozy."

"I see that," Anna said, stifling a laugh. "Quite cozy."

"Do you like it, Beth?" Terrence asked, his face solemn.

"Yes?" Beth said, nodding. Her gaze, however, wandered about the chamber, unfocused. "I-I have nothing to worry about."

Anna groaned.

Aunt Deirdre only smiled. "Of course not, my dear. You are going to marry my nephew, after all. And we are going to have special scones shortly."

Terrence laughed. "See, I rank right up there with special scones."

"Well, dearest . . ." Aunt Deirdre began.

Suddenly, a blood-chilling screech rent the air. Beth jumped and echoed the screech in a higher crescendo.

A portly, wild-eyed maid, came tearing through the hall, her hands waving. "I saw him! I saw him!"

"Oh, no," Beth moaned, then swayed.

"Beth," Terrence cried, clasping her to him.

"I saw him, mum," the maid sobbed and flung herself into the arms of diminutive Aunt Deirdre, who, wonder of wonders, maintained her stance.

"Now, Salome," Aunt Deirdre said, hugging the girl, who Anna realized was not portly, but well into her last months of pregnancy. "You know you couldn't have seen him."

"But I did see him," Salome cried. "I swear I saw him!"

"She saw him." Beth burst into tears. "We can't be married."

"What?" Terrence yelped.

"You couldn't have seen him, Salome," Aunt Deirdre said firmly.

"Why can't we be married?" Terrence cried.

"You know he ran off to America," Aunt Deirdre proclaimed.

Beth was caught in midsob. "He ran off to America? You mean he's gone?"

"Hightailed it the minute he heard Salome was increasing," Aunt Deirdre nodded. "The devil shied off from his responsibility when—"

"You mean . . ." Beth turned pale as she stared at the sobbing maid. "That *she* and *he* . . . But is that possible?"

Anna herself froze with shock. Reason asserted itself, however. "One moment, please. Just who is *he*?"

"Why, Salome's lover, of course—or ex-lover, that is," Aunt Deirdre said, frowning. She patted Salome's shoulder absently while she turned a concerned gaze upon Beth. "I can see you are a very tenderhearted girl, my dear, and you enter into other people's feelings, but you should not let this overset you. Salome is far better off without that no-good Peter Jenkins. Well, you can see that he is no-good, considering in what condition he left poor Salome." Salome hiccuped a heartfelt sob. "But Terrence is nothing like Peter Jenkins. He would never turn nasty and abusive just because you were with child. Terrence will make a wonderful father and husband. You should not fear marrying him."

"Oh, no. I do not fear marrying Terrence," Beth said, a deep red covering her cheeks.

"Then why can't we be married?" Terrence asked.

"I . . . I thought . . ." Beth halted, utter confusion and embarrassment rife upon her face.

"Beth thought Salome had seen the ghost," Anna interjected as gently as she could.

"The ghost?" Aunt Deirdre asked. Suddenly, she looked utterly confused. Then enlightenment dawned in her eyes. "You mean Charles Seeton? Gracious, no. Salome couldn't have seen him. He only appears at weddings. And as you can see, dear, Salome isn't anywhere near a wedding." Salome moaned and sniffled. "Oh, my, forgive me."

"I told you that, sweetheart," Terrence said to Beth in a comforting tone.

"Of course, you can hear him once in a while," Aunt Deirdre said, "and feel his presence. . . ."

"Oh, no!" Beth cried.

Terrence grimaced. "Only once in a while."

"How fortunate," Anna said, biting her lip. If she believed in ghosts, she would have been angry with Terrence's misleading ways. But since she didn't, one could not help but see the humor.

"But you will never *see* him," Aunt Deirdre said positively. She smiled. "Now that we have settled that, do let us hurry and prepare for tea." She patted Salome's shoulders. "Dearest, you know you are just suffering a bout of hysteria. It is very common in your delicate condition. But dry your eyes. Peter has run off and you will never have to see that mean man again."

"Yes, Miss Deirdre," Salome sniffed.

"There's a good girl," Aunt Deirdre said. "I know. Why don't you show the ladies to their chambers? Remember, we discussed their visit."

"Yes, mum," Salome said, dashing her tears away. "I remember it all. I-I won't fail you."

"I'll show Beth to her room, Aunt," Terrence said quickly.

"Yes, that is good," Aunt Deirdre said, nodding. "She needs your comforting. Then we will have special scones." A smile crossed her lips. "And Roark has promised to attend."

"Yes." Terrence smiled to Beth. "You will finally meet Roark."

"Will I?" Beth asked in a tone that showed that special scones *and* meeting Roark overwhelmed her.

"He's a great gun," Terrence said. "Just wait till you meet him."

"Yes," Beth whispered.

Anna refrained from comment with difficulty. "If you will show me to my room, Salome?"

Salome sniffed, drew a sleeve across her nose, and nodded. "Would you care to give me that basket, mum?"

Anna glanced at Salome. The basket of books was rather heavy. It would be a sin to burden the already heavily laden maid. "No, thank you. I shall carry them."

"Right this way, mum," Salome said.

Anna followed Salome. Or attempted to follow her. The girl intermittently sniffled and moaned while she led Anna at a brisk pace across the cavernous hall and into a lengthy gallery full of ancestral paintings, which Anna would have dearly liked to study, but she feared losing her guide. She all but loped past the master-pieces.

Salome finally led her to a set of steep stone stairs. Salome still moaned and sniffed. Anna, herself, was panting. She stopped to look back. Terrence and Beth surely should have been following them. They were no-where in sight. No doubt Terrence was permitting Beth to proceed at a regular pace. And perhaps even giving her a chance to observe the castle, Anna thought envi-ously. She turned back.

Salome was nowhere in sight. Fortunately, her sniffles could still be heard, though they were growing fainter. Either Salome was overcoming her bout of depression, or she was moving farther and farther away. Blowing at a strand of hair that had fallen into her eyes, Anna as-cended the steps. Apprehension stirred in Anna as she noticed during her climb that other stairs wended off from the main set. It was a stone rabbit warren—one she didn't particularly wish to explore at the moment.

Regardless of the stitch in her side, she picked up her speed and rammed directly into a moving body. A screech escaped her and she lost hold of the basket of books. It mattered not, for she also lost her footing. She teetered back and experienced the dreaded feeling of falling. A picture of all those cold, hard stone stairs behind her filled her mind.

Then she was jerked forward, slammed up against a hard wall of bone and muscle, and securely clamped there by strong arms. The stitch in her side yielded to pain. Wheezing, she looked up into a granite face and the darkest eyes she had ever seen. Anna could only stare. The man stared back.

The strangest emotion came over Anna. Her whole body leapt to life, as if a fire had flared up within it. Her soul felt as if it were taken up by a whirlwind. Fear and happiness were mingled within it.

The man slowly lowered his arms from about her, the oddest look upon his face. It almost looked like suspicion, which was ridiculous. Anna still stood frozen, staring at him as if she were spellbound. He stepped back cautiously, as if any sudden movement would precipitate a calamity.

Only when he was far enough away from her did Anna breathe. She hadn't realized she had ignored that function. For once in her life feeling faint, she stumbled over to lean against the stone wall. Her insides were in knots. She couldn't fathom what had come over her. She peeked at the man to see if she could gain a clue. He gazed at her with an unreadable expression.

She forced a smile. He must think her a want wit. "Th-thank you for saving me. If you hadn't, you might have had another ghost in the house . . . I mean castle."

The man didn't crack a smile. Anna flushed. He turned his gaze away. "Think nothing of it."

Anna blinked. A more offhand delivery could not have been possible. A laugh escaped her. "Of course not. It would have only been my life after all."

The man shrugged and walked down a step to pick up her books. Anna watched him. The strange emotions were fading, replaced by ire. As she studied the man, she knew with an instinctive certainty that he was brother Roark, the ogre.

He had somewhat the look of Terrence, though everything about him was darker and larger. Terrence's hair was brown. Roark's was black. Terrence's eyes were a light amber hue. Roark's were pitch dark. Terrence was tall and well built; yet Roark was taller and broader.

Funny, Anna thought, what the Fates did within a family. They had bestowed all the bold, strong looks upon the one brother, and then as if conscious of their overdramatics, they had reversed and bestowed all the gentler, refined ones upon the other. In the same way, they had been conservative when giving Anna plain, nondescript looks. Then the Fates, discovering they had hoarded, bestowed Beth with all the feminine beauty imaginable. Where Anna's eyes were a quiet hazel, Beth's were an intense sherry color framed by vivid golden lashes. Anna's hair was what could only be termed light brown. Beth had tresses of rich gold.

"Are you Terrence's bride?" Roark asked, picking up a book balancing on the step.

"No," Anna said. "I'm the sister."

His gaze raked her. He nodded curtly. "You didn't look like his type."

Anna flushed. "No, of course not."

Something flashed within his eyes. It appeared he might say something. Instead, he studied the book in his hand. A smile finally crossed his lips. It wasn't a warm one. "Definitely not his type. The sonnets of Shakespeare?" He leaned down and picked up yet another book. "And Byron. Who could live without Byron?"

Anna pushed herself away from the wall, anger flaring through her. "Give me those."

"With pleasure," he said, laughing. He tossed them to her. They fell at her feet.

Anna narrowed her eyes. "I had heard you were a woman-hater, but to hate poetry as well . . ."

Roark's eyes blazed. "I do not hate poetry."

"How fortunate," Anna said. That he did not refute hating women was telling.

"I merely find it rather useless," Roark added.

"Useless," Anna sputtered.

"Useless," Roark repeated. "Women—excuse me—people who sit around reading poetry generally want just that. Poetry. Which has nothing to do with life."

"Nothing to do with life?" Anna laughed. "You mean

that love and romance and the yearning of the spirit have nothing to do with life, correct?"

He grinned. "You do know your poetry."

She frowned. "Then just what is life without that?"

"Life," he said simply. "Reality. Not sighing and fantasizing about what isn't real."

"Oh, yes," Anna said in a cynical tone of her own. "No air dreaming, please. Common sense, reason, logic without emotions. What a fine reality."

"Better then being a pining sentimentalist," Roark retorted. He picked up another volume. Anna gritted her teeth as his brows rose. *"Poetry from a Lady of Devonshire?"*

"Yes," Anna said, reaching out to snatch at the book. "Just another silly sentimentalist from here who liked her poetry."

Of a sudden the temperature dropped. Anna, startled, looked quickly around. It was as if a north wind had whipped into the stairs and settled. She shivered. "Do you feel that?"

"Yes," Roark said. An evil grin crossed his lips. "It must be the ghost. Isn't that romantic?"

"Don't be ridiculous," Anna said.

"But it must be," Roark said. "It simply couldn't be a draft. That would be too logical, too commonplace."

"Do be quiet," Anna said, shivering again. "Does this happen often?' "

"Frightened?" Roark asked. "Perhaps you had best leave now. Before it is too late."

Anna glared at him. "I am here to help my sister prepare for her wedding. I'm not leaving."

"If there is a wedding," Roark said, his tone dry.

"There will be one," Anna retorted. "They truly love each other and *both* are faithful.' "

Something fleeting flashed through Roark's eyes. It looked like pain. Then his face became emotionless.

"We shall see. Dear ancestor Charles will no doubt have his say."

"So you believe in ghosts after all," Anna said, amazed at her need to taunt him. "Now who is being romantic?"

"I'm not," Roark said, his tone as arctic as the air about them. "I do accept unexplained phenomena, however—far more than I do love and marriage, I assure you. That is one thing I would agree with ancestor Charles upon, if he still existed."

Anna felt the challenge. "Beth and Terrence do love each other and they will be married, and if you try to—"

His brows rose. "To what?"

"To interfere in any way . . ."

"That's ancestor Charles's department," Roark said with a snort.

"I'm not worried about ancestor Charles," Anna snapped.

Roark's eyes blazed, though it was with malicious glee. "You're worried about me, are you? That I might manage to talk reason into Terrence or some such thing?"

"Yes," Anna said. She realized what she had said. "I mean no. I think you might try to ruin things, though, and if you do, I'll . . . I'll . . ."

"You'll what?" Roark asked, stepping closer.

No doubt he did so to intimidate her. Evidently it worked. Regardless of the cold air about them, she felt heat rush through her. "I-I don't know."

"You are a woman," Roark said, his tone low. Amazingly, he lifted his hand and ran it along her cheek. "I know you'll think of something."

Anna shivered. "What do you mean?"

"Nothing." Roark withdrew his hand. Then he actually glared at her, anger within his eyes.

Anna, totally at a loss and with no notion of how to react, settled for glaring back at him. Without another word, Roark spun and walked down the stairs. Anna was so intent upon fuming, that she hadn't realized she had let her one possible guide go. She gasped. "Roark . . . Your Grace!"

Of course, there was no answer. She plopped down upon the cold steps. She had met the Ogre. She shook her head and shivered. He was indeed just that. He hated not only women, but poetry and all the finer things in life as well. It was also all too clear he ranged himself against both Beth and her.

Anna gritted her chattering teeth. She had told Beth not to worry if the duke did not like her, and she most certainly would heed her own advice. Those strange and confusing emotions she had felt the minute she had met him, were evidently a warning. She would simply steer clear of him. For Beth's sake, she must be civil, but that would be as far as she would go. She suddenly noticed the temperature had become acceptable again. She laughed. She had heard old castles had their quirks, but this one excelled in them. Just like its inhabitants.

Anna heard a sniffle and looked up. Salome was returning down the stairs. Her reddened eyes widened when she discovered Anna sitting upon the steps. "Didn't you wish to go to your room, mum?"

Anna bit her lip and prayed for patience. "Yes, I think that would be pleasant. Only this time, you carry the basket."

It just might give her a lead this time.

Two

Anna grabbed her poetry book and dove under the covers of the huge tester bed. She might very well have been the romantic who air dreamed, but after that day, she most certainly deserved the right. She fully intended to escape into the beauty of poetry—and a snap of her fingers to the Ogre, at that.

Steering clear of Roark Seeton had been all too easy. The infernal man had refused to make an appearance. He had not come down for special scones. He had not come down for tea. He had not come down for dinner.

It galled Anna. No matter what their fight, he should not have punished the others because of it. Indeed, Beth had been crushed. Aunt Deirdre and Terrence had been disappointed, but they had taken his absence in stride. Aunt Deirdre had offered some pitiful excuse for Roark, alluding to his studies in science or whatnot, which must have detained him. Anna had pretended sangfroid for Beth's sake. She saw no reason to burden Beth with her unfortunate meeting with Roark Seeton. It would only disturb Beth, setting her at an even greater disadvantage when she met the Ogre.

Anna opened her book and forced her attention upon the page. *"My love for thee is true."* Clearly everyone had permitted Roark to become the hateful man he was. *"It grew within my heart, a simple, sweet bud . . ."* But hateful or not, he would not be permitted to destroy things for Beth. *". . . pure and undefiled."* He might spurn love and marriage if he wished. *"And only for thee, forever for thee . . ."* But he would not stop Anna's sister and Terrence from wedding. *". . . shall it bloom."*

Anna slammed the book shut. There was no use in trying to read. Then she froze. A gurgle choked from her throat. It should have been a scream, but fear strangled it. A man stood at the foot of her bed. Tall and dark, he wore a stuffed-and-busked doublet of amethyst satin trimmed in gold lace. The high-standing collar bore three rows of bronze-green pleating shot with glints of gold thread. A clock pattern of gold shot was embroidered along the side of each leg of the voluminous breeches tucked into the bucket-top boots peculiar to the Cavaliers of the seventeenth century, with their wide turnovers trimmed in gold lace. A short cloak of deep rose, edged in green satin, swung from one shoulder creating an air of martial swagger. Atop the man's head was a wide-brimmed hat adorned with a huge burgundy plume.

Anna's heart stopped. Dear God, it was the ghost! But she didn't believe in ghosts. She blinked and blinked and blinked again. Reason fought its way up through her pounding fear. Since it couldn't be a spirit, it must be a live man. As her vision cleared from the haze of shock, she also knew which man it was. There was no hiding the fact, even with the false beard he had donned and the extravagant dress. It was unimaginable that Roark Seeton had gone to such lengths to scare her, but the proof unquestionably stood before her.

She narrowed her eyes. Did he really think her such a twit as to be taken in by such a prank? Anna smiled grimly. She'd show him. She feigned a yawn. "Oh, hello there, Sir Ghost."

A brow shot up. "You can see me?"

"Of course I can see you," Anna said, chuckling. She had to give Roark credit, he'd successfully altered his voice. Indeed, his ability to throw it out and create almost an echo with it was true art. "Why shouldn't I see you?"

A strange light entered the man's eyes. "That I could not say, mistress."

"Thank you," Anna said, feigning innocence. "But aren't you slightly lost, Sir Ghost?"

He grinned. "Aye, wench, and so I have been for ages."

Anna stiffened. So the Ogre still intended to play the game. "I meant, don't you have the wrong room? I'm just the sister, remember?" she said maliciously. "You are supposed to appear to the bride."

He laughed. "You may be the sister, but such does not mean you are not the bride as well."

Anna drew back. How dared the man taunt her. "Oh, enough. Do let us have done with this charade."

"Charade?" he barked, appearing stunned.

"Yes," Anna said. "Charade. Isn't it clear that you have not frightened me as you intended? Though why you thought you could is beyond me. A more doltish thing I've never seen."

"Doltish?" His brows snapped down in a furious frown. "Doltish!"

"Yes, doltish!" Anna snapped. "I told you I don't believe in ghosts."

His eyes glowed and his smile was a challenge. "You don't?"

"No, I don't," Anna said, riled. "And even if I did, you would have to do far better then this, Your Grace. I'll not be taken in by a fake beard and trumped-up dress. Faith, how gaudy and overdone."

He frowned darkly. "Gaudy? Overdone? Fiend seize it, woman!"

"And no doubt moth-eaten," Anna said tartly. "So now you can cease your pathetic performance and be gone. Go play your tricks off on children or . . . or the village idiot."

He stared at her for a moment, but then laughed. His laughter filled the room. "Tongue-valiant shrew!"

"Shrew!" Anna gasped. "You call me that merely because I didn't fall for your little hoax? Well, let me tell you something . . ." He turned away. "Where are you going? I'm not finished talking to you!"

He moved across the room without another word. Enraged, Anna hopped out of bed. It was he who had entered her room and attempted to frighten her, and since he had failed, he thought to merrily leave, unscathed as it were. Well, she'd not have it!

She turned and quickly grabbed up her wrapper, struggling into it. She spun back. The infernal man had opened up what appeared to be a portion of the wall. "A secret passage! That is how you got in here. Some fine ghost you are."

He laughed again. "I go where I wish!"

"Go where you wish?" A disturbing thought struck Anna and she chased after him. "Just how many passages are there? There had best not be one to Beth's room. I'll not have you trying this farce on her. Do you hear me?"

Anna paddled across the room and lunged into the passageway. Cool air chilled her but she could hear him laughing. She stumbled through the darkened passage sliding her hand upon the wall. It felt cold and slimy. "Your Grace! Roark Seeton! Come back here this instant! I can't see!"

Anna heard him laugh, then saw a glow appear in the distance before her. Thank God, he had lit a tinder. She pushed the instant gratitude aside and doggedly followed behind. Matters were going to be settled between them—and settled now!

Anna finally emerged from the passage in relief. She blinked. She was in a darkened bedroom. One lone candle stood lit upon the bedside table. She treaded over to the bed. Her eyes narrowed. Outrage filled her. The sheets were drawn up, with only the dark hair of Roark showing. The audacity of the man. He was hiding under the covers and pretending to sleep. Well, he wasn't going elude her that way either.

"I've had enough of this!" Anna said. Bending, she grabbed hold of the sheet and flung it back. A shocked yelp escaped her. Gone was the gaudy, moth-eaten doublet. Gone were the voluminous breeches and the boots upon his feet. Indeed, gone was any fashion of clothing, modern or ancient. He was naked. Lean, stark naked!

"What?" Roark's eyes snapped open. He scrabbled up, a sleepy, disoriented look upon his face. "Who?"

Anna slapped her hands over her eyes, attempting to block out both the stunning, wicked image of a naked Roark, as well as the all-too-unsuspecting, innocent expression upon his face. "Please cover yourself!"

"Cover myself? Blast and damn!" Anna heard the movement more than saw it. "You! What the hell are you doing here?"

Anna peeked through the fingers of her hand. The sheet was drawn up, at least to his waist. Roark's sleepy eyes held a dark glower.

"I . . . I . . ." Anna moaned as a totally new and infelicitous reality sank into her conscience. No man could go from fully garbed and bearded to totally naked and clean jawed so quickly, not to mention extracting those ridiculous boots from his feet. Rocked to the core, she tottered to the bed and collapsed upon it. "I saw the ghost."

"You saw the ghost?" Roark asked, his brow raising. He laughed.

Anna's heart sank to her very toes. His laugh was in no way similar to the other man's. "Yes, I am sorry to say it, but I saw him."

Roark did not react as she had expected. He merely leaned back against the pillow, a satirical glimmer in his eyes. "So you came to me to comfort and protect you, is that it?"

"I did not," Anna gasped. "I . . . I followed the ghost here."

"Directly to my bedroom?" Roark asked, his tone far too male and confident. He chuckled. "I knew you'd think of something, but this is far more imaginative than I expected. Women have employed plenty of different stories to be able to get into my bed, but that a ghost—no, *the* ghost—lead them to me is by far the best."

"To be able to get into your bed?" Anna squeaked. She sprang up as if she had been sitting upon a bed of red-hot coals, which, in a manner of speaking, she had.

"Yes," Roark said. His gaze roved over Anna in a shockingly familiar way. "Into my bed."

"Why y-you conceited man," Anna sputtered. "Why would I want to get into your bed? You are rude and . . . and hate women."

"I could make an exception," Roark said, grinning. He patted the bed.

"Not for me, you don't!" Anna exclaimed, skittering back. "In fact, you can hate me all you want. Please do! Because I don't like you."

"You don't?" Roark asked. "Then why are you here?"

"I told you," Anna said, stamping her foot. "I saw the ghost. I thought it was you trying to scare me away! So I followed you—I mean, him—here." A shiver ran through her. "My God, I actually saw a ghost!"

Roark's brows snapped down. "You couldn't have. No one ever sees him, except at weddings."

Anna's laugh was hollow. "That is what I thought, but I saw him."

"You did not," Roark said. "Admit it. You came here to seduce me and then got"—his lips quirked—"cold feet."

Anna gasped. He wasn't gazing at her feet, rather he was looking at her chest. She hadn't realized her wrapper was completely undone. She quickly crossed her arms about her. "I d-did not. Th-think whatever you like, which I'm sure you will, but I did not come here to seduce you." Roark's gaze was passionate. "Or . . . or to be seduced." Anna spun and, forgetting all dignity, dashed across the room toward the secret passage. She skittered to a halt when she almost hit the solid wall. "Where . . . where is it?"

"Where is what?" Roark asked from the bed.

"The secret passage," Anna cried. She reached out and began pounding upon the wall in desperation.

"There is no secret passage," Roark said. "You can stop your charade."

"It's not a charade," Anna said, turning to him in fury and honest fear. "It was here! I swear it!"

"Calm yourself," Roark said, rising from the bed.

"No!" Anna squawked, closing her eyes. "Don't you dare come near me!"

"I'm just getting my robe," Roark said. "I wasn't expecting company, after all."

"Ha!" Anna scoffed. Nervous tears formed beneath her lids. "According to you, you always have woman slipping into your room. Apparently you dress—or don't dress—for them."

"But most of them aren't crazy women who've seen ghosts!" Roark said. His tone was surprisingly light and teasing. It acted as a tonic to Anna. In the absence of sanity, humor was a blessed thing. She drew in a deep, gasping breath. "No, I suppose not."

"In fact," Roark said, his tone wry, "the last woman who saw the ghost ran *away* from me, not to me. You can open your eyes now."

Anna did. Roark was dressed in a black silk smoking jacket. It fell open at the chest and molded to his broad, muscled shoulders like a second skin. It was better than nothing, but not by much. Blushing, Anna spun around and applied herself to searching the wall again. "It was here somewhere."

Roark carried the candle over and studied the wall. "Well, it's not now."

Anna glared at him. "You don't believe me, do you? You think I've just let my imagination run away with me, don't you? I mean, I'm a romantic flibbertigibbet. I must be imagining everything else."

His face darkened. "I'm not going to admit to anything. It is clear you believe you saw what you did. Shouldn't that be enough?"

Anna clenched her fists tightly. She wanted to scream. He was being reasonable, she had to admit, but she had seen a ghost! She had not only seen a ghost, but had also talked to him. She flushed. Heavens, she had even insulted him. She didn't need reason at the moment. She needed some further support, something to ensure her of her sanity.

She shook her head angrily. What was she expecting from this man anyway? She stepped past him. "You are right. There is no need to discuss it. Now if you will excuse me, I am leaving." She headed toward the bedroom door, then pulled on the handle. Sighing in exasperation, she turned. "Could you please unlock your door?"

"It isn't locked," Roark said, walking toward her.

"Yes, it is," Anna said.

"No, it isn't," Roark said. He reached out with the show of confidence, which let Anna know what a widgeon he thought her. He turned the handle. He frowned. "It must be stuck."

"Then unstick it," Anna retaliated, feeling her nerves unraveling further.

Roark jerked at the handle. He rattled it. He pounded upon the door and the frame, then tried again. "It must be jammed."

Anna groaned. "I shouldn't have insulted him."

"What?" Roark asked, pounding upon the door.

"I insulted the ghost," Anna said. "I told him his dress was gaudy and overdone."

"You what?" Roark halted a moment, brow raised.

"I thought it was you," Anna said.

"Thank you," Roark said in a dry tone. "But this isn't because of a ghost. It is merely an old door that has become jammed."

Anna felt a stirring of hope. "Then it happens often?"

"No." Roark frowned and tugged. "It started just now."

"Oh, just now. It is perfectly reasonable then." Sighing she walked toward the bed, then halted. The wickedest images flash through her mind: One was a replay of how she had seen Roark before; the other included her in the bed as well. Never in her life had she experienced thoughts of that sort, and so clearly at that. Dear Lord, her sanity *had* slipped all its moorings.

She spun around. Her voice quavered with desperation. "Can you break it down?"

Roark gazed at her, then at the door. It was large and solid oak. "I'm not that strong."

"Let us both try," Anna said, rushing toward the door. She slammed her shoulder against it. "Ouch!"

"We are not going to be able to do it," Roark said.

Anna pounded upon the door. "Help!"

"Miss Winston, stop it."

"Help!" Anna shouted. "We are locked in here!"

"Stop! You will hurt yourself," Roark said, grabbing hold of her shoulders and spinning her toward him.

"We are locked in here," Anna cried, panting. She looked up at him. Then, fearing he might read her unruly thoughts, she lowered her gaze. It wasn't a wise choice. Her eyes focused upon his exposed chest, mesmerizing her. His chest was well muscled, and a mat of dark curly hair covered it. How would it feel to the touch? she wondered.

When Roark's fingers dug into her shoulders, she tore her gaze away and looked up at him. But he wasn't looking at her either. His gaze was focused upon *her* chest. She flushed, her heart beating as madly as when she'd first seen the ghost. "Y-your Grace?"

They stood frozen for one tense and breathless moment.

"Let us try again," Roark said hoarsely. He jerked his hands from her shoulders.

"Yes. Oh, yes," Anna said.

Two desperate bodies immediately slammed against the door. It didn't budge.

Anna moaned. "Why does it have to be so infernally strong?"

"It was meant to keep enemies out," Roark grunted.

Anna stepped back, rubbing her bruised shoulder. She forced a laugh. "Well, it's keeping them in now."

"Yes," Roark murmured. His gaze seemed focused upon her hand movement. He looked swiftly away. "Let me try . . . alone. Go and cover yourself up." A disconcerted expression crossed his face. "I mean, go to bed. Get under the covers. I'm sure you are cold."

Anna did shiver, though her doing so had nothing to do with being cold. "Are you sure?"

"I'm sure," Roark said, his tone fierce. "And don't worry. I don't seduce crazy women who have seen ghosts. Just get under the covers, for God's sake."

Anna nodded. She scampered quickly to the bed, castigating herself as she did so. She truly was unsettled. Of course Roark wouldn't want to seduce her. He thought her totally unhinged. She crawled into the bed. She watched Roark as he knelt and studied the doorknob. He glanced at her. "Cover yourself up more. I mean, lie down and rest. This may take a while."

"All right," Anna said, obeying. She burrowed down, still watching Roark. However, her eyes fluttered shut. It was amazing, she mused. She had seen her first ghost and her first naked man. What an earth-shattering night.

That was her last thought.

Across the room, Roark set the poker down. It was no use. The door was too thick and he could not gain leverage to pry it open. He glanced over to his bed. Anna was fast asleep. Once again, he felt desire run through him, just as it had when he had caught her on the stairs earlier.

His anger rose. It simply made no sense. She wasn't beautiful. Nor was she sophisticated. He had seen the innocent, confused passion in her eyes at their meeting. The woman hadn't a clue.

She was just the kind of woman he avoided: a romantic who still believed in love and faithfulness and wanted the same from a man, an unreasoning air dreamer who lived by emotion and always tried to draw it from others and who searched for happily ever afters when there weren't any.

Roark clenched his jaw. Why couldn't she have come to seduce him? That was the kind of woman he could have taken to bed. That was the kind of woman he liked.

Instead, he was locked in with the other kind—and one who claimed to see ghosts at that.

Frowning, he stood and walked over to the most comfortable chair available, then fell into it. Just what had the woman seen—and not seen? What was real and what was not? With a woman like her, it would no doubt be impossible to determine.

Exhaustion dragged at Roark. He shifted, attempting to find a comfortable position in the chair. He would study both Anna's story and the jammed door once more in the morning. For now, he needed sleep. Faith, how he needed sleep.

Roark drifted off, only to awake, shivering. The temperature had dropped tremendously. His muscles ached with cold. Confound it, what an unseasonable May night it had become. He attempted to return to sleep, but the cold seemed ruthless.

His gaze roved to the bed. Anna slept soundly, a burrowed ball far upon one side. Roark rose, shaking. The bed was large, and there would be no harm in taking his portion of it. He crawled under the covers, grateful for the warmth.

Aunt Deirdre, always an early riser, padded down the hall. A slight frown marred her face. She had to speak to her dear Roark. His refusing to meet Beth and Anna had simply been too bad. She knew she had told him more than a dozen times that they were to arrive. Indeed, he had promised to meet them. He had also promised to behave civilly.

She sighed. It was such a shame. Ever since his failed wedding, Roark had become a different person. Before, he had been such a charming man, totally involved with life—a true darling of the *ton*. Then the ghost had appeared and that dreadful Tiffany Templeton had run off. Not that Deirdre had wanted Roark to marry the girl. Even she had known that their marriage would not have suited. Deirdre fully approved of ancestor Charles's appearance at the wedding. In fact, she had secretly prayed for his visitation.

She couldn't approve, however, of how Roark had changed. He had withdrawn from life and become interested only in his studies. It was a sad thing when the younger brother married before the older. It was famous that Terrence had found his mate, but Deirdre could not be happy until Roark also found his true love. She offered up her ritual plea to the heavens to send Roark a woman who would make him love and live again.

Aunt Deirdre sighed then. She believed in miracles and the wonders of the universe, only she wished the Almighty would respond posthaste to this matter. That Roark had become so withdrawn as not to come down to meet Terrence's fiancée and her sweet sister Anna was a clear sign that he was growing worse, not better.

However, she would have a good talk with him. Roark simply had to meet the two ladies. Breakfast would be an excellent time. Roark could not say he was studying the stars, for there were no stars in the morning. Quite satisfied with her thoughts, Deirdre reached Roark's door. She slowed when she discovered Salome ahead of her, with her hand upon the doorknob to Roark's room.

"Good morning, Salome."

"Good morning, Miss Deirdre," Salome said, sniffling.

"You are at your duties," Deirdre said cheerily. "I'm proud of you."

"Yes, Miss Deirdre," Salome said. "I be bringing His Grace hot water."

"You do that," Aunt Deirdre smiled, "and I will have a talk with him for a moment."

Salome nodded, then opened the door and entered. Suddenly, Salome's infamous earsplitting shriek arose.

"Oh, dear," Aunt Deirdre sighed, pushing into the room. "What is it now, dearest?"

A shriek splintered through Anna's sleep. Frightened, she snapped her eyes open. She attempted to start up, but discovered herself pinioned.

"What?" she gasped. Shrieks ringing in her ears, she stared directly into Roark Seeton's startled eyes. Her body was firmly pressed against his, his arms wrapped about her, his one hand curved possessively upon her hip. Aghast, she slapped at him. "What are you doing?"

"Nothing," Roark said, swiftly untangling himself from her. "I was sleeping."

"You aren't supposed to be sleeping! Not with me!" Anna cried.

She looked angrily to the source of the clamor. Her eyes widened. The door—that strong, unyielding, infernally jammed door—was wide open. Salome stood within the gaping portal, shrieking. Aunt Deirdre was beside her. The little lady actually wore a benign smile upon her face.

"Silence," Roark shouted.

Salome's wail clipped to a squeak. Her face turned blue; then she spun about and dashed from the room. Within seconds, her banshee wail arose once again.

"Dear me," Aunt Deirdre said, shaking her head. "Why ever Salome is carrying on so is beyond me. It is not as if she is an innocent." She smiled. "Roark, I was just coming to take you to task for not meeting our company, but I see you've met Anna, after all. I couldn't be more pleased."

"Pleased?" Anna asked. She glared at Roark. "I am anything but pleased. What are you doing in my bed?"

"Your bed?" Roark snorted. "You mean, my bed."

"Either way," Anna snapped, though a flush was rising to heat her. "What are you doing here?" A worse thought entered her mind. "And what *did* you do?"

"Now, dearest," Aunt Deirdre said. "Is that any way to talk to the man you just shared, uh, your love with?"

"I did not share my love with him—or anything else," Anna said. She cast a nervous look at Roark. "Did I?"

"Oh, for God's sake, of course not," Roark said, his tone surly with sleep and exasperation. "I told you, I don't seduce crazy women who've seen ghosts."

"Roark," Aunt Deirdre exclaimed. "That is not very kind of you. When you are married—"

"Married!" Anna gasped.

"Married!" Roark thundered.

"Yes, married," Aunt Deirdre said calmly.

Anna and Roark looked at each other. Their unified *no* was loud and vehement.

"Now, children," Aunt Deirdre said, frowning. "Without a doubt this happened fast, but miracles do happen."

"It's not a miracle," Anna objected.

"It's a bloody disaster," Roark said.

"Tsk, tsk," Aunt Deirdre said. "There is no need to deny your passion or love. Not for my sake."

"We don't love each other!" Roark said.

"We hate each other!" Anna said quickly. "Loathe each other, in fact."

"I assure you," Aunt Deirdre continued as if neither had spoken, "although I have never been married, I am quite enlightened. I am not at all embarrassed by what you have done."

Anna flushed. Aunt Deirdre might not have been embarrassed. She was, however, down to her very toes, in fact. "No, truly. We didn't do anything. It only looks as though we did."

A babble of voices suddenly rose from the hall. Indeed, it sounded as if an army approached. Salome's squawks of *help* and *sin* and *destruction* led the charge.

"Blast and damn," Roark muttered.

Another voice fought to the top. "Anna! Where are you? Anna!"

"Beth! Oh, no," Anna moaned. She couldn't face her sister. She slid down and covered her head with the blankets.

"Anna! Where are you?" Beth's voice was in the room. "Where is my sister? What has happened to my sister?"

"She's there, dear," Aunt Deirdre's voice said. "Under the covers."

Anna could just imagine Aunt Deirdre with her cherubic smile betraying her.

"Under the covers?" Even through the covers, the shock in Beth's voice was evident. "Anna, is that you?"

"Yes, it's me," Anna sighed. She threw back the covers and sat up. She cringed. Salome, Beth, and Terrence had joined Aunt Deirdre.

"See! See!" Salome howled, hopping up and down and pointing. Salome's fevered gaze held a glimmer. Misery certainly loved company.

"Get out of here, woman," Roark roared. Salome choked to silence. Making the sign of the cross, she backed slowly away. "And if you bring one more person here, I'll send you to America. This is not a posting house, for God's sake." Salome choked and fled from the room.

"That was slightly harsh," Aunt Deirdre said. "I know she is irritating—"

"Irritating!" Roark exclaimed. "Next she'll bring the kitchen help."

"Now, Roark," Terrence said, his face dark.

"Roark?" Beth gasped. She turned, shocked, and with widened eyes, exclaimed, "He's your brother?"

"Yes, dear," Aunt Deirdre said, beaming. "I am so pleased for you to finally meet my other boy. As you can see, Anna has already met him."

Beth looked at Roark, a far fiercer light in her eyes than Anna could have imagined. "What have you done to my sister?"

"I've done nothing, confound it!" Roark said.

"Truly, Beth," Anna said. "We only slept together. I mean, next to each other."

"We were locked in my room," Roark said.

"Children," Aunt Deirdre said. "Why tell such taradiddles. We are all adults here."

"But we were," Anna said. "The ghost did it!"

"Ghost!" Beth cried out. Terrence exclaimed loudly. Aunt Deirdre's surprised voice chimed in.

Anna winced. Then she gasped. The ghost stood across the room. He winked at her and said, " 'Tis enough to wake the dead, is it not?"

"You!" Anna said. "It's all your fault."

"It's not all my fault," Roark exclaimed. "You are the one who came here claiming you saw the ghost!"

"Claiming!" Anna glared at him. "I'm not claiming." She pointed. "Look! And tell me I'm just claiming."

Roark looked in the direction she pointed. "What are you talking about?"

"Him!" Anna exclaimed. "Can't you see him?"

"Who?" Roark frowned.

"The ghost!" Anna said angrily. "He's right there!"

"Oh, no! He's here!" Beth wailed and spiraled to the ground.

"Beth!" Terrence cried, kneeling down.

The ghost raised his brow. *"You* see me and *she* faints. Interesting."

"Beth is a sensitive girl," Anna said angrily.

"Yes, dear," Aunt Deirdre said, kneeling as well. "We understand!"

"Why can't they see you?" Anna asked.

The ghost shrugged. "Don't ask me. I'm only a ghost!"

"Beth," Terrence said, patting her cheek. "Are you all right?"

Beth's eyes fluttered open. Tears welled up in them. "He's here. He's come to stop our wedding."

"No," Anna said, glaring at the ghost. He's here to ruin my life."

"Tsk," Aunt Deirdre said. "No one's life is ruined. Yours and Roark's is just beginning." She patted Beth's shoulder. "And you shouldn't cry, dear. You will have your wedding. And so shall your sister."

"I don't want a wedding," Anna objected strongly.

The ghost laughed. "Remember, I said you would be the sister and the bride."

"We aren't going to be married," Roark agreed. "Not because of some supposed ghost!"

"No, we aren't," Anna said, glaring at the ghost.

"Of course not," Aunt Deirdre said. "You are going to be married because you have spent the night together and are thereby compromised."

"We didn't do anything!" Roark said angrily. "It was totally innocent."

"Very disappointing," Charles said. "I had expected more from a descendant of mine. I assure you, I would have done something."

"Lecher!" Anna gasped.

"What?" Roark exclaimed.

"I didn't mean you," Anna said, gritting her teeth.

"Then who did you mean?" Aunt Deirdre asked.

"She means the ghost, I believe," Roark said sarcastically.

"Oh, no," Beth moaned.

"The one right over there," Roark added, pointing in a completely different direction from which Anna had pointed.

Anna glared at him. "Stop it."

"He's over there then," Roark retorted, pointing wildly.

"Very well," Anna said, springing from the bed. "There isn't a ghost! I just made that all up because I'm crazy! Stark, raving mad." A sudden thought occurred. She grinned in triumph at the ghost. "In fact, I'm so insane, I am totally ineligible for marriage. I see things that aren't there. I talk to imaginary people. I read poetry! I'm unbalanced. No one would wish to bring that into a family."

"A gallant effort," the ghost said. He laughed and laughed loudly. Of a sudden, a cold wind whipped through the room, complete with sound effects. Beth squeaked and clung to Terrence, who sheltered her in protective arms. Roark stiffened, gazing around with narrowed eyes.

"Good God," Terrence muttered when the wind finally died down.

"Well," Aunt Deirdre said, a beatific grin crossing her lips. "Apparently Anna isn't crazy after all. That means she and Roark can be married."

Anna let out a howl of rage. Refusing to look left, right, or anywhere else, she stormed from the room.

Three

"Terrence, it is a beautiful estate," Beth breathed as they rode along another smooth road, the meadow grass upon its sides rustling in the breeze.

"Then you like it?" Terrence smiled down at Beth. The warmth and pride in his eyes were as bright as the sun. "It is home to me."

Beth gazed into his eyes, equally enthralled. "I love it."

Anna hid her smile, even as the feeling of relief soothed her. The day had, amazingly, turned into a pleasure. The contretemps of the morning seemed to have evaporated. Granted, everyone had tacitly agreed not to discuss the issue in any shape or form. Terrence, displaying a stroke of genius, had decided it was the perfect opportunity for an open carriage ride and offered to show Beth and Anna the estate.

Nothing could have been better. Riding along in the balmy late afternoon sunlight, one could not think of ghosts and such. Meeting the tenants and seeing that they were happy, open, and hospitable in their greeting, had erased the fear from Beth's eyes and brought back the glow of a woman in love.

Anna drew in deep breath of spring air. Things were growing and blooming. At that moment, the wilds of Devonshire were quite tolerable. A grudging admiration seeped into Anna. Roark might be a recluse, but apparently he was not so much of a recluse that he did not husband his property. Considering the size of the estate, that was no small task.

"Your tenants have been very kind," Beth said, blushing.

Terrence smiled. "These are only the beginning of their gifts."

Anna laughed. "The pickled pigs' feet from Mrs. Jameson, I do believe, are the finest gift."

"No," Terrence said, wiggling his brow. "The dram of spirits from Ed Thompson is the better choice. Perhaps we should uncork now."

"Terrence!" Beth squealed.

Terrence grinned. "You don't think we should?"

"No, of course not," Beth said, her tone aghast.

"Ed would be very hurt if he knew you spurned his gift," Terrence said, shaking his head in mock severity. He slowed the team of horses as they come upon a wooded crest. "I have no doubt he brewed it himself."

"Truly?" Beth asked.

"Yes," Terrence said, chuckling. He began turning the cart around. "The family has their own special recipe. It is famous in these parts."

"Gracious," Beth said.

Anna frowned, not really listening. She gazed at the road from which they turned. Large oaks lined it, spreading a green canopy above. Beneath, an array of colors teased the eye. It must have been wildflowers, the very wealth of them stunning, alluring. "Why are we turning back?"

"This is the end of our estate," Terrence said, completing his turn in a space Anna realized was well worn with the tracks of carriages doing the same before.

Anna looked back sadly. That tree-lined road beckoned. "Couldn't we go just a little further? Surely your neighbors would not object?"

"No," Terrence said. "That is the Anton estate."

"Who are the Antons?" Beth asked.

"Genevieve Anton was the woman who ran off with another lover," Terrence said, his voice sounding odd.

"I don't understand," Beth said, blinking.

Anna did. A quiver ran through her. "She was the woman who was supposed to marry your . . ." She froze. Who, or what, was she supposed to say? "Your ancestor?"

"Yes," Terrence said. "Charles Seeton."

"Then their marriage would have joined the estates," Anna said.

"It would have," Terrence nodded. "Instead she ran off with another, and Charles Seeton committed suicide." He looked to Beth, wariness within his eyes. "The only one ever in our family to do so, from his time to now."

"I believe that," Beth nodded.

"You still do not associate with the Antons?"

"No," Terrence said. His voice was calm. "Ever since that day, neither family has stepped foot upon the others land."

A deep, freezing chill ran through Anna. She looked back once more. No fence divided the land, but the forest was an unyielding bank, the line between trees and meadow drawn straight. The grass did not encroach upon the forest, and no tree—not even a meager sapling—dared to trespass into the meadow. The unbroken road that ran through it was well tended upon both sides, not a gully or bump on it. Anna almost choked. "The road is not very necessary for either of you then?"

Something flickered in Terrence's eyes. "Not really. It was only a shorter path to the main roads."

The chill settled into Anna's very marrow. She hadn't

even felt such a chill when she had accepted she had seen a ghost. That the dead still walked because they could not forgive or forget she could possibly believe. That the living, generation after generation, would not forgive and forget, would not leave the tragedy to the dead, she could not fathom.

She drew in a deep breath. She could not smell things growing and blooming.

She could not smell spring anymore.

Anna, Beth, and Terrence sat down to dinner at one end of the massive walnut trestle table, which extended the length of the cavernous dining hall. Roark had once again not shown himself. Anna grimaced as she smoothed the silk skirts of her favorite evening frock, its jacquard pattern dyed in a bronze floral on a muted olive background—a coloring she felt brought intensity to her hazel eyes. One could hardly have been surprised Roark didn't attend the dinner. Nor did Anna particularly miss him. Her hazel eyes snapped. After the episode that morning, she believed she could live very well without ever seeing him again.

However, Aunt Deirdre was also absent. Nor had she been present for tea, which did surprise Anna since again there were special scones. Salome had informed them Aunt Deirdre had gone into the village. Apparently Roark's threat that morning had performed a miracle, for Salome had delivered the missive with nary a sniff or sob. Everyone, however, had judiciously ignored the fact that the maid had donned five strings of rosary beads, which she constantly clutched. Anna had even suffered the maid gifting her with a string as well—no doubt an offering from one fallen woman to another. If Salome could find peace within religion, then the household might very well find some peace as well.

As for Aunt Deirdre's absence, Terrence had assured Anna not to worry. Aunt Deirdre rarely went into the village, but when she did, she often remained gone for hours, catching up with acquaintances and generally learning the village news down to the very last scandal. There would be no telling when she would return. Anna had accepted his statement far more readily than she would have earlier. Clearly an erratic form of hosting ran within the family.

Suddenly the large doors to the dining hall burst open. Aunt Deirdre entered briskly, a wide smile upon her face as she hurried to take up a chair at the table. "Hello, hello!"

Terrence laughed. "Hello, Auntie. You are home earlier than I expected."

"Yes, I am," Aunt Deirdre said, her eyes bright. "And I am just in time, I see. Salome told me Cook has prepared beef Wellington tonight. That is special indeed. We only have it once a fortnight."

Anna bit back a laugh. Here she had been thinking that the attendance of guests was rarely considered in the household; yet, unbeknownst to her, they had been receiving the royal treatment. She gazed at her beef Wellington with new respect. "It is very tasty."

"I can hardly wait," Aunt Deirdre exclaimed, her gaze eager as it settled upon the remaining portion of the specialty. She looked down then in disappointment at the absence of a place setting. As if upon cue, Salome entered, plate and cutlery in hand. "Oh, how wonderful. What a special ending to a special day."

Anna would not have applied the word *special* to the day. A myriad of other words, from *odd* to *confounding*, came to mind, but not *special*. However, Aunt Deirdre exuded such enthusiasm and pleasure, one could not help but smile.

Terrence himself chuckled. "Indeed. And what is the news in the village?"

"News?" Aunt Deirdre murmured, serving herself a hefty portion of the beef Wellington.

"Yes," Terrence said. "The gossip, the scandal."

Aunt Deirdre looked up and blinked. "Oh, no, dear. You know I never gossip. I show a natural concern for people and their lives, and I most certainly would never stop them from telling me whatever they wish. That is what friends are for, after all, but I never gossip."

"No, of course not," Terrence said with mock solemnity.

"Besides," Aunt Deirdre said innocently, "I was far too busy today for that."

"Too busy for *that?*" Terrence asked, his tone horrified. Beth and Anna laughed.

Aunt Deirdre only nodded her head vehemently. "Yes. I told you it was a special day and I have a special treat for you." She drew in her breath, looking like a child ready to burst. "I've invited the entire village to a dance to introduce your dear fiancées to them."

Anna blinked. Surely she had heard incorrectly. "Fiancées? As in plural?"

Aunt Deirdre frowned. "Plural? What do you mean?"

"You said fiancées," Anna said, her heart sinking.

"Of course, dear," Aunt Deirdre said, beaming. "I would never forget you and Roark. How could you think I would?"

"Aunt Deirdre," Terrence said, frowning, "you should not have done that."

"Why, dear?" Aunt Deirdre said, her expression confused. "A dance is quite the most acceptable way to introduce the brides to the village. We don't wish to wait until the weddings."

"Plural again!" Anna exclaimed.

"I beg pardon?" Aunt Deirdre asked.

"You said brides," Anna said.

"Of course," Aunt Deirdre said. "But what is this plural?"

Anna, feeling a rage fueled with fear, looked desperately at Terrence. "Terrence, please explain the word to her."

"Plural means more than one, Aunt."

"No!" Anna started.

"I was certain that's what it meant," Terrence said, frowning.

"It does," Anna said, sensing her sanity slipping. "I mean that she believes there will be two weddings!"

Terrence flushed. "Oh, yes. That."

"Yes, that," Anna said angrily. "Roark and I are not going to be married. We told you so, just this morning."

Aunt Deirdre's face fell. "Oh, dear, you two have not settled your lovers' tiff yet?"

"Lovers' tiff?" Anna exclaimed. "It is not a lovers' tiff."

"Dear, I know you are angry at this moment," Aunt Deirdre said, her face concerned. "But whatever is the matter between you and Roark can be resolved. It only takes patience and love."

"There is nothing between us, and there is no love," Anna seethed.

Tears welled in Aunt Deirdre's eyes. "Please do not break my boy's heart again. You have brought him back to life. Do not hurt him."

"I-I . . ." Anna expelled a frustrated breath. "I have not done anything of the sort."

"Talk to him," Aunt Deirdre said. "Please work this out."

"Very well," Anna said, her eyes narrowing. She stood abruptly. "I will talk to him. This moment, in fact. Where is he?"

"He must be in the tower," Aunt Deirdre said, then

glanced over to Salome. "Dear, do show Anna to the tower."

Salome appeared to shake. "The tower, Miss Deirdre?"

"Yes, do be a good girl," Aunt Deirdre said. "I should escort Anna, I know, but I would also like my beef Wellington. It is very special."

"But the tower?" Salome wailed.

Aunt Deirdre frowned. "I know Roark never wishes to be disturbed when he is working, but this is more important. Do show her."

"Yes, Miss Deirdre," Salome said. Shaking, she turned to Anna, her gaze as frightened as if she were preparing to lead Anna to the executioner. "Right this way."

Anna felt a sudden qualm, but anger pushed it away. "Thank you. If you will excuse me."

Silence reigned as they departed. Anna, seething, followed Salome, who rattled her rosary beads and whispered a litany of pleas. The maid let loose her beads but a moment to pick up a candle before leading Anna into the long gallery.

Unlike the previous day, Salome did not trundle along at breakneck speed. Despite her turmoil, Anna could not resist glancing at the fine paintings upon the wall. She halted with a gasp when her gaze fell upon one.

"What is it, miss?" Salome said, her eyes wide and frightened. Surprisingly, she did not burst into tears.

Anna, however, felt she might become a watering pot at any moment. There, painted to the exact detail, was the man whose spirit she had seen. Oh, if only she had viewed it the day before! She wouldn't be in such a predicament. She might have realized she was seeing Charles Seeton, the ghost, and not Roark Seeton masquerading as said infamous ghost. She would have then

been aware how strong the family features ran through
the generations. She would not have dashed after a
ghost to Roark's bedroom. Then they would not have
been discovered . . . and then . . . Anna sighed. She
had enough troubles without turning into a bedlamite
with the hopelessness of *what ifs* and *if thens*. Such could
only lead to madness.

"Nothing. Nothing at all, Salome. Proceed."

Salome nodded and they continued. They once again
ascended the wide stone stairs, only this time turning
onto one of the narrower stairways curving off from it.

Salome halted and turned. "This will lead you to the
turret." She leaned close, handing Anna the candle.
"Pray. Pray."

Anna narrowed her eyes. "Why?"

Salome's voice fell to a whisper. "It is *the* turret. It is
where the ghost took his own life."

"He wasn't a ghost at the time," Anna said, despite
herself. Salome blinked. "Oh, never mind."

She brushed past Salome and followed the winding
stair until she reached a heavy door of hefty oak slats
banded crosswise with iron rods. She swung the door
wide open. She entered a darkened chamber smelling
of mildew and old wood. A solitary threadlike beam of
light confined itself to one small inky portion of the
room, where it had dared to trespass through a moth-
eaten hole in the heavy black sacking nailed over a narrow slit of a window. Each of more than a dozen such
windows were likewise covered along the stone wall
curving around the circumference of the chamber.
Anna held her candle aloft and peered around, spying
Roark across the chamber. He was bent over a huge
scope set onto a wood scaffold built into an embrasure
leading to the battlements.

She stepped gingerly across the rough wooden floor-
boards, cautious of the wood pegs that had over the

years swelled outward with moisture above the floor-boards creating stumbling blocks she all too soon discovered. "My lord, you must speak to your aunt. She is crazy."

Roark glanced up at her, then turned his gaze back to the scope. "You say she is crazy? You are the one who has seen a ghost. Blow out the candle."

Anna started back. "I beg your pardon?"

"Blow out the candle. It distracts."

Anna, disgruntled, blew out the candle. Moonlight filtered into the turret. Without the candles glow, it suddenly felt eerie. "You know, this is very macabre."

"What is?" Roark asked.

"You studying up here," Anna said. "Where the ghost—I mean Charles Seeton—killed himself."

"The tower is the best height and angle for me to study the stars," Roark said. He made an adjustment upon his scope. An odd smile hovered upon his lips. "It also ensures me privacy. Very few venture to come here."

Anna stared at Roark. The man had chosen this room on purpose. It was one more barrier against the rest of humanity. "I see."

"What did you want?"

Anna drew in her breath. "Do you know what your aunt did?"

"No, I do not know what my aunt did. But I take it I am to find out—that is, if I am to continue while the moon is still aloft.

"She has invited the entire village to a dance to introduce Beth and me to them."

"That is nice," Roark said, his tone distracted.

"As your and Terrence's fiancées," Anna barked with force. "Plural!"

"I see," Roark said.

Anna's mouth fell open. "Is that all you can say?"

"Hush," Roark murmured, his gaze glued to the scope. "This is important."

"Important!" Anna gasped. "What could be more important than the fact that your aunt has announced our engagement?"

Roark glanced over to her. He stepped from the scope. "Look."

Anna studied him suspiciously, then peered through the telescope. She gasped. A luminous sphere appeared before her vision. She gazed and gazed at it. "It is beautiful."

"The sphere you see is only visible at this time," Roark said in a soft voice. "Once every century."

"Gracious!" Anna said. "Truly?"

"Truly," Roark said with gentle amusement.

"But why?" Anna asked.

"Because it is the only time in its orbit that it draws close enough to the earth to be visible."

"And most people still don't see it," Anna whispered, mesmerized, "Or even know about it."

"No, they don't," Roark said. "Each star has its own shape and color. Each follows its course, its revolution, even if it takes a century."

"I see now why you study the stars. They are so beautiful and pristine in their orderly course," Anna said softly. She thought of Charles Seeton, who had flung himself out of the same opening from which she was blessed to view a beautiful orb set on its course, decade after decade, to arrive at this appointed place and time once a century. She sighed. "While life is so unset, so unpredictable, so . . . so fleeting." She drew in a deep breath and turned toward Roark. She no longer wanted to view such distant beauty. "Thank you for permitting me to see this."

Roark stared at her, a strange look in his eyes. He

stepped close, and his hand just slightly brushed her arm. "I will talk to Aunt Deirdre. Do not worry."

Roark strolled into the breakfast room. Everyone was assembled. The conversation died, and all looked toward him in surprise.

He smiled. "Whatever could be the matter? You are acting as if you've seen the ghost."

"Close enough to it," Terrence said, grinning.

"No, the ghost has a beard," Anna claimed, smiling sweetly.

Roark chuckled as he took up his chair.

Aunt Deirdre sighed. "It is so nice to have you with us, dear."

"Indeed," Roark said. With Anna's eyes directly upon him, he smiled. "I heard you partook of a very busy day yesterday, Aunt."

"I did," Aunt Deirdre said, nodding with excitement.

"Anna informs me you invited everyone to a dance to introduce Anna as my fiancée."

"Also to introduce dear Beth as well," Aunt Deirdre said. She cast a beaming look to Beth, who blushed. "We certainly cannot overlook her."

"Indeed," Roark said. "Especially since she is the only bride there will be in the family."

Aunt Deirdre's face fell. Her gaze skittered from Roark to Anna. Tears welled up in her eyes. "Oh, dear. You two have not settled your disagreement."

"There is no disagreement," Roark said. "In fact, that is the one thing we do agree upon. There will be no wedding between us."

"But you two love each other," Aunt Deirdre said.

"We don't," Anna said.

"Yes, you do," Aunt Deirdre said.

"No, we don't," Anna repeated. She then bit her lip and cast Roark a frustrated, helpless look.

Roark frowned severely at Aunt Deirdre. "No, we don't. And there is no reason for us to do so. What you thought you saw yesterday morning was completely circumstantial. Moreover, totally innocent. I did not compromise Anna in any way whatsoever. If you had not seen fit to announce the engagement, this all could have been ignored for the ridiculous incident it was."

"But it was not a ridiculous incident," Aunt Deirdre objected.

"Yes, it was," Roark said. "But in either respect, it certainly should have been held within the confines of the family. If Anna and I had intended to announce our engagement, it should have been our prerogative."

Aunt Deirdre turned white. "I am so sorry, dear. I hadn't considered. I was only so pleased and excited you two had found love."

"We have not found love," Roark snapped. "Good God, Aunt, we just met!"

"I know," Aunt Deirdre said, nodding. "But love can happen within a moment. I am sure that is what happened to you, and for you to deny it would be terrible." A sob escaped her.

"Please don't cry, Aunt Deirdre," Beth said in a watery voice. "Please don't."

"But it makes me so sad," Aunt Deirdre said, another sob escaping her.

"I know," Beth said. She burst into tears. "It makes me sad too."

"Beth!" Anna exclaimed, utter shock upon her face.

"I'm sorry, Anna," Beth cried. "But you were"—she lowered her voice—"in bed with him."

"But nothing happened!" Anna shouted.

"I know, or at least I think I know. Oh, I am so confused," Beth wailed. "Between the ghost and seeing you with Roark, I am just so confused. You were right. We should never have come here." She jumped from her chair and dashed from the room. "Never!"

"I am so sorry," Aunt Deirdre rose, shaking her head. "Look what I have done!" She too fled from the room sobbing.

Terrence, his face grim, stood. "Now look what you have done."

Roark started. "What *I* have done?"

"I have always believed you to be an honorable man," Terrence said stiffly. He turned on his heel and stalked from the room.

Roark cast a glance at Anna. "I certainly did not handle that well."

"You said what had to be said," Anna said, her tone firm.

Roark laughed. "Indeed, but apparently not diplomatically. I fear that such is not my long suit."

A slight smile twitched at Anna's lips. "No, I believe not."

The door to the breakfast room burst open. Roark glanced up, then stifled a curse. There stood Clarise Bentford, becomingly framed in the pointed arch of the doorway. He had not seen her for over three months, but she was as stunningly beautiful as always. She was decked in an emerald green morning dress; its copious deep green flounces enhanced her deep green eyes and luxuriant, perfectly coiffed red hair. Her eyes glittered with anger and her magnificent chest heaved.

"You lying bastard!" Claire cried.

Roark heard Anna gasp, her normally calm hazel eyes were wide and shocked. Roark grimaced and stood. "Good morning, Clarise."

"You told me you would never marry," Clarise said, stalking into the room like a hungry lioness. "You lied to me."

"I did not lie," Roark said.

"I gave you my heart, my soul, my body," Clarise said, flinging out a hand wildly. "I even begged you to marry me."

"Clarise, do not be so dramatic," Roark said sharply. Her tendency to overreact was one of the reasons he had broken the liaison with Clarise. She enjoyed a fierce temper.

"You told me you would never marry," Clarise said. "That is what you said. You said you would never give your heart away again."

"If you will excuse me," Anna murmured, rising.

Clarise spun around. Her eyes narrowed to feline slits. "Who are you?"

"I'm nobody in particular," Anna said, flushing. "Roark—I mean, His Grace can explain."

"You are the one!" Clarise said. "Aren't you?"

"Who?" Anna asked.

Clarise stalked up to her. The difference between the two women was impossible to overlook. Manicured and attired in the highest kick of fashion to accent her vivid coloring and curvaceous form, Clarise was perfection itself. Anna, in turn, wore a serviceable dove gray muslin tied with a single soft-apricot ribbon below a bodice encompassing a neat, adequate figure.

"You! You are the fiancée."

"No, I'm not," Anna said. "That is what Roark can explain."

"He doesn't need to," Clarise said, laughing. " 'Tis clear why he is marrying you."

"It is?" Anna asked, blinking.

"Of course," Clarise said. "It is for your money."

"Oh, no," Anna said. "It wouldn't be for my money, he has—"

"Of course it is. Don't expect to gull me," Clarise purred. "It surely isn't for your beauty."

"Clarise!" Roark barked. Her scathing remark reminded him of the other reason he had broken off their liaison. Clarise was a bitch.

Clarise turned and glared at him. "Well? You cannot make me believe it is. I didn't just fall from the hay wagon!"

"He isn't trying to make you believe so," Anna said. Her voice was small and dignified, but it was clear she had shrunk into herself. "You do not understand—"

"That it was love at first sight for us," Roark interrupted as a sudden anger flared through him. Anna had not appeared a wilting violet in any of their confrontations, but now she timidly bowed before this cat.

"What!" Clarise screeched.

"What?" Anna gasped.

"Anna seduced me," Roark claimed, moving quickly around the table.

"I did not!" she yelped.

"With her beauty," Roark finished and smiled wickedly at Clarise.

Clarise all but choked in rage. "Impossible!"

"No, not impossible," Roark said, coming to stand beside Anna. "I desired her from the moment I saw her."

The expression upon both women's faces were priceless. Both were equally stupefied and disoriented. Roark bit back a laugh. He hauled a limp Anna to his side. If she would not stand up for herself, he would do it for her.

"I cannot wait until we are wed."

"But we are not—" Anna whispered.

Roark took immediate action. He bent and sealed the truth upon her lips with a firm kiss. He took in the very breath of her intended words so swiftly did he kiss her. Then he took in more, much more. He took in the feel of her stunned, pliant body, which fit the very curve of his arms. He took in a sweet, electrifying taste from her lips beneath his. An emotion, undefined and as vast as the stars he loved to study, overwhelmed him.

Almost desperately, without thought or intention, he drew her body closer to his, bending it to his lines. He deepened the kiss, seeking the vastness, filled with the excitement he felt before finally seeing a new star or a shooting comet. Only that too disappeared as all too human sensations teased him. He could feel the fabric of Anna's sensible dress with the heat of her body beneath it. He could taste innocence, yet with a passion as strong as the ages, upon her lips. The scent and very essence of the woman filled him.

Desire—earthy, strong, and hot—flared through him. It coursed and thrummed through his veins, racking his body. It was all too close, all too alive. Her body, her emotions, just . . . her. He agonizingly tore his lips from Anna and pushed her away.

"Insanity," he said.

Anna stood a moment; then she tottered over to a chair before the breakfast table and fell onto it. Her eyes were dazed, wide, and passion filled.

"You *are* insane," Clarise said.

Roark blinked. He was suddenly brought back to earth. No, earth was the moment before, when stars and comets that arrived once in a century did not matter. Earth was the moment before, when he found exhilaration in a once in a lifetime experience. No, he was back to reality. He shook his head to clear his thoughts. His lips became firm. Only the taste of Anna was still upon them. He clenched his jaw and focused on Clarise. Her face was mottled, her beauty distorted by anger. He forced a smile. "Yes, I am."

"That you could want her, love her, instead of me," Clarise said, her eyes hard as the gemstones they resembled. "Look at her!"

Roark couldn't look at Anna. Not after that kiss. Not when desire ran through him as it did.

"You are supposed to marry me," Clarise said lowly. "I am beautiful! Not her!"

A sound like the wind filled the room. The temperature dropped swiftly.

"No, not again," Anna groaned.

"What?" Clarise asked. "What is this?"

The wind appeared to circle about Clarise and only Clarise. Her skirts twirled. Then her perfectly coiffed hair appeared to lose its pins. It flew straight up and out, strand by strand, as does a cat's when attacked. One untoward hank of hair thwacked the center of her face. Since her mouth was wide open expounding curses only a Newhaven sailor would employ, she appeared ludicrous, whipped by her luxuriant locks, which were her pride and joy.

She spat and shouted a few more blasphemies to the good Lord and every other creature upon the planet. She turned and struggled to the door, the wind buffeting her. At the last second, her back skirts were blown up, exposing her stockings, garters, and fine silken drawers. In effect, the wind was a definite boot to Clarise's backside.

Roark, overcome, doubled over with laughter. "What a draft there is today."

"How can you laugh?" Anna said, appearing ruffled. Roark wondered how Clarise could call Anna anything but pretty. Not beautiful, no. But with a flush high upon her cheeks, and warm embarrassment in her eyes, she was adorable. "It is not amusing."

"I don't know," Roark admitted, chuckling. "For once, I must agree with Charles. Clarise deserved it."

"I'm not talking about that," Anna snapped.

"You aren't?" Roark asked.

"You told Clarise we are going to be married! You

confirmed it rather than denied it. And after you . . . you . . ." She halted, her flush deepening.

Roark grinned. "I kissed you? Yes?"

"Well . . . well . . ." Anna said.

"Well what?" Roark asked.

"She may very well believe it," Anna said. "You've only agitated—I mean aggravated—the situation."

"I know," Roark said. He stifled another laugh. He couldn't help it. He felt more lighthearted than he had in years.

"What are we going to do?" Anna almost wailed.

Roark shrugged. "My advice is that we stop fighting it."

"What?" Anna sprung up. "Are you insane?"

"Perhaps. I believe it is catching," Roark said, his lips twitching. "But at this moment, everyone is far too fraught over it all. I suggest we go along with the engagement."

"What?" Anna gasped.

"For the present," Roark said. "Only until after Beth and Terrence are married. Then we can break it off."

Anna's eyes were wide with shock. "You are actually suggesting that we pretend to be affianced?"

"We won't need to pretend," Roark said. When Anna flushed deeply and looked away, he knew she was thinking of the kiss. A surge of pure male satisfaction filled him. It was clear that his kiss had unsettled her far more than any of the other strange happenings had to date. "What I mean is, it appears, no matter how we act, the family believes we should marry. Surely within these two months they will have time to see it is anything but true, and they will approve when we do break the engagement."

"Perhaps," Anna said, biting her lip. She looked at him with clear reproach. "But that won't happen if you . . . if you . . ."

"If I kiss you," Roark said in a helpful tone.

"Yes," Anna said. Her chin tilted up. "You gave Clarise the wrong impression."

Roark grinned. "I know I did."

Anna's eyes narrowed. "You are doing this simply to escape her, aren't you?"

"No," Roark said. "I had already *escaped* her months ago. I don't know why she felt it necessary to come here and enact this scene."

"She's in love with you," Anna said. "And you broke her heart."

"I did not," Roark said. "She knew exactly what kind of liaison it was. I never offered marriage."

Anna gasped. "You rake!"

"Rake?" Roark asked. He exploded into laughter.

"Yes, rake," Anna said, her tone totally offended. "You have fooled everyone. They think you a recluse and a woman-hater, but you are nothing more than a rake in sheep's clothing."

"Am I?" Roark asked blandly.

"Yes," Anna said. Her eyes narrowed. "And I'm not sure I want to aid and abet you in any fashion."

Roark smiled. "Then what are we to do? Keep Aunt Deirdre and Beth in constant tears?"

Total frustration washed Anna's face. "No, I suppose you are right. We must wait until this storm has blown over." She flushed. "So to speak. But then, no matter what, we will end our engagement."

"Most definitely," Roark said.

Anna looked at him suspiciously. "This is still not funny. The way things are transpiring, we could end up forced into marriage."

"No. Even if we went down the aisle, I'm sure ancestor Charles would appear to rescue us." He looked at Anna calculatingly. "Hmm, he's never blown a bride's skirts up before. It might just be worth having the ceremony to see that."

"Rake!" Anna gasped, then quickly left the room.

Roark sat down and laughed once more. Yes, indeed. He hadn't felt so lighthearted in years.

Four

Anna slammed the door shut to her room and leaned against it, expelling a frustrated sigh. Never had she been happier to escape a dinner table. Her lips ached—literally ached—from being forced to smile.

Roark had taken the situation in hand and had not only apologized to the family for upsetting them, but had informed them that their disagreement had been settled. Anna and Roark were indeed engaged, but wished for a longer engagement due to the circumstances. They also suggested that preparing for one wedding at a time might be the best. Furthermore, they did not wish to overshadow the wedding of Beth and Terrence in any manner.

Anna shook her head. If she hadn't seen it, she would never have believed it. The family, Beth included, had swallowed his story, lock, stock, and barrel. They had exclaimed and congratulated them in sheer, unquestioning delight. How they could have accepted such twaddle, and with such credence, Anna could not comprehend.

"It's him," Anna murmured, anger welling up within her.

They all trusted and believed in Roark. She could understand how Aunt Deirdre and Terrence wished to see Roark married, even to the point of ignoring all logic. However, Beth had been no better. She had hugged Anna and whispered that she could marry happily, secure in the knowledge that Anna would not be left alone. That Anna's marriage would be within Beth's new family only made it all the better.

Anna flushed. She had never even known such had been a concern of Beth's. She accepted that the years had past her by. Indeed, by society's standards she was clearly on the shelf. Raising Beth, though, had been a worthy and sufficient enough goal. In truth, Anna had refused to consider her own future. Apparently, her younger sister had not, though Beth was far wide of the mark if she thought Roark to be Anna's future. She had no way of knowing Roark was nothing but a rake in disguise.

"Oh, that man!" Anna stormed across room to the cherry-wood armoire.

"Which man?" a deep voice queried from behind.

Anna squeaked and spun around. Ancestor Charles sat negligently upon her bed. It was rather unsettling. He left no impression upon the mattress where he rested. "Oh, it's you. You frightened me."

Charles chuckled. "Good. I was beginning to think nothing frightened you." He turned, lifted his legs onto the bed, and rested his back against the headboard. "Who is *that* man? Me or Roark?"

"Roark," Anna declared angrily.

"Ah, I thought it might be me." Charles sighed. "Thrown into the shade by my own blood, b'gad."

"No," Anna pronounced, glaring at him. "You are *that* ghost!"

Charles grinned as if extremely proud of himself. "Am I?"

"Yes," Anna said. "You both behaved abominably this morning."

"Not I," Charles said. "That redheaded she-devil of

a wench deserved what she got and more. A harlot and termagant if I have ever seen one."

Anna flushed, but decided it would be useless to castigate a man more than two hundred years old upon the use of his language. "That shrew was Roark's, er, lady."

"Lady? Anything but," Charles quipped, laughing. He arched his brow. "Is that what has you in a pother?"

"Yes," Anna said. She jumped. "I mean no!"

"You mean yes," Charles said, grinning. "Od's blood, woman, what did you expect?"

"I expected more proper behavior," Anna retorted. "Everyone thinks Roark a recluse who spurns women."

"Recluse he may be," Charles said. "But he ain't a monk, thank God."

"No, he's a rake," Anna retorted.

"A rake?" Charles asked. Languidly, he stretched out his legs, crossing them at the ankles. He picked up a pillow, plumped it, and stuffed it behind his back—an all-too-human action, odd in that the pillow showed no reaction. He folded his hands behind his head and reclined back, looking for all the world like a pasha in his harem.

Anna started. Even in a satin doublet and those ridiculous, voluminous breeches, he looked extremely like Roark. She flushed. "I would appreciate it if you would not make free with my bed in such a manner."

Charles brow rose. "S'death, but you are a prude."

"I am not!" Anna snapped. When Charles suddenly disappeared, Anna blinked in disbelief.

"Yes, you are," Charles's voice said. Anna gasped and turned to see him sitting upon the chair. His legs were crossed, and he held one wrist up in a dainty manner. "Is this better?"

"No, it isn't," Anna retorted, her eyes narrowed.

"For shame," Charles said, his tone reproachful. "I but strive to please, lass."

"What a clanker," Anna sputtered. When Charles raised his brow, Anna said in clarification, "That means a lie."

"I know what you meant," Charles said, laughing. "I am privy to all the changes in the Kings English, I assure you. You could say it has been a study of mine for quite some time. Though this is the first chance I've been able to speak it with anyone."

"What?" Anna frowned.

"Only you, lady, have been able to see me and talk to me," Charles said. "Except at the occasional wedding or two, that is. 'Tis an event I have no control over." He chuckled. "And no one ever remains to converse."

"What a fortunate woman I am," Anna said bitterly.

"So you are," Charles said, laughing. "I am glad to help you in any way I can."

"Help me?" Anna said. "You've done everything but help me. Only look what your malicious pranks have caused. Now I must pretend I am engaged to *that man!*"

"As I said, I but strive to please."

"I am not pleased to pretend to be engaged to that rake," Anna argued, stomping her foot.

"Now who is telling *clankers, whoppers, taradiddles,*" Charles asked, demonstrating his command of the King's English to its fullest. *"Balderdash?"*

"Enough," Anna groaned.

"I saw that lusty kiss between you and Roark," Charles said, his eyes gleaming. "You cannot say he does not stir your blood, mistress."

Anna stared at Charles. Roark had more than stirred her blood—he had turned it into molten lava. What his kiss had done to the rest of her parts, she most certainly did not wish to discuss further. She lifted her chin and dredged up as much dignity as possible. "That is of no significance."

"No significance?" Charles hooted. "Forsooth, woman. I'm the one who's supposed to be dead. Such passions ain't common. 'Twas obvious with you two, even upon the stairs." He chuckled. " 'Twas hot enough. Bgad, I thought it benevolent of me to cool it down for you."

"That is not true," Anna said.

"Yes, it is."

"Very well," Anna said in exasperation. "I do not care what you think. The simple truth is Roark and I do not like each other. He's a rake!"

"Gads, woman, do have done with that," Charles said. "Just what other kind of man would you wish? Never say you want some puling infant who doesn't know what to do with a woman."

Anna flushed. "What I want or do not want in a man is none of your concern."

"I have not much else to concern myself with at the moment," Charles retaliated, grinning. "Plenty of time on my hands as 'twere."

Anna choked. "I do not wish my life turned upside down merely because a ghost is bored.

" 'Tis that kind of manner which has kept you *just the sister,*" Charles said in a mimicking tone, "and not a bride."

Anna sucked in a bitter breath. Charles had sheared too close to the bone. "I am very sorry you have too much time on your hands. Indeed, I am sorry you killed yourself and *are* a ghost, but I refuse to be your entertainment."

"I did not kill myself," Charles roared.

Anna started back. "What?"

"You heard me fine and well, lass," Charles said, his eyes shooting sparks. "I am not now, and never have been, such a cowardly weakling as to take my own life. Such a grievous sin I would not commit."

"You didn't?" Anna asked, her voice thin.

"I did not," Charles said. He stood, the sound of wind rushing through the chamber. "I was pushed from that turret. And if I had seen the craven blackguard who did it, 'tis he who I would have haunted and tormented into the very bowels of hell."

Anna, stunned, tottered to the bed and sat down. "I am sorry."

"Sorry?" Charles said, his voice low. "No, mistress. You do not know what sorry is. 'Tis I who am bound. 'Tis I who neither live with the living nor find the rest of the dead. I had thought there to be at least heaven or hell. I would take either, madam, over what existence I suffer now."

Unwanted tears stung Anna's eyes. "That is why you remain then. You cannot rest until you know who your murderer was. You cannot rest until your honor is restored."

The fire left Charles's eyes. "Sounds like rot to me."

Anna blinked, then a sudden giggle escaped her. "Oh, I am sorry. Ah, I mean, forgive me."

A wry grin crossed Charles's face. "No, forgive me, lass. I have been surly and rude."

"It is understandable," Anna said. She frowned. "We must find out who murdered you."

"We?" Charles asked, raising a brow.

"Of course," Anna said, her mind racing. "That is what holds you here to be sure. Once we discover who it was and can let the world know you did not commit suicide, you will be free."

A solemn expression crossed Charles face. "I do not think the world will care anymore." He offered her a courtly leg. "But I thank you, mistress, that you do. I have not had someone care for me in a very long time."

A bitter laugh escaped him. "Even in life, those I thought cared did not. But finding my murderer might release me from this torment, and if you can help, I would be forever grateful."

Charles disappeared and Anna hoped he had truly left, for tears she could not stop streamed down her face.

Anna finished her breakfast in a state of abstraction. All the previous night her dreams had been filled with phantom murderers of Charles Seeton.

"Anna, are you feeling well?" Beth asked in concern.

"Yes, dearest," Aunt Deirdre said. "You have been frightfully quiet."

Anna bit her lip as she noticed all eyes were turned upon her. Aunt Deirdre's and Beth's were deep with concern. Terrence's were curious. Roark's were unreadable. Where to start? She drew in a breath. "I fear I must tell you something."

"What dearest?" Aunt Deirdre asked.

"What?" Beth asked.

Anna looked at Beth, who appeared nervous. After debating a moment, Anna firmed her resolve. "Charles appeared to me last night."

"Charles?" Aunt Deirdre asked, bemused.

"The ghost," Beth moaned.

"So you are on a first-name basis with him now?" Roark asked, raising a cynical brow.

Anna glared at him. "Yes, and he didn't kill himself. Someone murdered him."

"Good gracious!" Aunt Deirdre exclaimed. "Never say so."

"Yes," Anna said, focusing her attention on the tiny lady, who alone was the only one not staring at her as if she had lost her mind. "That is why he haunts the castle."

"Oh, the poor man," Aunt Deirdre said, her tone sympathetic.

"Poor man?" Roark asked, his tone dry.

"Yes," Aunt Deirdre said. "It is one thing to be forced to haunt this earth because of something you've done, but it seems grossly unfair to have to haunt it due to someone else's misdeeds."

"My thoughts exactly," Anna said eagerly. "We must discover who killed him."

"Good Lord," Roark said, rolling his eyes heavenward.

"But how?" Aunt Deirdre asked, frowning.

"I don't know," Anna said, frowning. "That is the problem."

"Indeed," Roark said, snorting. "Solving a two-hundred-year-old murder, if there was a murder . . ."

"If?" Anna asked, glaring.

Roark shrugged. "You are taking the word of a ghost—and one who seems to be overly capricious, I might add."

"Now, dear," Aunt Deirdre said. "You cannot say that. He always seems to know what he is about. He's never been wrong when he's appeared at the weddings."

Roark's face darkened. "No, he hasn't."

"So why would he be wrong in what he is telling Anna now?" Deirdre said, her tone reasonable. "But just how can we help him?"

"I thought I would first study any family records you have," Anna answered.

"Family records?" Aunt Deirdre asked.

"Good luck," Roark said, laughing.

Anna cast him an angry frown, then returned her gaze to Deirdre. "Where do you keep them?"

"Well . . ." Deirdre said, then halted in contemplation. After a moment, she sighed. "I'd say they are in no particular place."

"What do you mean?" Anna asked.

"They are most likely everywhere," Aunt Deirdre said.

"What Aunt Deirdre means," Roark said, his words dripping with condescension, "is that our forebears have never been historians. We haven't kept tidy records over the past hundred or so years in anticipation of solving the murder of one of our ancestors."

Anna expelled a breath. She was appearing stupid, and it didn't help to have Roark point out her shortcomings so adroitly. "I did not expect that. I was only attempting to determine a place to start looking."

Roark leaned back in his chair, then waved expansively. "Have at it. Our castle is your castle. Accept it as being at your disposal. Every crumbling crevice."

Anna's chin jutted out. "Thank you very much for you kindness. I will accept your munificent offer."

Roark's face turned thunderous. "Don't be a widgeon. You can't hope to discover anything of purpose."

"I can try," Anna said.

"Very well." Roark stood. "If you will excuse me, I have work to do. Do come and tell me when you've discovered that signed confession—you know, the one left by Charles Seeton's murderer. I'm sure you'll discover it in some priest's hole or perhaps in the dungeon."

"You have one?" Anna asked, amazed.

"Of course," Roark said dryly. "We wouldn't want to disappoint you." Then he turned and walked from the room.

"Do you need our assistance today, Anna?" Aunt Deirdre asked, her tone hesitant. "We had thought to go into the village. I wanted dear Beth to look at Mrs. Brewster's pattern cards."

Anna flushed. "No, of course not. But if you do not mind, I would like to remain here."

"I understand," Aunt Deirdre said. "You are such a kindhearted soul. Salome can help you if you wish."

Anna winced, then forced a smile. "Thank you. I'm sure she will be of great assistance."

Roark sighed and threw down the chart he had been studying. No, truth be told, it was the chart he had merely been staring at unheeded for the past thirty minutes. Blast and damn, he wasn't accomplishing anything. His mind persisted in straying to Anna. The woman was beyond crazy. She not only claimed to have seen the ghost, but believed she was holding heartfelt conversations with him.

Granted, Roark could no longer deny that the unexplained phenomena occurring periodically might as well be accepted as the ghost of Charles Seeton. There was far too much human motive and personality behind the activities that had been transpiring to see them as random phenomena—not to mention the fact that Charles Seeton appeared to have too wicked a humor to keep it impersonal.

Yet Anna was the only one who claimed she could see Charles Seeton. Was such a claim real as well? Or was only part of it real and the other portion of it an extension of Anna's overactive imagination? Did she really believe Charles Seeton have been murdered? Worse, did she really believe she could uncover who had committed a murder two hundred years earlier?

"Harebrained, totally harebrained," he muttered to himself.

Roark stood abruptly, then halted. Why had he stood? He frowned. Realization struck. He was going to find Anna. He shook his head. Why? He knew the answer.

It wasn't safe for her to be scouring the castle alone. Faith, there were places he and the family hadn't been in years. There could be danger for her.

He laughed when he realized that she could get lost and never find her way back to daylight. He had best see to her.

Anna sat upon an old trunk, squinting at a spidery script sprawled across a yellowed parchment. Furniture cluttered the large chamber; some of it was so old that both its design and intended use were a curiosity. The rough stone floor—at least the patches of it that could be seen beneath the mounds of discarded items—was layered with dust. Moth-eaten tapestries lay beside even more moth-eaten clothes. Chamber pots were toppled next to rusty swords and dented armor.

Anna had grinned in delight when she'd discovered the lofty, cavernous room. Salome had indeed been of service in bringing her here, though both of them had been mightily winded after the several long flights of stairs. Anna had thought carefully upon the matter and decided that, if the Seetons were true to most of humanity, unwanted items deemed as requiring too much effort to destroy generally migrated to either the bowels or to the rafters of an establishment. Since Roark had mentioned that the bowels of this establishment consisted of dungeons, she had assumed the equivalent of the rafters of a castle would be the place to begin.

Anna giggled. Even castles apparently had attics. No doubt in earlier times, this cavernous room had performed a more strategic and furious purpose than the storing of ancient clutter, but at present it was merely that. She could envision vats of heated oil raised to the rafters to be let loose down upon the walls of the castle keep. Today no large vats were to be spied; but true to a family that kept a ghost hanging around, the Seetons had also kept everything else around. Aunt Deirdre was more right than Anna had first thought. The records of this family were certainly all over the keep.

She refocused her attention to the parchment before her. Her eyes widened and a blush rose to her cheeks. A surprised laugh escaped her. She read on avidly, chuckling despite herself.

"What do you find so amusing?" a deep voice asked.

Anna tensed and looked up. Roark stood between a rotted oak highboy and a crumpled mass of plate mail. She blushed to a fiery red. For once she would have preferred it if it had been Charles popping in on her. Unwittingly, her hands quickly covered the parchment. She frowned. "What are you doing here?"

Roark grinned. "I came to help you."

A surprised, and very unladylike, snort escaped Anna. "Indeed?"

Roark frowned. "I realized that it is not safe for you to be left alone."

"You consider me to be that dangerously insane?" Anna asked, galled to her very bones.

"No," Roark said. "But there are portions—indeed a vast terrain of this castle—that have not been tended for years and could be unsafe." As he gazed about, a smile, quite pleased and smug, crossed his lips. "I am correct. You have found such a place."

Anna clenched her teeth. "I thought it a very likely place to discover old records. And I believe I am quite safe. I am sure I do not need your protection."

Roark grinned and leaned against the highboy. When the highboy tottered, he straightened up. "You never know."

"I do," Anna said. "I would imagine a ghost to be the most dangerous thing about and I have already met yours. He does not mean me any harm."

Roark's eyes darkened. "Nor do I. That is why I am here to watch over you."

"I do not need you to watch over me. I shall do fine by myself."

Roark studied her closely. When his gaze fell to the parchment in her hand, his brow rose. "Have you found the murderers confession already? How callous for you to be laughing over it."

"I-I . . ." Anna bit her lip. "It is not a confession."

"What do you have?" Roark asked, walking toward her.

Anna clamped the parchment tightly to her lap. "Nothing. Now will you please leave? I assure you, I am perfectly safe and I most definitely do not need your help."

"Do let me see," Roark coaxed.

"No."

Roark grinned and said in a firm voice, "As lord of this castle, I wish to see what you have found."

Quicker than Anna expected, he leaned over and snatched the parchment from her. She would have clutched to it, but respect for its fragile antiquity froze her fingers.

Roark cast her a teasing glance. "Thank you ever so much."

Anna, flushing as he turned his attention to the paper, stood quickly. She scuttled away, determined to distance herself from the situation.

Roark broke into laughter when he reached the identical section of the page that Anna had been perusing. "Why, Anna, you have fooled me. I thought you were interested in poetry and romantic high flights. Now I discover this is what you read."

"I only read it to see what it was," Anna objected.

"And you were laughing over it," Roark said, knowingly. "You are not the prude I thought."

"I am not a prude. You Seeton men are all alike."

"We Seeton men?"

"You are no better than your ancestor," Anna said.

Roark's eyes flashed with amusement. "Never say ancestor Charles called you a prude as well."

"It is of no consequence," Anna claimed stiffly.

Roark laughed. "He did then! I grow to respect him more and more."

"I am not a prude," Anna said. "It is your family that is . . . licentious. That piece was written by some lecherous ancestor of yours."

Roark studied the paper again. "Why so it was. One Elliott Seeton. Like the rest of us Seeton men, he was rather talented."

"Talented!" Anna exclaimed. "You are not talented. You are just all rakes!"

"But that takes talent," Roark grinned.

Anna clenched her teeth. "It does not. Now if you will excuse me, I have work to do." She all but tromped through the clutter before her. "I do not need you."

Her words were cut off. Where Anna expected stone floor, she found rotted wood beneath the blanket of dust—indeed, splintering rotted wood. It cracked and groaned, and suddenly Anna was falling. She felt as if she were falling for a lifetime, which was ridiculous since a lifetime would have prepared her for the jolt of landing upon hard stone again.

"Anna, are you all right?" Roark's voice called.

Anna blinked. She was sitting in a square room formed completely of stone: a stone slab floor, four craggy walls with no windows or doors, and a stone ceiling arching upward to the remains of the wood panel she had fallen through. Wincing, she peered up to Roark. Thank God, she could see him above, peering back down at her. "What? Where am I? What is this?"

"Are you all right?" Roark repeated.

Anna blinked again. "Yes. Yes I am. But what is this place?"

"How the devil should I know?" Roark said. "You swear you are all right?"

"Yes," Anna shouted. "But what is this?"

A loud sigh drifted down to her. "I don't know. Perhaps it is a priest's hole."

"A priests hole?" Anna squeaked. "Highly unlikely."

"Very well," Roark said, his voice irritated. "It clearly is a trapdoor. Now who it was meant to trap or hide . . ."

"It wouldn't be priests," Anna said angrily. "Not in your family."

"I said I don't know," Roark retaliated. "Ask ancestor Charles. Perhaps he knows."

"Very amusing!" Anna said bitterly, slowly rising to a stand. She checked the use of her limbs and dusted herself off, wincing. The chamber was quite clean, other than the dust, the remaining splinters of rotted wood, and a structure that showed somewhat the shape of a ladder. She looked up again, judging the distance. "Blast!"

"What?" Roark asked.

Anna bit her lip. "Nothing. Nothing at all."

"What is it?" Roark's voice was filled with concern.

"Nothing," Anna repeated. "Only . . . will you . . . could you . . ." She halted, seething.

Roark chuckled. "Could I *help* you perhaps? Could you possibly need me?"

"Never mind," Anna said, stalking over to one wall. She checked the height by stretching her hand upward. Hope blossomed. The room wasn't so deep as she had first thought. She studied the edge of the opening above. It looked to be within an arms distance. So was Roark's grinning face. She ignored that. She reached up her hands. Not good enough.

"I know that you are perfectly safe and can take care

of yourself," Roark said. "But would you perhaps like me to lend a hand?"

Anna seethed. Only diabolical people would have built such a hole for no reason, and Roark certainly showed every sign of being a descendant of them. In her estimation, that branch did not fall far from said tree. "No, I will manage." Anna drew upon all her strength and jumped up, her arms outstretched. She hoped to shorten the distance and grasp the ledge.

"You are doing fine," Roark said in an encouraging tone. "It is clear you don't need my paltry help."

Anna, rage fueling her efforts, jumped higher. Once again, she missed any handhold. She also landed much harder. Her left foot caught on a piece of rotten wood and Anna went down completely, a screech bursting from her.

"Anna!" Roark shouted. "Are you all right?"

Anna gritted her teeth. Her ankle throbbed. She forced herself to stand and caught her breath painfully.

"Anna," Roark said, "answer me! Are you hurt?"

Anna sighed. "Please help me."

"Here, take my hands," Roark said.

Anna looked up. Roark had hung himself over the ledge and stretched out both of his arms. Grimacing, she reached up. She winced inside even more, for the distance between her reach and his was such that she had to stand on tiptoe. She felt Roark's strong hands gripping hers; then he was hauling her body up. She dangled for a moment at the ledge before Roark heaved back, drawing her full-length to him. They toppled, with Roark's arms securely about her. His hold tightened.

"Where are you hurt?"

"I'm not hurt," Anna panted.

"Yes, you are," Roark said, "or you wouldn't have accepted my help."

"Very well," Anna said, feeling decidedly foolish—and decidedly hot. "I twisted my ankle."

"Damn it, woman," Roark said, his voice booming. It rumbled through Anna's rib cage, he held her so close.

"Don't yell at me," Anna said as sudden tears formed at the corner of her eyes.

"I'm not yelling," Roark blasted into her ear.

Anna blinked back the sting. "Yes, you are."

Roark halted. He expelled a breath. "I am." The open sincerity in his eyes stunned Anna. "I'm sorry." His hold became gentle, and his hands rubbed her back. "How painful is your injury?"

Shock waves coursed through Anna. "Not that painful. My ankle is only twisted."

"Are you sure?" Roark asked, his voice dipping to a deeper octave. His hands kneaded the muscles of her shoulder. "You look as if you are about to cry. Please don't. I didn't mean to make you cry."

"I'm not crying," Anna said. Her nerves sang at his touch. The warmth in his gaze lit an answering glow within her. "You don't need to apologize. It wasn't your fault."

"Yes, it was," Roark said. "I shouldn't have teased you the way I did."

Faith, he hadn't teased her before . . . not the way he was doing that moment with his arms about her and his hands roaming over her back.

"It was my fault." She quivered. Memories of the kiss they shared flooded her mind. Unwillingly, a thrill shot through her. Fear followed. She couldn't allow him to kiss her. Her fragile equilibrium wouldn't survive it.

"It was my fault," Anna said again. "You may yell at me now."

"Yell at you?" Roark asked, his voice husky.

"Yes," Anna said. "Only . . ."

"Only what?"

"Don't kiss me," Anna whispered.

Roark looked as if she had doused him with a bucket of water. "I wasn't going to kiss you."

Anna started. Gracious, she had actually said the words aloud! "Forgive me. I am just overset."

His arms fell from her. "I wasn't going to kiss you. No matter what you think, I would not take such advantage of you."

"No, of course not." Anna said. If only she could crawl back into that hole.

"I am not the rake you make me out to be," Roark said. After rolling away from her, he stood abruptly.

Anna sat up. "I said I was sorry."

Roark's face darkened. When he held out his hand silently, Anna clasped it just as silently. Words were a certain danger between them at the moment. As he slowly drew her up to stand, Anna winced.

"Can you walk?" he asked.

Anna tested her weight on her left ankle, and she sucked in a breath. "Indeed."

Roark frowned. "Shall I carry you?"

"No!" Anna almost shouted.

The slightest smile touched Roark's lips. "You may yell at me now."

An answering smile teased Anna's lips. "I'm not yelling."

Roark gingerly placed his arm about her. "Let us go."

"Yes," Anna said gratefully because she wanted the entire situation behind her.

They left the immense chamber, going around the multitude of objects in a silent pact of determination. To her chagrin, however, Anna found she had to lean heavily upon Roark for support. By the second flight of stairs, she was clutching Roark's jacket. By the third flight of stairs, she had wrapped both arms about his firm waist. Roark's arm was no longer on her shoulder, but curved around her side, with his hand firmly upon her hip.

Still they did not speak. Anna racked her brain for something to say, but she couldn't come up with one decent remark. She gave up and merely tried to control her panting. She wanted to believe her panting was from the exertion and pain, and not from the sheer tension of being so closely entwined with Roark. When they arrived upon the last flight, Roark groaned, and Anna was forced to speak.

"What?" Anna asked. "What is it?"

"Confound it. I'm carrying you, and do not argue."

He promptly scooped Anna up into his arms. Anna didn't argue. In fact, she was so worn out she but sighed and laid her head upon his shoulder. The scent of Roark filled her nostrils.

"See," Roark said, his voice hoarse. "I can be a knight errant as well as rake."

With that, Anna's knight errant proceeded to carry her at an amazing pace—almost as if he ran a race, in fact. Anna blinked in bemusement after they quickly arrived at her bedroom door. She felt no more than the merest featherweight as Roark shifted her and opened the door. He carried her to her bed and set her down upon it.

Anna smiled at him, although she never doubted her lips in all probability quivered as much as her insides did. "Thank you. You truly have been a knight errant."

"Thank you," Roark said, his voice odd. "You should rest."

"Yes," Anna said. "Yes, I will rest."

"I will send Salome to you for anything you need."

"I shall not need anything," Anna said. Od's blood, what a clanker, whopper, taradiddle, balderdash! She needed Roark to kiss her. "I only need . . ."

"Need what?" Roark asked quickly.

"Rest," Anna said, flushing. "As you said, rest."

"Very well," Roark said. "I shall leave you . . ."

"Yes." Anna nodded. Her thoughts screamed, *No, kiss me.*

". . . now," Roark said.

"What?" Anna asked.

"I am leaving you now." Roark walked toward the door. But once there he stopped. "Damn it!"

"What?" Anna asked.

He turned, his face fierce. "I'm no knight errant."

"You aren't?" Anna asked, wickedly hopeful.

"Never have been," Roark said, stalking back to her. "Never will be."

He sat, then jerked Anna into his arms. Their lips met as swiftly as their bodies did. They kissed fiercely, their hands and arms tangling, as both sought to hold and explore the other. Anna was drowning, submerged in a tide of emotions and sensations.

She had never known passion before. Yet it filled her so completely she felt as if she had always known it. She flowed to its demands, pliant as Roark pushed her back against the mattress, eager as his large body covered hers. Anna reached up and clasped his shoulders, her fingers splaying over his corded muscles. She arched in need when Roark deepened the kiss and caressed the length of her with a sure, demanding hand. But their kiss ended abruptly when a sudden, keening howl arose.

"What the devil!" Roark said, his voice a rasp.

As a chant, low and fervent, flooded the room, Roark, cursing, rolled away and sat up. Anna, dazed and blinking, lifted herself onto her elbows.

Salome stood in the middle of the room, her hands mangling a rosary strand. Her eyes were wide and frightened as she murmured a litany.

"What in blazes are you doing?" Roark growled.

"I came," Salome said, "to cleanse the room."

"Blast and damn!" Roark muttered.

Salome jumped. Her litany rising in pitch, she darted over and flung her rosary beads upon the bed.

"For God's sake," Roark muttered.

Salome clearly thought the same thing. With a new chant, she dragged four other strands of beads from about her neck and showered Anna and Roark with them. Then she wisely fled the room.

Anna stared down at the beads. Flushing, she peeked at Roark, whose face was a mixture of shock and exasperation.

"Why does everything have to be an infernal drama in this house?" he said.

Anna, despite her embarrassment and her blossoming guilt, laughed. "I don't know."

"I'm sorry, Anna." Roark smiled wryly, sincere contrition in his eyes. He swiftly moved from the bed, shaking his head. "I guess I am a rake, after all. I promised you I wouldn't take advantage of you, and I did."

Anna bit her lip. He was stronger than she. She knew full well she had been an active participant, but admitting she was a wanton hussy was something she couldn't bring herself to do.

"I promise you," Roark said, his eyes darkening, "it won't happen again. I want you to be able to trust me."

"I do," Anna said quickly. "I mean, I will."

"Thank you," Roark said, relief crossing his face. "I will leave you to rest now. And I think I'll send for the doctor."

"A doctor?" Anna asked. "Why?"

"For your ankle," Roark said.

"Oh, yes. Of course," Anna said, flushing. She had completely forgotten about her ankle. Indeed, it had been some moments since it had caused her any discomfort. "I don't think it necessary, though.

"I will feel better if our doctor examines your ankle," Roark said.

"If that is your wish," Anna said.

"It is." Roark smiled and left the room.

Sighing, Anna brushed the rosary beads away and lay down. She closed her eyes in determination. She didn't need a doctor to examine her ankle. She needed one to examine her head!

Five

Anna sat comfortably ensconced in a tattered chair, reading through a diary of one of the late Seeton wives. It was a very dry account. The major excitement in the woman's life appeared to have been pig butchering. In regard to that activity, Matilda Seeton delivered far more detail than Anna thought wholesome.

Sighing, she glanced over to Roark. He held possession of another dilapidated chair. The trunk of papers they had unearthed was closed, acting as a makeshift table upon which the remainders of their lunch rested.

It was the fourth day into their search. That morning Roark had surprised her with a picnic lunch and even a bottle of wine. Anna smiled. He had been correct. It was ever so much more comfortable that way, rather than interrupting their studies to trek all the way back through the castle for a nuncheon. Though the doctor had informed Anna she had only twisted her ankle, Roark still showed concern for her injury. It might be under false pretenses, but Anna found she enjoyed the cosseting.

"Find anything of interest?" Roark asked with a smile.

"No," Anna said, blinking.

Roark truly had the easiest of smiles. It did not fit with the image of the bitter recluse, nor with the image of that unyielding man she had first met. The relaxed man she had come to know over the past four days, the man who appeared as eager as she to dig through ancient history, who would discuss any subject on a whim, was like a secret unfolding to Anna—though, indeed, a very confusing, compelling, and perhaps dangerous secret.

"Matilda did enjoy her pig butchering though," Anna said a moment later.

"Did she?" Roark asked, laughing.

Anna flushed. "What are you reading?"

A glint entered Roark's gaze. "A journal you do not need to see."

"Why?" Anna asked.

"Sir Peter seems to be of Elliot Seeton's ilk," Roark said, grinning. "You will never let my family live down its licentious reputation if you read this."

"Oh."

Heated memories flooded Anna, and they had nothing to do with Roark's ancestors. Roark had indeed shown Anna a relaxed and easy manner, which, as much as it delighted her, also made her tense. True to his word, he had not made one advance toward her since that time in her bedroom. Apparently those kisses, which had rocked her and made her intensely aware of him, had been of little consequence to him. She peeked back at Roark. He had taken up his glass of wine and was once again studying Sir Peter's account.

"Do you think we are going about this the proper way?" Anna asked, frowning.

An odd look entered Roark's eyes. "I'd say the most proper way imaginable."

"Yes, but we don't seem to be progressing very much," Anna said, sighing.

"It takes time." A wry smile twisted his lips. "That is what I remind myself."

"You are right," Anna said, smiling.

Roark laughed. "I thought you would agree."

"You warned me discovering Charles's murderer would be difficult," Anna said. "But I had expected at least to find some clue. There hasn't been even a trace of writing from his family."

"Most of his generation were not literate, and those who were rarely spent their time writing," Roark said. "Nor would they have cared to admit one of their members committed suicide."

"True," Anna said, "but—"

"Hello," a voice called. "Roark, you here?"

"Terrence?"

"Anna?" Beth's voice called out.

"Beth?" Anna said, completely surprised.

Terrence finally appeared with Beth, who clutched his hand tightly. All four were rather astonished to see each other.

"Terrence, what are you doing here?" Roark asked after a moment.

Terrence grinned. "Came to see what you two were doing, that's what. Haven't seen you for days."

"Still on the hunt," Roark said, grinning. "Haven't found a clue about old Charles."

"We can help," Terrence said eagerly. "Can't we, Beth?"

Beth cast a somewhat frightened look about. She wore a dress of the palest yellow muslin with a Brussels lace overskirt—truly a hazard in such a place. "Yes."

Anna smiled. "I'm sure you have more important things to do than help us."

Beth's face brightened. "Oh, yes, we do. Anna, the dance is only five days away. We must attend to our wardrobes. And we still have the wedding lists to do, Terrence."

"Thought we did that," Terrence said, strolling over to Roark.

"No, Terrence," Beth said. "That was for the rehearsal dinner."

"Was it?" Terrence asked absently, peering at the wine bottle. "Any of that left?"

"Yes," Roark said.

"Good!" Terrence, heedless of his buff unmentionables and blue serge coat, hunkered down upon the stone floor. He reached for the bottle and gave Roark a wolfish grin. "Got this rather cozy up here, what?"

"Cozy?" Beth asked, her gaze skittering about in disbelief.

Roark laughed. "There is no reason we cannot have at least some creature comforts while researching."

"That's my man," Terrence said. "So you haven't found a clue? Then what have you been doing?"

"Discovering a wealth of information about our family. Some of it quite damning." Roark cast a teasing look toward Anna. "Anna's come to the conclusion that there were nothing but rakes, rogues, and lechers alight in the family tree. Not a righteous soul among the lot."

Anna pulled a face. "The ladies seemed to be acceptable on the whole, though Matilda seemed overfond of pig butchering."

"Pig butchering," Beth gasped, her tone horrified.

"Rather to be expected. Having the occasional odd one, that is," Terrence said, grinning. "Seen old Charles lately, Anna?"

"No," Anna said, "not at all."

"Anna," Beth said, frowning. "you have a large black smudge on your cheek."

"Do I?" Anna quickly rubbed her cheek. "Why didn't you tell me, Roark?"

"I thought it was rather charming."

"I don't think it very kind of old Charles," Terrence said, frowning. "Here you are doing all this for him, and he's left you in the lurch, as it were."

"How long has it been there?" Anna asked, still scrubbing her cheek.

"Only for an hour or so," Roark said.

"An hour or so?" Anna squeaked.

Roark smiled and looked at Terrence. "Perhaps he won't appear again until we've discovered something of import."

"Hmm," Terrence said, "could be. Could be."

"And you've something on your shoulder, Anna," Beth gasped. "Is that a cobweb?"

Anna left off attending to her cheek to swipe at her shoulder. "I don't know."

"It would help if he'd appear again," Terrence said.

"Stop it," Beth cried.

Anna froze in her action. "What?"

"I don't know why you would want that ghost to appear again." Beth's voice quavered and a high flush covered her cheeks.

Terrence's face darkened. "Well, it might help Anna."

"Why should it help her?" Beth asked. "She wouldn't be here in this dreadful place with cobwebs all over her if it weren't for him. I am sick of hearing about him!" She stamped her foot. "He's ruined everything. Everyone cares more about him than the wedding."

"That isn't true," Terrence said, his face outraged. "All we've been doing is wedding stuff. We go and look at china patterns. All of them with flowers. This flower with that curly thing, or that flower with that scrolly thing. It took two infernal days. And I still couldn't tell the difference."

"I thought you liked what we chose," Beth gasped.

"Next the silver!" Terrence said, his tone disgusted. "Big bowls, little bowls, and a thousand tiny forks! That took a whole day!"

"But—"

"And we are always making lists of people. Who have

we forgotten? Who might we offend? As far as I can tell, we've even invited the traveling tinker," Terrence said hotly. He glared at Beth, who had turned deathly white. "So don't tell me I don't care just because I asked after old Charles!"

"But you don't," Beth said, her face crumpling. "I'm just trying to make everything perfect for the wedding, and I'm sure I don't know why, because that dreadful ghost will appear and ruin it—I just know it. And you won't care one wit. In fact, you'll probably be glad for it!" Sobbing, Beth turned and stumbled away.

"Beth, wait! Blast it!" Terrence bolted past Anna and Roark, clunking and clattering as he tripped and kicked over the unfortunate objects in his path.

"Oh, dear," Anna said, contrition wrenching her heart. "Beth is right. I have not paid much attention to her."

"Do not let it concern you overly much," Roark said, his tone amused. "You are far better off here—and much safer, I assure you."

"Safer?" Anna asked, lifting a wry brow. "Why? Because you are here to protect me?"

"I wouldn't say that," Roark laughed. When an almost wolfish glimmer rose in his eyes, Anna's heart jumped. "However, better that you are here, rather than caught, as it were, between those two."

"But—"

"They are suffering wedding nerves, Anna, and nothing more," Roark said. "Every couple has them."

"Did you?" Anna asked, then flushed deeply.

"No," Roark said with a bitter smile. "Though I should have if I had been a wiser man. I didn't know at the time what old Charles did."

"Yes," Anna said. They fell silent a moment, and a stray thought flitted through Anna's mind. Unfortunately, she chuckled at it before she realized she had.

"You find that amusing?"

"Yes," Anna said, then choked. "Well, no. But . . . yes."

"Do make up your mind," Roark said, his tone dry.

"I am sorry. I suddenly imagined you spending two entire days dithering over china patterns."

A slow grin crossed Roark's face. "Perhaps that is why I didn't suffer the jitters. I simply refused to choose china or anything else for that matter. Regardless of how besotted I was, I at least knew enough to draw the line there."

Anna forced a smile, though the thought of Roark besotted did strange things to her stomach. She absently brushed at her shoulder. "Of course."

"Anna," Roark said in a gentle tone, "Do stop that."

"What?" Anna asked, frowning.

"Forget about the cobwebs and the smudge on your cheek," Roark said, laughing.

"You mean it is still there?" Anna quickly rubbed at her cheek. "Why didn't you tell me? I must look ridiculous.

"You are only smearing it all the more," Roark said, chuckling. "Besides, what does it matter how you look? It is only you and I here now."

"Yes, of course," Anna said, her hand slowly falling from her cheek. She quickly focused upon her journal. Of course, he didn't care how she looked. He wasn't besotted with her so it did not matter.

Anna sat in her bed, her legs drawn up to her. By the end of the evening, Beth and Terrence had settled their disagreement. Once again they were the loving, adoring couple. Neither of them had taken his gaze off the other. They were besotted. Anna sighed long and deep.

"Ah, a lover's sigh?" Charles voice said.

Anna started slightly, but only slightly. "It was not a lover's sigh, and where have you been?"

"Oh, here and there," Charles said with a shrug, "and then nowhere in between."

"I have been waiting for you to appear," Anna said, her tone accusing.

"Have you?" Charles chuckled. "I seem to remember, when last we conversed, you requested me *not* to appear to you—and in a very unkindly manner at that, mistress."

"That was before I knew—" Anna halted, flushing. "That was before I started looking for your murderer."

"Yes," Charles said, turning solemn.

"I am sorry," Anna said with sincerity. "But Roark and I are making no progress whatsoever."

"I would not say that, lass," Charles said, amusement flaring in his eyes once more. "I rather thought you did some strong *progressing* but a few short days ago."

Anna's heart sank. His meaning was all too clear. "You saw that?"

"I but glanced," Charles said, his tone sanctimonious. "Then, gentleman that I am, I took myself away. Unlike that banshee of a maid, I am not one to ruin sport."

"Sport." Anna sighed. "That is what it was then."

"Nay, vixen," Charles said, chuckling.

"Vixen?" Anna asked, offended.

"Yes, vixen," Charles said. "Like all of womankind. If you ladies would but determine your minds, we men would not suffer so."

"What do you mean?" Anna asked.

Charles grinned. "At first it is *thou shall not kiss me* and *where is thy honor, sirrah?* Thus we poor wretched males, seeking to please, restrain our lusty natures. And what do you dainty ladies say to that? *Fie, thou doest not kiss me anymore. Alas it was just sport.*"

He spoke so comically, Anna had to laugh. "Perhaps."

" 'Tis no perhaps," Charles said with mock severity. "You are a vixen."

"Then I am a vixen, but not a very good one, I fear."

"You shall be," Charles said, devilment in his eyes. "For I am here to instruct you, milady."

Anna leaned forward eagerly, then froze. Was she actually turning to a ghost for advice about love? Doing so seemed quiet improper, if not a little underhanded.

"Well?" Charles asked, his brow arching. "I have seen both love and betrayal, both the little tricks of love and the little games of deceit. What would you have of it?"

"Very well," Anna said, throwing her reserve to the winds. "I would not want to be a true vixen, but I would not mind to know the tricks of love—at least one or two."

Charles roared with laughter. "Aha! You are caught out, mistress."

"What?" Anna asked, stiffening with indignation.

"You chose the tricks of *love*," Charles said, satisfaction clear upon his face.

Anna blinked, a flush rising in her cheeks. "You tricked me."

"Not I," Charles said innocently. "You but spoke your mind."

"So what are the tricks of love?" Anna said, knowing when best to retreat or at least to divert further accusations.

"Simple," Charles said, leaning back in his chair with a superior look. "Follow your woman's heart."

"That is it?" Anna asked, deflated. She frowned at him. "You definitely tricked me."

"Nay," Charles said, shaking his head. "What of this

afternoon? You were none too pleased to be found with a besmirched face and cobwebs about you."

"Is there nothing you do not see?"

"You looked a veritable monkey, scrubbing at your face," Charles said, grinning.

"Oh, no," Anna wailed.

"Yet Roark thought it charming," Charles said. "Did he not?"

"He must have said that to be polite," Anna groaned.

"Nay," Charles said. "A woman without artifice is a delight. A man does not wish to wed a courtesan. As for your sister, that bratling should have had a rod taken to her for her behavior."

"Oh, no," Anna said. "Beth is always the sweetest of girls. Her behavior this afternoon was very unlike herself."

"S'true," Charles said. "And I shall forgive her, for 'tis she who will help you buy a dress for this dance— one which will not charm Roark, but heat his blood to boiling."

"Oh, dear," Anna said.

"Own it, wench. That is what your heart wishes." Charles laughed. "B'gad, but it will do Roark good. The lad has not suffered the pangs of desire for far too long."

"You sound as if you enjoy it," Anna said, stunned.

"All men enjoy watching other men suffer at the hands of love," Charles said. A shadow crossed his face. "Then they do not feel so alone in their folly."

The oddest wave of grief and pain overwhelmed Anna. Suddenly Charles disappeared. He reappeared far across the room, standing by the fireplace. Anna found she could breathe again. The pain was gone. More likely it had been drawn away. She forced a laugh, pretending that nothing had transpired. "I think it will be my folly to try to play the siren. I am not beautiful like Beth."

Charles studied her. "Nay, you are beautiful. But your mind is always looking for the beauty that is not seen. Indeed, you attend so much to that, you forget to dress yourself."

"I beg your pardon?" Anna said in mock offense. "I have never gone about without my clothes."

"You should." Charles raised a hand at her shocked gasp. "Nay, do not begin a tirade. 'Tis only that you and your generation trusses yourselves up like swaddled babies. Your bodies never see sun or moon. 'Tis unhealthy. But enough. Each to his own time. Just make sure your sister dresses you for the dance to her taste and not yours. For once, she can be of some service."

Anna bit her lip. "Do you not like Beth?"

"I like her fine," Charles said with a shrug.

"She truly loves Terrence," Anna said, hesitantly, "and Terrence loves her."

"I have told you, lass. I myself do not have a choice in whether I appear or not at a wedding. It is beyond my control."

"Truly?" Anna asked, confused.

"Aye. I have seen much, and I can hold my own opinion on what I see," Charles said, frowning. "Still, it never changes. I only appear at those weddings where one has betrayed the other. I have seen the most ill-matched couples plight their troth in that chapel, but to them I will not appear. Only do I appear to the ones who are unfaithful. A cruelty of fate, would you not say?" Charles said, his voice bitter. "Betrayed in my time and drawn to betrayal forever after."

A chill rushed through Anna. She remained silent, for there was nothing that could be said.

Charles appeared to shake off his mood. "Though

there have been some diverting moments because of it. I remember a couple that even I thought was a true love match. Not a hint of scandal anywhere. Never a sign within these walls of my ancestor's fickleness. Alack, I appeared at that wedding to all our surprise. Especially the groom's, I assure you. He was not only being unfaithful to his betrothed, but he was doing so with twins, both of whom were in the ceremony. Ah, that was a day."

"Then you cannot promise you will not appear at Beth's wedding," Anna asked, frowning. "I wish I could assure her of that."

Charles shrugged. "I cannot offer that promise. Though I doubt your sister is the unfaithful type. Not like the trollop Roark had chosen. Faith, and they called her lady."

"They still do," Anna sighed. "How could he not have seen?"

"Love is blind," Charles said, snorting. "It will refuse to see what it does not wish to see—until it is too late, that is. I assure you, 'twas galling to watch that strumpet work her ploys and games. Roark was the only one who believed her. I awaited that wedding day most heartily."

"It is unfortunate you could not have warned him before the wedding," Anna said with a sigh. "He could have been saved that embarrassing scene."

"At least his bride showed herself," Charles said with a snort. "But I did not have the power than that I do now. If I had, I would have blown that strumpets skirts up for the world to see what most of the men attending already had. But for poor Roark."

"You are learning more and more," Anna said, nodding.

"No," Charles said. " 'Tis something about your arrival."

Guilt tore at Anna. "I believe I am here to find your murderer. That is what it is. But I don't know how to go about it. Have you no clue as to who wished you dead?"

"Do you not think that over the decades I have not wondered?" Charles laughed, a sadness within it. He shook his head. "Though it is all blurred to me now. My friends. My enemies. Even my family."

"And Genevieve?" Anna asked softly.

Charles stilled. "One never forgets betrayal. That memory remains as clear as the day it happened. Decades cannot tarnish it. Would that I had such a strong memory of my murderer. I remember those first hundred years. I sought to listen and discover from everyone who entered this castle. Alas, there never was anything. All believed I had thrown myself from that bloody turret on purpose."

"Your brother inherited from you, did he not?" Anna asked hesitantly.

"That he did," Charles said, his gaze solemn. "He did not seek to take my place, I know. In truth, he sincerely grieved my death. I did not realize the ties until later. Nor those friends who were not friends. 'Twas a small funeral, befitting a man who had taken his own life."

Charles's image merely faded away. Anna did not call him back, nor did she say good-bye. He would return again. He must. Just as she must discover who had murdered him. Somehow, she and he were bound. Time demanded something from them both. Only finding out what it demanded was the mystery.

"Now we must attend to your dress for the wedding," Beth said, her eyes snapping brightly.

"What?" Anna asked, appalled.

She sat among rolls of cloth, pattern cards, laces, and spools of thread. Her mind reeled. She was totally exhausted. The only thing that fortified her was the cup of tea the little assistant had brought her just then. She drank from it readily, wincing. She had been poked and prodded, measured and remeasured. Faith, she could not even remember what they had ordered.

"Indeed, yes," Mrs. Brewster, the dressmaker said, her eyes as bright as Beth's. She scratched away hurriedly at the list. Apparently she would not lose count.

"I believe that . . ." Beth said in a slow considering tone.

"Yes?" Mrs. Brewster asked eagerly, leaning forward.

"That . . ."

The door to the dress shop opened and a lady attired in ruby red entered with a gentleman. Anna could not help but take note, for though the lady was dark haired, she possessed the look and confidence of Clarise. The tall blond gentleman accompanying her was dressed equally well. The couple displayed all the polish of the *ton* and would have been better suited for a London drawing room than the small dress shop.

"That it should be of light rose silk," Beth said, "and figured with seed pearls."

Anna's attention promptly veered back to her sister. "Seed pearls?"

"Oh, yes," Mrs. Brewster exclaimed. "That will be lovely."

"Seed pearls?" Anna asked again. "Will that not be costly?"

"What does its cost matter?" Beth said blithely.

"Excuse me," a voice called. It was the woman who had entered. "I will require service."

"Yes, madam, I shall be with you in a moment," Mrs. Brewster said, quite absently, never taking her gaze away from Anna and Beth. "It truly would be perfect for you, Miss Winston.

"I have no doubt," Anna said, flushing as she heard the woman in red muttering to her partner. "But I—"

"Anna," Beth said, all but stamping her foot. "I will not have it. You have an absolute fortune at your disposal, and this one dress will certainly not matter one wit."

"One dress?" Anna laughed. "Mrs. Brewster, just how many dresses have we ordered up so far."

Mrs. Brewster pursed her lips and studied her list. "Only four . . . No, there is the peach satin and the mauve net."

"That makes six," Anna said, casting Beth a look of justification.

"It is of no significance, Anna. You said you wished my assistance."

"Yes, to buy a dress for the ball," Anna said. "Not to commission an entire wardrobe. I've lost count of what else we ordered."

"Four silk petticoats," Mrs. Brewster dutifully rattled off. "That modish French corset with the pink rosettes . . . Oh, it will be so chic."

Anna heard a male chuckle and she swallowed hard. "That will be enough, Mrs. Brewster. I believe the tabulation sufficiently proves my point."

"Oh, but I assure you. The corset is so necessary, so *de monde,* when the waist is dropped back down to its normal position. I assure you soon it will be *de trop* to wear the Empire waist. The corset is truly vital."

Again, a baritone chortle could be heard cross the room.

"That is fine, Mrs. Brewster. I will take all of it." Anna hurriedly interrupted the modiste's litany before she reached any further undergarments on the tab.

"Yes," Beth stated firmly. "You need those things, just

as you need the dress for the wedding. I want you dressed fittingly. Please? You know expense is not an issue."

"Madam," the woman in red said, her tone sharp, "I am still waiting!"

"Oh, yes," Mrs. Brewster said.

Anna glanced over. The woman's face was dark with displeasure. Clearly, she was not a woman accustomed to being ignored.

Mrs. Brewster, however, did not seem overly concerned. She waved a hand at her assistant. "Sally, do attend the . . . lady."

Anna's eyes widened, for her tone was quite dismissive. The woman's eyes blazed as Sally approached her. "I refuse to tolerate this shabby behavior." She spun on her heel and stalked from the shop.

Her partner was left standing there. He seemed totally undisturbed by his position, however. He smiled warmly at Sally, who flushed with embarrassment. "You must forgive, Sarah. She is never patient, even at the best of times." Bowing, he strolled to the door. He halted then and, turning, looked directly at Anna. He had the bluest of eyes. "I do hope you buy the dress. It sounds perfect for you."

Beth crowed. "See, Anna! You must permit me to order this dress."

Anna sighed and agreed. It took another hour of heavy discussion, upon Beth and Mrs. Brewster's part, that is, to finalize the plans for the ball dress. The skirts had to be widened, and perhaps the sleeves needed to be puffed out. Gratefully, Anna made her escape. Loaded down with carefully stacked boxes, she was escorted by Mrs. Brewster to the door. Sally and Beth were arming themselves with even more packages. Their day of shopping had started with just one dress for the dance and now it seemed they should have commandeered a train of mules for their purchases!

Anna exited the shop, relieved to see the light of day again. Suddenly she exclaimed as she ran into a man and her boxes flew in all directions. "Oh, dear! I'm so sorry," she exclaimed. Her eyes widened when she recognized the tall blond man from earlier.

"Hello again," he said, smiling down at her.

"Hello," Anna said, blinking.

He laughed. "Did you buy the dress with the seed pearls?"

"Yes. Yes, I did," Anna murmured, quickly bending down to retrieve her boxes.

The man graciously assisted her. He handed her a box, grinning. "You have made quite a haul, I see."

"Yes. Thank you," Anna said, taking the box from him. "I do seem to be a cause of trouble for you."

"Not at all," the man said. His blue eyes smiled at her in the most admiring fashion.

Flustered, Anna reached for another box. "Then your friend is not overly upset?"

"Cousin!" the man said quickly.

"What?" Anna asked.

"Cousin," the man said, his tone firm, his gaze seeming unnecessarily serious. "She is my cousin. Nothing more, I assure you."

"Oh, of course," Anna said. She nodded her understanding since it appeared important to him. Her boxes once again stacked, Anna stood.

The man still held on to one last purchase. He gazed down at Anna, smiling. "I hope you will not consider me forward, but I could not help overhearing you mention a ball as well. Could it perchance be the one the Duke of Whynhaven is giving?"

"Why, yes, it is," Anna said, shifting her boxes to a more secure hold. "How did you know?"

The man laughed. "Who in this backwater—I mean in the village—does not know of it? It is the only thing talked about these days. My aunt, who I am visiting with for the nonce, is counting the days, I assure you." His blue eyes deepened. "As I find myself doing so . . . now."

"That is nice," Anna said, lacking anything better to say.

He still held the one last box. "May I ask if you are one of the ladies in whose honor it is being given?"

"I suppose I am," Anna said. The conversation could become tricky if she did not take care. She glanced behind. Just where was Beth?

"Then you are engaged?" the man asked, sighing.

"Not exactly," Anna said, evasively. She did not wish to lie, but there certainly was no reason to attempt the truth.

The stranger's eyes lightened and he smiled in what appeared to be relief. "You are not?"

"I mean," Anna said quickly. "There is no official engagement as of yet between Roark—I mean, the Duke—and me."

"I am glad to hear it," the man said, his tone almost embarrassingly warm. He offered her a formal bow. "I know the ball is meant to introduce you to this fine village, but forgive me if I do not wait. My name is Julian Rothman."

"I am pleased to meet you," Anna said, politely. "And I am Anna Winston."

"Anna," he murmured. "You have a lovely name."

"Thank you." Anna heard a commotion from behind.

Beth was emerging from the shop. Her arms filled with packages, she had the most delighted expression upon her face. "I am sorry to have kept you waiting,

Anna, but I remembered a few last details that simply had to be attended."

"Indeed," Anna said, then shook her head. Beth had always been swift to deny her intelligence, but evidently when it came to clothing, her dear sister had a mind like a steel trap.

Beth smiled, though with a hint of embarrassment. "I also ordered you one more dress I realized you simply must have. Please do not be upset with me."

Anna stared, then laughed. "I am not. Only I do hope you did not deck it with diamonds."

"No, of course not," Beth said, her tone aghast.

"That would be very costly," Julian Rothman said, his eyes alight.

"Cost?" Anna said, chuckling. "That would not be the issue. It is the weight of the dress I am thinking about. It would sink me, I am sure."

Beth stared at both of them, a worried frown upon her face. Then she smiled. "I see, you are teasing me. You know very well diamonds are not stones you should wear, Anna. You must have color, you know."

"Ah," Anna nodded, not knowing anything of the sort. "Then rubies will have to do."

"No, rubies are ill-fated stones." Beth considered a moment. "I think perhaps topaz."

Anna rolled her eyes. "Oh, do come along, Beth, before you have us returning to Mrs. Brewster."

Julian placed the final last box upon Anna's stack. "I shall see you at the ball then . . . Anna."

"Anna!" Beth gasped. "You are right. We must attend to your jewelry."

Smiling wryly, Anna nodded to Julian Rothman. "Good day, sir. If you will excuse us, my sister will now demand I go to the jewelers."

"Of course," Julian Rothman said, stepping back. "Au revoir."

"Can we, Anna?" Beth asked, as eager as any child.

"Why not?" Anna said in a blithful tone. Her exhaustion faded away. She had never bought jewelry before, but it was something she rather thought she would enjoy. Then she chuckled. If she was not careful, it would be Charles Seeton who told her the dress she wore was gaudy and overdone.

Six

Roark covertly watched Anna as she sorted yellowed slips of paper, all of different sizes and condition. The huge, ornate Jacobean chair she sat upon dwarfed her. Sunlight danced through the massive pier window, its diamond-shaped fretwork creating a myriad of patterns across the desk and the stacks of documents it held. He knew outside the library walls servants scurried to finish final preparations for the dance that night. Aunt Deirdre careened through the halls, confusing both the family servants and the extra staff acquired for the momentous occasion with her quick, conflicting orders and sudden inspirations. After all, those brilliant visions that popped into her head at the most auspicious moments simply had to be done. In the library, however, there was safety and sanctuary.

Anna perused a document drawn from the far left stack. Her expressive face revealed each change in thought as she read the aged vellum. A romantic she might be, and an air dreamer, and perhaps totally crazy; but no one, once they knew her, could deny her intelligence. In a woman, such intelligence was indeed stunning.

A strand of her soft brown hair slipped from its haphazard confinement and fell across her face. She slowly, absently pushed the lock back. It was a small movement, made somehow more graceful for its unconsciousness. A tension ran through Roark—a tension he had been growing very accustomed to of late.

Anna was truly beautiful. How he had not seen it earlier, was beyond him. How other people could overlook her beauty was a mystery. Even with the ink smudge upon her cheek—the kind of smudge that always occurred when she became engrossed in study—she was beautiful.

Roark smiled slightly. Perhaps that was the answer in itself: Anna was beautiful because of the ink smudge. She was so natural, so completely enveloped in life, that her looks were clearly her last consideration. She possessed no artifice.

An unwanted memory flashed through Roark's mind. The first time he had seen Tiffany Templeton his heart had stopped dead. Of alabaster complexion, with golden hair, Tiffany had appeared an angel. She had the lightest laugh—the kind of sweet, feminine laugh that lifted a man's spirit. Her eyes were cornflower blue; they teased and delighted with secret promises. Only too late had Roark discovered that her appearance was carefully crafted artifice. Tiffany's angelic looks hid a trollop's soul. Her wide blue eyes hid a deceiving, greedy heart.

Roark pushed his thoughts away. He had thought Tiffany the epitome of womanhood. She had been his first love. She had taught him about women and love. Only when Roark looked at Anna did his heart begin to thaw. Only with Anna did he begin to wonder if he had truly learned what a woman was and what love entailed.

Anna glanced up from her paper, capturing his gaze. Quick concern filled her eyes. "Is there something wrong?"

"No, nothing at all."

Fortunately the library door opened at that moment,

and Aunt Deirdre bustled into the room. "Ah, there you are. Thank heavens, you two have not wandered astray."

Roark laughed. "We knew better than to do so on this day of all days."

"I am sure I would not have had the strength or breath if I had been forced to hunt you down in the dungeons or whatnot." She looked to Anna, her eyes glimmering. "Anna, Beth says it is time for you to prepare yourself for this evening."

Anna gasped. "So soon? The dance is still six hours away."

Aunt Deirdre laughed. "Beth said you might say something like that, but she told me I must hold firm and demand you go to her directly."

"Oh, yes," Anna said. An odd, almost embarrassed expression crossed her face. Anna rose swiftly, rubbing her hands upon her skirt. "If you will excuse me."

"That's a good girl," Aunt Deirdre said, nodding her head. "You have ink upon your cheek, dear."

Anna gasped and swiped at it. Reproach filled her eyes when she looked at Roark. "Why will you never tell me when I have a smudge?"

Roark forced a laugh. "I had not noticed.' "

Once again, that odd look crossed Anna's face. "Of course. If you will excuse me now."

As she hurried from the room, Roark found himself smiling. Then he noticed Aunt Deirdre grinning at him with smug satisfaction in her eyes. She walked over and settled into the chair Anna had deserted.

"I am so glad you two have found each other," she said.

"We have not found each other," Roark said with a surprising lack of vehemence. Indeed, his remark sounded suspiciously like a polite nothing.

Apparently Aunt Deirdre thought the same, for she

giggled. "I do wish you two would reconsider. I understand you do not wish to steal Beth and Terrence's thunder, but I think you are being too conscientious. I'm sure they would not mind if you announced your engagement to Anna as well tonight."

"It is not time yet," Roark said, then started. He had said the words with far more truth to them than he had intended.

He stood abruptly. What was he thinking? He'd best beat a hasty retreat before he disclosed even more to his aunt. There would be six more hours to while away before he saw Anna again. He wondered what Anna was thinking. He wondered what was behind those nervous looks she had cast his way.

Anna walked down the stone steps in trepidation. Beth followed behind, happily chattering away. Anna could not pay attention. She felt extremely odd, totally unlike herself. The last look in the glass before she and Beth had departed her room had verified she certainly did not look like herself.

Her brown hair was a mass of ringlets cascading from the top of her head and delicately framing her face. Or at least, that was what Beth had said was the intended effect. Anna knew her cheeks were brighter, her eyes a deeper shade of hazel, for once appearing more green than brown. Never before had Anna worn any form of paint. Beth had assured her it appeared completely natural. It did not feel so upon Anna's face, however.

Anna's pale willow green dress was cut to outline her figure, its décolletage far lower than what she was accustomed. Strange, the fashionable ball gowns Beth often wore had never appeared improper to Anna, but now that she was clothed in one with a neckline similar to Beth's, it seemed far more scandalous. Even the collar of emeralds did not seem to conceal enough of her exposed flesh.

Furthermore, Anna's corset positively stifled her. Beth had demanded it be cinched far tighter than Anna had ever thought possible. She stopped Beth short of following the advice inscribed on the placard Mrs. Brewster had folded in with it. *"It is suggested the fashionable lady lie facedown on the floor in order that her dresser might then place a foot in the small of the back to obtain the necessary purchase on the laces."* She was certain Beth had obtained the necessary purchase on those dratted laces. In fact, Anna feared she would expire before she reached the main hall. Worse, even with all the added hours of preparation, they were late. Anna was never late. She detested being late. All eyes would turn to her in impatience, making her feel like a truant child.

They entered the great hall, where they would form the reception line. Roark, Terrence, and Aunt Deirdre were already assembled.

"There you two girls are," Aunt Deirdre said, fluttering her hands expansively as they approached. "We were worried . . . Anna!" Her eyes widened. "Anna, is that you?"

Anna flushed deep red. Everyone gaped at her, though, to be sure, there was no sign of impatience in their eyes.

"Yes, it is." She looked quickly to Roark. Her breath wheezed from her. He was the most handsome man imaginable in his formal, evening attire. Then her heart sank. He appeared more thunderstruck than awestruck. "Is something wrong?" She attempted a teasing smile. "Do I have a smudge on my cheek?'

"No," Roark said. His tone was not inviting. "You do not."

Terrence laughed. "You've bowled big brother over, I think. You look lovely."

"Doesn't she?" Beth said, rushing over to Terrence. "She looks just the way I've always known she could look."

"She is quite transformed," Roark said, his expression cool.

"Thank you," Anna said hesitantly. She was unaccustomed to compliments on her looks. She could not be certain, but she didn't think they should sound as forbidding as the way Roark delivered them.

"You look beautiful." Aunt Deirdre shook her head. "Roark, I do think you should announce your engagement tonight. Anna will be besieged by the men, and they should know she is yours. It is only fair to them."

"Oh, no," Anna gasped, then glanced at Roark, whose eyes had narrowed. "I did not mean for that to happen. I mean, I did not dress like this for—" She halted. What could she say? She *had* dressed like this for Roark; she *had* wanted to demand his attention. However, she hadn't planned to force a proposal from him. Her thoughts had never gone that far. She turned pale. She could not be so positive of the purity of Charles's intentions or strategies. "No, indeed not. We have already discussed this matter. Tonight is for Beth and Terrence."

At that moment, to Anna's relief, Salome dashed into the hall, quivering and shaking. "The guests are arriving! The guests are arriving!" Her behavior was the same as if she had announced that infidels were beating down the inner gates.

"That is nice, dear," Aunt Deirdre said, her tone soothing. "Thank you for telling us. You may leave us now and go to your room. The other servants shall attend us tonight."

"You did not . . . ?" Salome asked.

"I promise you," Aunt Deirdre said. "I did not invite that no-good Peter Jenkins to my dance. You will not see him. Now hurry and leave." After Salome had nodded and departed, Aunt Deirdre shook her head. "As if I would invite a footman to my dance. Even if he was not in America. I do hope motherhood will settle Salome down." Her voice changed to that of a general marshaling his troops. "Enough of that. Do let us go and greet our guests."

Anna stood beside Roark, forcing a smile and nodding at each new arrival. Aunt Deirdre had transformed herself into the lady and matriarch of the castle within an instance. She graciously introduced Beth as Terrence's fiancée. Then she would say fondly, "And this is Roark, who you know, and Anna, dear Beth's sister. She is soon to be a member of the family as well." No amount of growls or glares from Roark swayed Aunt Deirdre from her introduction, for she innocently argued it was quite a proper introduction. Anna would be an in-law regardless, would she not?

Roark had apparently conceded the battle, for he remained stolidly silent beside Anna, only speaking when necessary to the guests. No one appeared offended by his aloofness. Except Anna, of course. She felt both confused and ugly, though the glances from the other men belied that notion. They at least seemed to approve of Beth's handiwork. Much good it did her.

Anna, with the grimmest determination, kept her smile from wavering as she held her hand out to the next guest in line.

"Hello, Anna," a male voice said, warm and welcoming. "I'm sorry. I mean Miss Winston."

Anna blinked, quickly focusing upon the man before her. An embarrassing second passed, but then she remembered—it was the man from the dress shop. "Hello," She floundered. "Julian! Mr. Rothman."

His eyes were as warm as his voice. "So you chose emeralds. They are magnificent. And I am glad you ordered this dress as well. I doubt the rose silk with seed pearls can be any more alluring."

Anna smiled, a pleased flush rising to her cheeks. "No, this one is simple compared to the rose silk, I assure you."

"I can only hope to see you in your future glory, though it would seem impossible," Julian said, his blue eyes admiring her. "Do you not agree, Your Grace?"

Roark's gaze was arctic. "Indeed, she is the epitome of womankind, after all."

Anna looked at him. There it was again. His words should have been a compliment, but they sounded infernally like an insult. "Thank you."

"You are welcome," Roark said, promptly turning his gaze to the next person waiting in the line.

Anna looked at Julian, ready to withdraw her hand. "I thank you."

"Do say you will honor me with a dance," Julian said, gripping her hand more tightly rather than releasing it.

"I . . ." Anna hesitated. She held no real desire to honor the man with a dance.

"She will be delighted to dance with you," Roark said promptly, his gaze narrowed.

"I look forward to it," Julian said, not once looking in Roark's direction, but staring at Anna steadily.

"Thank you," Anna said, then jerked her hand back.

Julian, offering her what could only be described as a besotted smile, sauntered away. Anna bit her lip, seething. She tolerated greeting a Miss Someone-Or-Other with Mr. So-And-So. Then, unable to withstand the tension any longer, she hissed lowly to Roark, "I believe I can choose my own dance partners, Your Grace."

"I simply did not wish for you to have to pretend," Roark said, his tone dry.

"Pretend what?" Anna asked. They both greeted Squire Petersham and his wife. Anna smiled her best to them, then repeated more forcefully, "Pretend what?"

"Pretend you did not wish to dance with him," Roark said. "I now understand why you are dressed the way you are. All this preparation was for your Mr. Rothman, was it not?"

"What?" Anna exclaimed. Roark was so very wide of the mark, Anna could only stare at him.

"Mrs. Doherty," an old woman boomed. Mrs. Doherty grabbed Anna's hand and pumped it. "Pleased to meet you, I am. This here is my man, Franklin."

"Hello," Anna said, nodding. She then greeted Mrs. Doherty's man Franklin.

The couple left, Mrs. Doherty saying, "Pretty gal, but short of hearing, what?"

"Why would I dress like this for Mr. Rothman?" Anna said, lowering her voice. "I have just met him."

"Indeed?" Roark asked, his tone disbelieving.

"Yes, indeed," Anna snapped. She greeted the next person in line, a shy young debutante who squealed when Anna accidentally shook her hand with the force of Mrs. Doherty before. The girl rushed away, nursing her hand to her.

"You only just met him?" Roark said. "But he knows the dresses you have ordered and the dresses you shall wear? Just what other apparel of yours does he know of so personally?"

Anna gasped at Roark's nasty implication. Rage flared through her. "Oh, he knows of all my different dresses and even of this blasted new French corset I am wearing."

When Roark's face turned darkly threatening, Anna

flushed deeply. Never in her life had she been so indiscreet. What kind of wild anger had caused her to say such a thing, she could not imagine. By the look on the old gentleman's face standing waiting to meet her, he could apparently not imagine either.

"Is it red?" the old geezer asked. No, evidently he could well imagine.

"Forgive me," Anna said to the old gentleman, turning that very color.

"Sure, sure," the old man said. "But I do hope it's red." He winked at Roark. "Don't you, Your Grace?"

Roark remained silent, and the old man toddled off, chuckling.

"I'm sorry," Anna said. "But what you said was unforgivable as well. I met Mr. Rothman at the dressmaker shop. He was accompanying his cousin. He overheard Beth's and my conversation. That is all."

"I find that difficult to believe," Roark said.

"I had already ordered this dress," Anna said in exasperation. "I wanted to . . ." Anna froze. She could not believe her eyes. Clarise approached them, accompanied by no less than a man who was clearly a member of the clergy and a woman who surely must be his wife.

"To what?" Roark asked, his voice hard.

Anna swallowed hard. The hounds of hell could not force her to admit that she wanted to impress him. Considering who approached, her thoughts were a mix between blasphemy and undeniable hurt. Never would she have thought Roark would have invited Clarise. She glared at Roark and then pinned on her overtaxed smile.

"Good evening, Clarise."

"Clarise," Roark said, his voice sounded surprised. "Reverend Bertram and Mrs. Bertram."

Ah, his surprise was not at Clarise's attendance, but that she was accompanied by a godly couple.

"Good evening, Your Grace," Reverend Bertram said. His eyes held a fervent glow and his gaze darted about the ballroom quickly.

"I hope you do not mind I attended the dance," Clarise said. Her eyes glowed as fervently as Reverend Bertram's did, though surely hers glowed on a a different spiritual level. A pool of green fire, her gaze was focused directly upon Roark. "When I received the invitation, I could not remain away."

Anna bit her tongue. The words forced their way out regardless. "That was very brave of you, Clarise, considering what happened the last time you came to visit."

Clarise shrugged, her smile smug. "Of what do I have to be afraid?"

"The righteous shall always prevail," Reverend Bertram said in a ringing pulpit voice. "Evil must be cast out."

"Amen," his wife said, nodding.

Anna's eyes widened as realization struck. Clarise's company with such a couple suddenly made sense. She had not come unprepared, in a manner of speaking. The reverend and his wife were to be her protection if Charles decided to become frisky.

"*Miss* Winston," Clarise said. "You have not met my cousin, have you? He is a very prominent reverend in these parts."

"How do you do?" Anna murmured. Not only protection, but supportive relatives at that.

Clarise fluttered her lashes at Roark. "I do hope you will dance with me, Roark, to show me all is forgiven?"

"Of course he will dance with you," Anna said in sheer perversity. When Roark frowned at her, and she raised her brows in innocent inquiry. "To show his good . . . spirit, to be sure."

"Thank you," Clarise said, smiling at Roark instead

of Anna. She nodded and the unlikely trio proceeded past them.

"Why did you say that?" Roark growled.

"I'm sure you want to dance with her," Anna said, clenching her teeth, "since you invited her."

"I did not invite her," Roark said. "Aunt Deirdre must have."

"You could have told Aunt Deirdre not to invite her," Anna retorted.

"I had not thought of it," Roark said angrily. "But since I have your approval, I will dance with her."

"Just as I have your approval to dance with Julian."

Frustration crossed Roark's face; then a blankness replaced it. He turned from Anna and together they silently greeted the remainder of the guests. Both departed once Aunt Deirdre decided it was time to join the festivities. Anna had no difficulty in gaining dance partners. Indeed, at the close of every dance, there was another man waiting. Filled with rebellion, she determined to enjoy every moment of her unusual success.

Her determination flagged unfortunately, for Roark was receiving fully as much attention from the ladies as she was from the gentlemen. He was casting them all that rare smile of his—the one she had foolishly thought she had brought back to life. Worse, the lady gaining most of his attention was Clarise. No matter who he danced with, Clarise navigated back to him, like a bee to a flower—or more like a vampire circling back for its next meal.

"I believe you promised me this next dance," Julian said, who now sat beside her.

Anna glanced at him and smiled rather gratefully to him. She suddenly realized that his pattern was no different than that of Clarise. He was there no matter what. Only *his* attention to her was a balm to her wounded heart. Her new dress and her six hours of effort had

had no effect upon Roark, but they were clearly enough for Julian. Anna's heart wrenched. She had been a fool to think she could attract Roark, not when a woman like Clarise was present. Her looks might have improved to passable, but certainly she'd never reach beautiful. "So it is."

Julian rose and led her to the dance floor. The strains of a waltz struck up and Julian grinned. "Ah, this is what I've been waiting for all evening."

Anna laughed. "Have you indeed?"

He grinned as they began to dance. "I could not be certain Lady Wynhaven would be forward enough to play a waltz. But I had hoped so."

Anna laughed. "Aunt Deirdre is most certainly forward enough in every fashion."

"For which I am forever grateful," Julian said. "I could not wait to hold you in my arms."

Anna flushed. "You are much like Aunt Deirdre."

"Forgive me," Julian said, his blue eyes darkening. "But ever since I saw you in the dress shop, I have not been able to think of anyone else or anything else."

Anna didn't know what to say. Then her eyes widened in surprise, because the vision of Charles appeared directly behind Julian. He did not bother to touch the floor; rather he floated and bobbed. Her mind quickly recalled Reverend Bertram's presence. "Oh, no! What are you doing?"

Julian pulled her closer. "I know I should not have said it, but I cannot contain myself around you."

Charles shook his head. "For such a prudish generation, I've always been amazed that you will permit such promiscuous acts in public."

"This is not promiscuous," Anna objected before she thought.

"No, no," Julian said eagerly. "I am so glad you understand."

"Own it," Charles said. "Such embracing you call *dancing* is a prelude to sex."

"This is not a prelude to sex," Anna gasped.

"No," Julian said, "but if you wish it to be, it shall. You have my heart."

"What? What did you say?"

Julian blinked. "I said you have my heart. I shall do anything you wish."

Anna stared in astonishment. "But you just met me."

"Forsooth, the lad closes in swiftly," Charles chuckled as he bobbed behind Julian, totally disconcerting Anna as others dancers whirled straight through him. "He's randy for you."

Anna attempted to ignore Charles. "I do not know what to say."

"Say only what is in your heart," Julian said, his blue eyes intent.

"Tell him to bugger off," Charles suggested with a smirk.

"I could not," Anna gasped.

"My sweet Anna," Julian said. "I know I ask too much too quickly. But there is no time. If you have, or had, an understanding with the duke . . ."

"He's a jumped-up popinjay," Charles said. "Tell him to bugger off."

"He's not a popinjay," Anna said, flaring up, "And I won't tell him to bugger off!"

"No, of course not," Julian stammered. "I would never expect you to say such a thing to him. Ever!"

Charles laughed. "The man is a fortune hunter, b'gad."

"He's not a fortune hunter," Anna refuted.

"I didn't say that!" Julian's expression changed to curiosity. "Never say the duke is all to pieces too—I mean, that he's all to pieces."

"Why would you think he's a fortune hunter?" Anna asked Charles.

"I didn't. I thought *you* said that!" Julian said.

"Because, mistress," Charles said. "The man accepts whatever you say. He flatters you for a purpose."

"Enough," Anna said, frustrated to a breaking point. She'd not had much flattery to date, and to have it pointed out at such a moment hurt even more. "Just tell me what you want."

"I want whatever you want," Julian said. "I want to make you the happiest woman I can."

"Blast and damn, I forgot," Charles said. "At the end of the dance you must follow Roark and Clarise."

"Why?" Anna asked in exasperation..

"Why, because my heart is yours," Julian said.

"That jade is up to something," Charles said. "She's begging to be private with Roark. I scent a trap."

"I'm sure I don't care what Roark does," Anna said, shrugging her shoulders in what she hoped was a blasé, rather than a petulant, manner. "Not a rap."

"My God," Julian said, breathing in deeply, "you have made me the happiest of men."

Charles looked anything but happy. For a ghost, his eyes could narrow rather dangerously. "Either you do what I tell you, milady, or I shall do something myself."

"Why should I do anything for Roark?" Anna asked, her chin jutting out. "It is clear he is enamored of Clarise. I do not matter one wit to him."

"He is a fool," Julian said, his tone vehement.

Anna focused upon Julian for a moment. His words rang a sweet chord within in her. "Thank you."

"I warn you, mistress," Charles's voice demanded her attention once more as the strains of the waltz faded, "if you do not do my bidding, I shall be forced to take extreme measures, though I am loath to cause a scene at an engagement ball."

"I will not be coerced," Anna said obstinately.

"I would never dream of coercing you in any fashion," Julian said, his tone reverent.

Anna glanced over to Roark and Clarise across the room. True to Charles's word, Roark and Clarise were leaving the dance floor and moving toward the exiting doors. "Oh, very well, I'll go."

"You'll go?" Julian asked, his arms dropping from about her. "Go where?"

"Though I warn you," Anna said to Charles as she turned and stalked toward the same exiting doors, "do not expect too much."

"Expect too much?" Julian asked, following behind. "I swear, it shall only be whatever you wish and desire."

Anna grimaced and glared at Charles, who floated beside her with a blatantly satisfied smile upon his face. "What I wish is that certain people would permit me to live my own life and not interfere and interrupt."

"You are a free spirit then," Julian said, an oddly eager tone to his voice.

Anna winced and Charles laughed. "Do not mention spirits to me." She looked around the hall they had entered in irritation, but there was no sight of Roark or Clarise. "Now where do we go?"

"Anywhere you wish," Julian said, his laugh filled with excitement. "You are leading the way, my sweet Anna."

"Gads but he doesn't give up," Charles muttered. He disappeared, then blinked back. "This way."

"This way," Anna mimicked and followed.

Julian laughed again. "I have never met a woman like you before."

"Yes, I am quite insane," Anna said bitterly as she trod down another corridor, Charles floating farther ahead and impatiently waving his hand.

"Never," Julian said, sounding breathless. "Just reckless and exciting."

"Not exciting enough," Anna said, thinking of Roark. She couldn't believe she was following a ghost bent on playing chaperon. Charles pointed to the door of a room, then popped out of sight. Anna drew in a deep breath and swung the door open, entering before she lost her courage.

She froze. For all her brave and careless talk, she hadn't truly expected to see Clarise in Roark's arms. She hadn't expected to feel the wrenching pain the sight caused her.

"Alone at last!" Julian exclaimed as he entered behind Anna. He halted. "Er, wrong room. We're not alone."

Apparently the entwined couple came to the same conclusion. Clarise swiftly pulled back from Roark. She crossed her arms about her chest in a semblance of demureness. Her voice was husky. "Roark, we have been discovered."

Anna stood completely immobilized. She feared the rage within her would rip her apart. If she had possessed Charles's powers, she would have caused a typhoon to tear through the room. She braced herself for the ignominy of seeing the triumph in Clarise's eyes when the other woman turned to find insignificant Anna watching. Instead, Clarise's eyes opened wide in surprise and confusion when she looked at Anna. "You!"

Anna's lips trembled, but she forced a smile. She could not bring herself to look at Roark. "Yes, me. Who else would it be?"

Clarise actually bit her lip and looked away. She uncrossed her arms in what appeared a fit of pique.

"Aye, Anna," Charles's voice said. Anna looked swiftly about to discover Charles standing not far from Clarise and Roark. He actually rubbed his hands together as if he were watching a famous theatrical show. "Put her to the pillar. Ask her again who she did expect. 'Twas not you to be sure."

"What are *you* doing here?" Roark asked instead.

Anna turned a blazing look to the perfidious man. He actually had the brass to use an accusatory tone upon her. "A certain *friend* of yours demanded I come."

Roark's eyes narrowed. He flicked a sarcastic glance to Julian behind her. "No need for such a story, Miss Winston. You were looking for a private room. My apologies that we upset your plans."

"I was not looking for a private room," Anna gasped in outrage. "I—"

"Clarise!" a male voice bellowed. Reverend Bertram charged into the room. The man of God waved a wooden crucifix in his hand. Anna blinked. Just where had he hidden that before? His wife stumbled in directly upon his heels, shoving out a Bible before her. An even more interesting question would be where she had secreted that tome. The only one missing now was Salome.

"Ha! I was right!" Charles laughed. "Blast and damn her to hell, I was right."

"Don't curse," Anna murmured.

Reverend Bertram halted, his gaze darting about the room. "Yes, daughter, yes. We must fight evil with righteousness."

"Where have you been, Horace?" Clarise all but snarled. The anger flashing from her eyes lacked a certain righteousness.

"We tried to follow directly, as you asked," Bertram's wife said, her voice shaking. "Only we took a wrong turn for a moment."

"I did not ask you to follow," Clarise said, her cheeks flaring, though her eyes showed she lied.

"But we are here," Bertram thundered, rattling his crucifix. "To exorcise what evil spirit may be present."

"He need but exorcise his harlot cousin from hence," Charles murmured with a chuckle.

Anna blinked. She had thought the reverend accompanied Clarise as her protection, but he had also been meant to be her dupe: He and his wife had been appointed to catch Clarise and Roark in a compromising situation—one in which, as a reverend, he would have the power to demand restitution. Anna looked at Charles, stunned. "B'gad, you were right."

"Who are you talking to?" Roark said, his eyes narrowed.

Anna swung her gaze to him. Her anger flared high again. Although Charles forced her to save Roark from a scandal, the fact that Roark had willingly put himself in the position of needing to be saved was telling. Worse, Roark appeared more angry and indignant than anything else. Most likely he was merely upset because he had been interrupted from his disgusting pursuit.

"No one, no one at all." Anna lifted her skirts and cast Roark a look of disdain. "I do apologize if we interrupted. We shall leave you now."

"Anna!" Roark said, but his anger was a mere backfire compared to hers. "This is not what it appears."

"I am sure that I do not care. It is no concern of mine," Anna spat. She heard Julian sigh in relief. Then she saw Clarise's eyes brighten with delight.

"Nay, wench," Charles growled, "stand and fight, for God's sake. Don't leave your man to another woman."

A dry chuckle rose in Anna's throat. In retaliation for her pain, she looked to Reverend Bertram and his wife. "You have my permission to try and exorcise them all. Start with whomever you bloody well want to."

Anna ran from the room and down the hall, unwanted tears spilling from her eyes. Even through the blur, she could not avoid the vision of Charles standing before her. She skittered to a halt.

"Gads, woman!" he roared. "You are acting like a child, not a woman full grown."

"A child!" Bile rose within Anna's throat. "I am not a child. Do not tell me I am a child. It is all your fault!" Enraged, she lunged forward with her fists flailing, but she fell directly through Charles. She felt something in that passing—a sincere confusion and outrage. It only made her wilder. She spun, panting.

Charles was still there, frowning darkly. "My fault?"

"Yes, yours," Anna said. " 'Follow your woman's heart,' you said. 'Learn the tricks of love,' you said." Suddenly everything she had done on Charles's advisement, everything she had done to win Roark's desire, seemed humiliating. "It's all poppycock! You men are all arrogant, lascivious, no-good, beasts!" With vengeful intent, Anna pulled off a shoe, and flung it at Charles.

There was no need for him to duck since the shoe merely flew through him. He stiffened. "Here now, vixen!"

"Vixen? That 'twas your advice too, wasn't it?" Anna said nastily. She snatched off her emerald necklace and lobbed it at Charles. The necklace flashed and sparkled straight through him.

"I told you rightly," Charles said.

"Rightly?" Anna shouted. "This dress, this entire wardrobe, did nothing." She clamped the thin and expensive fabric at her shoulders. "Do take this dress . . ."

Of a sudden, Anna felt an object hit her skirts. Stunned, she looked down. A crucifix lay at her feet. She looked past Charles. Reverend Bertram, his wife, Julian, Roark, and Clarise stood crowded together, their expressions all variations of astonishment and fear.

"Begone, demon! Possess this woman no more," Reverend Bertram said. He tore the Bible from his wife's hands.

"No, wait! There is no need for that," Anna said,

dragging in a ragged breath. She glared at Charles. "You heard the reverend. I do not want to see you ever again."

"Do not be a bratling," Charles said.

Anna clenched her fist. "I told you. I do not want to see you."

"Very well," Charles said. "My lady's wish is my command." Eyes blazing, Charles disappeared to the sound of rushing wind.

Mistress Bertram squalled and the good reverend, shouting, flung the Bible wildly. It ricocheted off the wall.

"Just what the devil were you two up to?" Roark asked, totally ignoring the dramatics. Clarise had taken advantage of the situation and was clinging to him.

"What were *we* up to?" A sharp laugh escaped Anna. To date, she'd had rosary beads showered upon her, a crucifix thrown at her, and a Bible flung at her. And the man responsible for it all dared to make accusations. It was more than enough. "I do not wish to speak to you ever again."

"Anna," Roark said, his face clouding. He made an attempt to step forward, but Clarise held firmly to him.

"Now, if you will excuse me," Anna said with dignity. "You have done well, Reverend. I believe I am saved from those who have sought to possess me."

"Praise the Almighty!" Reverend Bertram cried, throwing up his hands. "Praise the Almighty."

"My God," Julian said, shaking his head. "What a spirited woman!"

Seven

Anna sat alone in the breakfast room, sipping a strong cup of Darjeerling tea. She had intentionally come downstairs late in order to miss the family at breakfast. Roark most likely had not attended, but Anna hadn't wanted to take a chance. She had not lied when she said she didn't want to see him. Considering the mood she was in, she didn't want to see anyone.

Perversely, she felt bereft. Her life had taken a sad turn indeed if she felt bereft merely because she had ordered one interfering ghost and one philandering rake to get out of her life. She sighed, setting her teacup down and staring into it. It was fortunate she could not read tea leaves. She would never wish to glance at her future, especially since it seemed rather grim and lonely at the moment.

"Anna," Aunt Deirdre's voice said.

Anna started upon finding Aunt Deirdre watching her, her blue eyes filled with concern. "Forgive me. I did not hear you enter."

"I know," Aunt Deirdre said. "I've been standing here for a while. Is anything wrong?"

"No," Anna said quickly. What a clanker. Her entire life was wrong. "I have a headache." Another lie, but it was certainly better than confessing she had a heartache instead.

Aunt Deirdre's eyes lighted. "Then I shall tell the gentleman in the parlor you cannot see him?"

"What gentleman?" Anna asked, frowning.

"Julian Rothman." Aunt Deirdre frowned. "He says he knows you."

"Yes, I met him . . . last night," Anna said, knowing better than to go into any lengthy detail with Aunt Deirdre.

"Yes, that is what he said." Aunt Deirdre nodded. "The dear boy thanked me for the enjoyable evening quite properly. He stays with his own dear aunt, Lydia Talboth."

Anna smiled. Evidently Julian had not escaped Aunt Deirdre's inquisition. Anna stood, her mood lightening. After the previous night and the grand display she had made, she had not expected to see Julian again. That he would so bravely return to the castle showed a sincere interest. "Does he? I shall see him."

"Yes," Aunt Deirdre said, following behind her. "Lydia is such a sweet lady, but she has had a very sad life. She is a widow, you know."

"Indeed," Anna said, not really listening.

"Yes," Aunt Deirdre said. "I have been trying to decide whose boy Julian is. Lydia has two brothers. One is quite respectable, but the other is a different kettle of fish altogether."

"You don't say?" Anna murmured and entered the parlor. A pleased grin crossed Anna's lips when she saw Julian sitting upon the sofa. He was dressed in buff unmentionables and a perfect-fitting tan riding jacket; his cane and beaver hat rested beside him. He held in his arms a large bouquet of red roses.

Julian's blue eyes gleamed with admiration. "Anna—I mean, Miss Winston, thank you for seeing me."

"It is my pleasure." Anna flushed. "I was not certain you would wish to see me again after last night."

"That was quite a brouhaha, was it not?" Julian said, grinning.

"A brouhaha?" Aunt Deirdre asked from behind.

"Then you were not frightened," Anna asked hesitantly. "or overset by what happened?"

"What did happen?" Aunt Deirdre whispered.

"You mean all that talk about demons and possession?" Julian asked.

"Demons and possession?" Aunt Deirdre asked. "Gracious, whatever are you two talking about?"

"Reverend Bertram attended last night," Anna said in a low voice. "He was under the misapprehension that we had demons present."

"Demons here?" Aunt Deirdre exclaimed. "How ridiculous. Why ever would he think such a thing?"

"I don't know, Aunt Deirdre," Anna said, casting her a stern look. "He is probably the superstitious sort who believes in demons and ghosts and whatnot."

"Oh," Aunt Deirdre said, her eyes widening. "I see."

"They were a queer lot," Julian said, laughing, "but Anna took care of them readily."

Anna blinked. "I did?"

"She gave the old reverend exactly what he wanted," Julian said. "Made him think there was a demon there, than let him think he had cast it out. It was brilliant. Else you'd never have gotten shed of them, I have no doubt. They'd always be poking about with their sour faces, looking for spooks and whatnot."

"Oh, my." Aunt Deirdre said, "we most certainly wouldn't want that."

Anna smiled weakly at Julian. "I am so glad you understood."

"I am an enlightened man," Julian said. "I know far better than to believe in superstitions."

"Do you?"

Julian walked toward her. "The only thing I am possessed of is admiration for you." He held the bouquet of roses out. "These are for you."

"Thank you," Anna said, taking the flowers in her arms, then breathing in their sweet scent. "They are beautiful."

"Not as beautiful as you," Julian said.

Anna stifled a gasp as the top rose of the bouquet began to rise in the air. She grabbed it quickly, but eased her hold as thorns stung her. The rose darted forward and slapped Julian in the face. He reared back, a stunned expression upon his face.

Anna forced a nervous laugh. "Fie, sir, you are such a flatterer!"

Julian rubbed his cheek, grinning. "You are a playful lady, I see.

"Very playful." Anna cast Aunt Deirdre a beseeching look. "Aren't I, Aunt Deirdre?"

"Oh, yes," Aunt Deirdre said, "and very mischievous."

"I was hoping you would go for a ride with me," Julian said.

"I . . ." Anna started, but the bouquet in her arms exploded from her arms, roses showering down upon them.

"Good God," Julian said, staring.

Anna, her arms empty, clapped her hands together. "What a famous idea. I would be delighted to ride with you. I am so excited."

Julian plucked a rose from his shoulder. "Er, yes."

"Such an enthusiastic girl, our Anna," Aunt Deirdre said.

"Let us go," Anna said. "Immediately."

"Do not concern yourself with the roses," Aunt Deirdre added quickly. "I shall tend to them. Oh, no!"

Aunt Deirdre dashed past the two to where Julian's

cane and hat floated high in the air. Aunt Deirdre jumped up and down, attempting to grab them.

"No," Anna said quickly to Julian, who had begun to turn around. To his surprise, she clutched him by the shoulders. "We cannot leave Aunt Deirdre to pick these up. Help me!" She applied all the pressure she could muster to his shoulders. Julian stumbled to his knees.

"Ouch!" Julian exclaimed, for Anna had forced him onto a rose stem.

"Oh, I am sorry."

"No, no," Julian said. "it is of no significance."

"You are so kind," Anna said.

Aunt Deirdre had caught the beaver hat and was just then clamping on to the cane. "Got them! Oh dear!" The cane in Deirdre's hand started to drag the little woman along, its tip pointed directly at Julian's unguarded back side.

"Move!" Anna cried, then pushed Julian over and jumped aside as Aunt Deirdre stumbled past.

"What is the matter?" Julian asked, his eyes wide.

"Nothing," Anna said. "Only you missed a rose. Yes, you missed a rose."

"What?" Julian asked, frowning.

"Beware! Coming through." Aunt Deirdre attached to the cane, was driving directly at Julian.

"Enough!" Anna grabbed hold of the cane. It took both her and Aunt Deirdre to halt the propelling stick. Even then, it bobbed through the air like a dancing sword, weaving a pattern of which the most demanding of fencing instructors would be proud.

"*En garde?*" Aunt Deirdre said in a hopeful voice.

"Oh, do stop," Anna said. Then she pinned a smile upon her face. "Aunt Deirdre is so very playful herself."

"I see," Julian said, crawling backward and standing.

"Dearest, I don't think you can go with him," Aunt Deirdre said. "You forgot you have an appointment."

"What?" Julian asked, his gaze confused.

Aunt Deirdre cast Anna a pleading look. "Besides, a carriage ride right now would be frightful. I'm sure there would be a storm or something. Yes, it is coming on to rain."

"There is not a cloud in the sky," Julian objected.

"It's going to storm," Aunt Deirdre said in a portentous voice. "I feel it in my bones."

"All right, I will not go," Anna said in exasperation, and the cane immediately stopped its animosity.

"But—" Julian said.

"Aunt Deirdre's bones never lie," Anna said solemnly. "I'm sorry."

"Perhaps another time," Aunt Deirdre said, offering Julian his cane and hat quickly.

"Yes," Anna said, grim determination in her voice. She hurried over to Julian and took up his arm. "Only you must leave now."

"I must?" Julian asked.

"You must," Aunt Deirdre said, nodding her head vehemently. She scurried over and took him by the other arm.

The two ladies marshaled Julian from the room and bodily escorted him to the castle door. When they closed the heavy door, Aunt Deirdre sagged against it. "Good Gracious, but Charles's has been naughty."

"Naughty? I'd say he has acted like a bratling." Anna's eyes snapped furiously. "When I said I didn't want to see you again, I meant I wanted you to stay out of my life."

"Well, dearest," Aunt Deirdre said. "He is right in a fashion. You should not be entertaining other gentlemen when you are engaged to Roark."

"I am no longer engaged to Roark!"

"Oh, no," Aunt Deirdre sighed. "Did you and Roark have another dustup?"

Anna laughed dryly. "Yes, a brouhaha at that."

"What happened dearest?" Aunt Deirdre asked in concern.

"Ask Roark." Anna smiled grimly. "I must dress."

Aunt Deirdre blinked. "But, dearest, you are dressed."

"No," Anna said firmly. "I am not dressed for going out."

"You are going out?" Aunt Deirdre asked, frowning. "But, dearest, aren't you exhausted? I know I am."

"No," Anna said, primed rather for battle. "If I am not able to see Julian upon the premises, I shall see him away from the premises, where there are no busybodies to try to interfere with me."

"Anna," Aunt Deirdre gasped, "surely you would not do anything so brazen."

"Would I not?" Anna asked, laughing. "Everyone else in this castle is brazen, why should not I be?"

"Roark," Aunt Deirdre called.

"Yes, Aunt?" Roark asked, looking up from a chart as she entered the turret. Only Aunt Deirdre never feared the place. Well, she and one other. Forcefully, Roark brushed aside that thought before he put paid to the peace he had worked so diligently the whole morning through to obtain. He would *not* think about her. "What is it?"

"You must stop Anna," Aunt Deirdre said, her blue eyes worried. "She is intending to be brazen."

"Brazen?" Roark asked, frowning. Apparently he would not be able to push aside the subject of that morning's thoughts easily. Indeed, she did have a way of returning. Again.

"Yes," Aunt Deirdre said with a nod. "She says she

might as well be brazen like everyone else. What does she mean?"

Roark bit back a curse. "Nothing."

"Does it have anything to do with the brouhaha last evening?" Aunt Deirdre asked.

Roark started. "Anna told you what happened?"

"Not exactly, dear," Aunt Deirdre said. "Julian Rothman was talking about it—something about demons and Reverend Bertram."

"Julian Rothman?" Roark asked, eyes narrowed. "When did you speak to him?"

"This morning. He came to ask Anna if he could take her for a ride."

"He did, did he?" Anger and jealousy flared within him. Forcing the emotions away, he shrugged and even managed a laugh. "It is not brazen if Anna drives out with him."

"Oh, no, dear," Aunt Deirdre said, shaking her head. "They couldn't go for a drive. Ancestor Charles would not permit it."

"What?" Roark asked, astonished.

"Yes, he was very naughty," Aunt Deirdre said. "In all my days, I have never seen so much involvement from him. It took Anna's and my best efforts to protect Mr. Rothman and escort him from the house before something serious happened. That is why Anna did not go for a drive with Mr. Rothman."

Roark chuckled. "Bully for Charles."

"So I thought." Aunt Deirdre sighed. "Only now Anna is determined to go to visit Mr. Rothman. She declares, if she cannot see him here, she will see him outside the castle. I fear Ancestor Charles has set her back up past all reason. You must stop her."

Roark ignored the turmoil of emotions ripping through him. "I cannot stop her."

"Why not?" Aunt Deirdre asked. "You are her fi-ancé."

"Not anymore." Roark laughed sharply. "I fear I am in her black books as much as old Charles is."

"What did you do? Surely it was not so bad."

Roark sighed. If he did not explain to Aunt Deirdre, she would only persist in badgering him. "Anna found me kissing another woman."

"What?" Aunt Deirdre asked, turning rather pale. "I cannot believe it."

"Too bad you aren't Anna. She believed it immediately," Roark said dryly. He flushed, feeling like a total heel. "Clarise Bentford begged me to give her a private moment to apologize for her past behavior in a certain incident."

"Clarise Bentford? I did not think you knew her other than in passing."

Roark shifted uncomfortably. "No, I've known her slightly better than that, but that does not matter. Suffice it to say, I permitted her a private interview and she flung herself upon me and started kissing me."

"Gracious, the hussy." Aunt Deirdre sighed and shook her head. "I had prayed you would once start to live and again be a part of life, but not quite to this degree."

A laugh escaped Roark. "To be sure."

Aunt Deirdre looked sternly at him. "If what you say is true, you must go to Anna and explain this to her."

"I will not," Roark said, stiffening.

"If you love her, you will," Aunt Deirdre said.

"I do not love her," Roark said angrily.

"Very well, you do not love her," Aunt Deirdre said in the sternest voice Roark had ever heard. "But if you did, you would go to her directly. You have broken her trust."

"Her trust!" Roark asked in defense. "What about

my trust? It is she who is going to brazenly visit a man she has just met."

"Yes," Aunt Deirdre said, nodding, "a man who seems intent upon gaining her trust and perhaps even her love. But since you do not want that, I would not fault Anna for seeking one who does." She walked to the door. She would not look at Roark. She did not need to do so because he could read the sadness and grief in her body. "I know you think there is a good reason for you to turn love away. I used to think the same. But now after all these years, I cannot believe it anymore."

"Aunt Deirdre," Roark murmured, guilt ripping through him. Never had she spoken in such a manner to him.

"When it is true love and yet you are untrue to it, it does not fade, Roark. It only grows deeper and nothing takes its place—except regret."

Beth and Terrence sat upon the sofa, holding hands. When Beth sighed, Terrence asked, "Are you happy, love?"

"Oh, yes. Yes, of course I am." Beth laid her head upon his shoulder.

"Imagine," Terrence murmured. "We shall be married within two weeks."

"Yes," Beth said, sighing again.

"All the wedding plans are in order," Terrence said. "They are, aren't they?"

"What?" Beth started. "Oh, yes. Yes, they are."

"What is the matter, darling?" Terrence asked, frowning.

"Nothing. Nothing at all," Beth said quickly.

"Something is troubling you. It isn't . . . ?" Terrence's voice grew hesitant. "It isn't the ghost, is it? I mean, he hasn't done anything for a week or two, has he?"

"No, he hasn't," Beth said. "And I am so very grateful for that."

"Then what is it?" Terrence asked. "What is the matter?"

"It is Anna," Beth finally said.

Terrence frowned. "And Roark."

"I cannot believe she is happy," Beth said, straightening up. "I simply cannot—not with that Mr. Rothman."

"I know," Terrence said, pursing his lips. "I can't say why, but I don't like the fellow. I don't trust him one whit."

"Of course not," Beth said. "Even I would know better, but Anna is so very innocent where men are concerned. You cannot believe the books she can read. And she understands them! But with men, she is completely unwise."

"Have you talked to her?" Terrence asked.

"Yes," Beth said. "I've tried to tell her she cannot trust him. She's only known him for two weeks after all."

"Good, good," Terrence nodded. "That is good."

Beth shook her head. "No, it isn't. She declares Julian always behaves like a perfect gentleman."

Terrence snorted. "I find that hard to believe. It is just an act, I'll lay odds."

"I tried to suggest that," Beth said. "But Anna grew quite incensed. She said I was not being fair to Julian, and why would I ask her to be cautious of Julian when I had showed no such concern with her marrying Roark after she had only known him a day?"

"But that *was* different," Terrence said, his tone offended. "We found them in bed together and—well, it's different. Roark ain't Julian Rothman. No matter what happened, he can be trusted."

"I know," Beth said. "That is exactly what I told Anna."

"You are the sweetest and best woman ever," Terrence said, a warmth flaring in his eyes.

"Thank you." Beth blushed.

Terrence cleared his throat. "What did Anna say when you told her that?"

"She said she didn't wish to talk about Roark," Beth said. "She simply refused."

Terrence nodded. "Roark did the same thing."

"Then you have talked to him?"

"I tried to," Terrence said, an embarrassed look crossing his face

"Oh, dearest," Beth said, gazing at him with pleasure. "You are such a wonderful man. I am so glad you talked to him."

Terrence flushed deeply. "Well, I made mincemeat out of it. Roark would have none of it. He declared he didn't care what Anna did, and furthermore, it wasn't any business of his or ours."

"What?" Beth exclaimed, aghast.

"You must understand Roark," Terrence said. "He was hurt badly when Tiffany Templeton ran from the wedding."

Beth shivered. "You mean when that ghost appeared."

"Yes." He watched Beth closely as her face twisted in alarm. "He was hurt as deeply as I would be if you ever left me."

Beth's eyes warmed. "I would never leave you."

"I know that," Terrence said, his voice deepening. "But you ain't Tiffany Templeton. If you say Anna is stupid when it comes to men—"

"I did not say that," Beth objected.

"Well, unwise then," Terrence said. "Roark ain't much better. He knows the stars and all that, but he doesn't know women."

"I understand," Beth said, her brow wrinkling.

"So when Tiffany left him, he decided all women are like her."

"Anna is nothing like her!" Beth exclaimed.

"I know that," Terrence said. "And truth is, Roark knows it too. But he never likes to be proven wrong. Never liked it when we were young and still doesn't."

"But they are making each other miserable," Beth said.

"I know," Terrence said. "If I have to watch the two try to ignore each other one more time or watch them looking at each other when they don't think anyone sees them . . ."

"And if I have to listen to Anna talk about Julian as if he is a wonderful man when it is clear he is not and that she loves Roark . . ."

"Well, I think I'll . . ."

"Just cry," Beth said.

Terrence paused. "Something like that."

"What are we to do?" Beth asked.

"I don't know," Terrence said, frowning. "Even Aunt Deirdre has lost hope. It almost makes me wish . . ."

"Wish what?" Beth said, her voice hopeful.

"What do you wish?" Beth said. "Please tell me."

"Well, I know you don't want to hear it," Terrence said. "But it seemed to me things were better with Anna and Roark when old Charles kept popping in and about."

"No, oh, no," Beth said, shaking her head and glancing about in fright. "Don't say that. Whatever you do, don't say that."

"Forgive me," Terrence said. "I won't say it again. I promise."

* * *

Roark walked down the darkened hall with a candle in hand. He had chosen to take dinner in his rooms. Only to himself would he admit he was avoiding Anna, though his efforts were most likely unnecessary. No doubt she was once again out for the evening with Julian. The familiar emotions of anger and jealousy rose within him. Those feelings were making themselves at home—indeed, giving themselves free reign to run hither and yon within his being. He squelched them. What Anna did was no business of his, none whatsoever.

Roark frowned as he saw a flash of light ahead of him in the hall. He strode forward. The light had disappeared. Roark halted, regardless. By the light of his own candle, he could see a section of wall that appeared to be at an odd angle, as if it had inched forward from its neighboring stone. He walked over and studied it. It was evidently a door to another secret passage.

"What game are you playing now, Charles?" Roark murmured. Instinct warned him to avoid the passage. He turned and walked past it. Sheer curiosity, however, brought him to a standstill. By God, it was his house, and if there were hidden passages within it, he should know about them. Perhaps Charles had something of import to show him. It was no secret within the household that Charles had fallen into disfavor with Anna just as Roark had. That bond alone should have been his security.

Roark slowly pushed the panel farther open and entered the passage. He inspected the walls, which were made of smooth stone. There were no cracks or crevices of any significance. He continued until he came to the end, where another panel stood ajar. He was intrigued, despite himself. Perhaps it led to a secret room. He stifled a laugh. No doubt it was the priest's hole and would contain the truth of Charles's murder.

He slowly pushed open the door. It was no priest's hole. Indeed, he knew the room well, yet the sight before him drew him forward as if he had discovered a treasure cave. Anna sat before the fire, rubbing a towel over wet hair. She wore a loose silken robe, which clung to her, its dark patches testifying that her body beneath was still damp. A large tub set to the side was conclusive evidence she had just risen from her bath.

Roark sucked in his breath. The thought of her naked only moments earlier shot heat through his body. His reaction was as strong as if he had caught her out in her bath. The robe she had donned could be so slowly removed, exposing each curve just as slowly. Her skin would be fresh and moist, tasting of soap and water. Roark actually groaned.

Anna froze, turned her head. "Roark!"

"Hello," Roark said, his voice hoarse. "Excuse me. I had no intention of coming here or interrupting . . ."

Anna suddenly jumped as if he had shot her. Her gaze skittered wildly about the room. Roark had come to know that look of hers well. It helped him to focus upon something other than the wild thoughts in his mind, the aching tightness in his body. "It is Charles, isn't it? What did he say?"

Anna's face turned rosy. She worried her lower lip. "He said if you hadn't dawdled you would have been interrupting something a damn sight better."

Roark bit back a groan. He didn't need that thought reinforced. "We've been set up again." He turned back toward the passage door, but smooth wall met his gaze. "Where is it?"

"Where is what?" Anna asked. Her tone sounded as if she already knew the answer.

"The secret door." Roark had been so mesmerized

by Anna he had never heard the panel shut. Fool! He should never have stepped from the passage in the first place. "I came through a secret passage."

"I believe you," Anna said, sighing. She passed a hand across her eyes in a weary gesture. "Try the door."

Roark, muttering a curse, strode to the door and jerked at the knob. It did not budge. "It's locked."

Anger flared in Anna's eyes as she said to the room at large. "That is not very original, is it?"

The temperature in the room dropped instantly. Anna shivered and crossed her arms about her, for which Roark was grateful. The air was cold—and Anna definitely showed it in her silken robe—but an inner heat coursed through him. He growled in frustration. "Let us out, damn it!"

"Yes," Anna said, stamping her foot. "Let us out! Don't be ridiculous. And if you are going to speak to me, you might as well show yourself." She waved a hand. "You know very well that, when I said I didn't want to *see* you again, I meant I wanted you to stop interfering entirely, not merely to remain invisible. Now let us out." Anna listened a moment. "No, I won't!" Anna began to pace and her face held the most truculent of expressions.

Roark sighed in exasperation. "What did he say?"

"Hmm?" Anna asked, whirling about for another turn.

"You know I can't hear him," Roark said. "What the devil did he say?"

Anna halted, her face totally indignant. "He wants us to apologize to each other."

Roark clenched his teeth as he glared at Anna. "I have nothing for which to apologize."

"Nor do I!" Anna said.

"No, indeed not," Roark snorted, disbelief written in his expression.

"I don't," Anna said. "*I* was not the one who was kissing Clarise."

"No," Roark said, "you were the one looking for a private room to be alone with your Julian."

"I was not," Anna said. "I was following you, because Charles demanded I do so. He thought Clarise was setting a trap for you."

Anger swelled within Roark, but a fairness forced him to say, "He was right."

Anna sniffed. "Indeed?"

Roark glared at her. "You know full well he was right. I took Clarise to that room only because she was becoming overset. She begged me to permit her to explain herself. I thought she would create a scene if I did not heed her. The minute we entered, she threw herself at me."

"And you welcomed her with open arms," Anna said, her tone dry.

"I did not." Roark stepped toward Anna and then halted. "You may believe me or not, but I did not."

A flush rose in Anna's cheeks. "You danced with her all night long."

"And you danced with Julian," Roark said, the memory pulsing jealousy through him.

"I only did so because—" Anna halted.

"Because why?" Roark asked.

"I know I am not beautiful. But I had dressed my best for you, and you told me I should dance with Julian."

Roark sucked in his breath as if Anna had punched him in the stomach. "Anna . . ."

"But that is of no significance now, is it?"

Roark stopped dead in his track. "No, I suppose not."

Anna's gaze skittered around the room. "All right,

Charles, we've apologized. Are you satisfied?" She frowned. "Yes, yes, we are friends now"—Anna looked at Roark, her eyes wary—"aren't we?"

Roark forced a smile. "Yes, we are friends now."

"See," Anna said, her own smile weak. "Now open the door." There was a pause. Then Anna gasped. "What? You cannot mean it!"

Roark's brows rose as Anna's face turned red. "What does he want now?"

She stared at Roark with an aghast expression. "He wants us to seal our friendship with a kiss."

Roark barked a laugh. "That devil drives a hard bargain."

"We are not going to kiss," Anna said, her tone positively mulish.

Despite the situation, or perhaps because of it all, Roark smiled. Anna's face, blue lipped with cold, was set in determined lines. When she shivered, a tenderness overcame him. "Let us simply get it over with before you freeze."

Anna glared at him. "You cannot be serious. I refuse to kiss anyone merely because some conniving, perfidious ghost tells me I must. I am not a performing monkey."

"For God's sake," Roark laughed, "the man is right. Let us kiss as friends and be done with it."

Anna paused a moment, then started, and Roark asked, "What did he say?"

"He said I could have all night to decide," Anna said. Roark watched her closely. "Then let us be about it."

"Very well," Anna said.

Roark, grinning, walked toward her.

"Wait!" Anna held out a hand. "Charles, I want your promise that, once Roark and I kiss, you will open the door. Promise me." She paused, then nodded. "Very well." Anna dashed up, placed a quick peck upon

Roark's cheek, and pedaled backward a goodly distance.

"There, we've kissed," she said, smiling with clear relief. Her smile disappeared just as swiftly as she had kissed Roark. "What do you mean that was not good enough?"

Roark's humor faded. "He means that was a paltry and stingy kiss for friends. Are you afraid, Anna, that you might in some way be unfaithful to Rothman?"

"Julian has nothing to do with this," Anna said.

"Then prove it," Roark said. "To me and yourself."

"Very well," Anna said, her eyes suddenly frightened.

Roark realized he had been insane to issue the challenge, for it could be his undoing as well. Anna walked hesitantly forward. Her hazel eyes were more green than brown, her wet hair clinging in tendrils about her face. She stood upon her toes and placed her cool lips to his. They remained thus, but Roark could feel the quiver of her lips as they grew warm beneath his.

When Roark slowly reached out and drew her body close to his, Anna sighed. It was an echo of his soul. She had been out of his arms for far too long. He caressed her curves with painstaking slowness, the cool silk of her robe only the slightest tease between his hands and her warming flesh beneath. He gently plundered her mouth. He was already hot with arousal, but he didn't want to move fast. He wanted to know this woman, to discover her every secret. If it took all night or a lifetime, he did not care.

He moved his lips from hers, tracing kisses along her cheek and down the column of her neck. God, it was as he imagined it. Her skin was soft, damp, and fragrant. He heard Anna moan low in her throat. He slid his hand to the collar of her robe. He had to see her, but slowly. She was a treasure to uncover.

"No." Anna pushed him away, clasping the folds of her robe together. "This is wrong."

"Wrong?" Roark asked, his voice coming out hoarse with shock. It was right. Nothing had ever been more right in his life. How could she turn away from it? How could she deny what should be? The answer entered his mind, shooting jealousy through already taught nerves. "Wrong because of Rothman?" He clasped her shoulder. "Is it right when he kisses you like this? Do you feel this with him?"

Anna's eyes shimmered with passion—and tears. "Get out." She jerked free of him, her chest heaving. "I don't care if you must leap from the window. Just get out!"

Roark stiffened. An angry, bitter laugh escaped him. He'd had women use him before—and betray him before. He should have known better. "No, one man taking that form of exit in the family is enough. There isn't a woman alive who is worth it." He turned and strode toward the door. He didn't hesitate, but grabbed the handle and pulled. The door opened.

He stalked out, reminding himself what a fool he had been. Clearly Charles had realized the same thing.

Eight

"Anna," Lydia Talboth asked, "is anything wrong?"

Anna's gaze flashed first to Julian, then to his aunt. Lydia was a small, sparse woman with sandy hair and blue eyes. She was a sweet woman with a certain nervousness to her movements. It was clear she worshiped Julian, a nephew whose plumage was far brighter than hers would ever be. However, Anna often caught a worried, almost frightened, look in Lydia's eyes at times. What trials in her life had caused such timidity?

"No," Anna said, knowing she lied. "I fear I have the headache, that is all."

"What can I do to help, dear?" Lydia asked. "Would you care for a powder?"

"No," Anna said.

All day she had suffered because of one taxing question—a question that had circled and buzzed in her mind like an irritating fly. The previous night Roark had asked her if Julian's kiss made her feel the same as his. In truth, Anna did not know the answer.

Feeling some guilt, she looked down at the blackberry cobbler Lydia had baked. She knew full well her visits with Julian had caused great concern with the family. Though she had assured Beth and Aunt Deirdre that Julian was the perfect gentleman, she had purposely left out the information that she was also carefully chaperoned by Lydia Talboth at all times. It would have destroyed her image as a brazen woman and no doubt would have made Roark laugh if he knew.

Anna remembered the day she had arrived upon Lydia's doorstep. She had come with such grim determination to see Julian and stake her independence that the wind had been taken from her sails when she discovered Julian had not returned home. Yet Lydia had kindly offered her tea until his arrival, and they had instantly developed a liking for each other. When Julian did appear, Lydia had remained steadfastly in the room, silently staking her own claim as chaperon. Anna, her temper cooled, had been grateful for Lydia's staunch support.

Ever since then, the pattern have been set. Anna arrived at Lydia's cottage in her own carriage and left in her own carriage. Whatever activity was planned included Lydia. Julian had made certain joking comments, but both ladies ignored them and never pressed the issue. He was indeed a true gentleman—just as he had been when Anna explained that she did not wish him to visit the castle for it would cause a certain amount of unrest. He had only winked at her, nodded, and said he understood and would do whatever she wished.

Anna winced. She didn't understand herself now. Julian admired her, courted her insidiously, and did whatever she wished, no matter what it was. She told herself she had grown to care for him, but she was uncertain. She had resolved that there was nothing between her and Roark, and there would never be anything. As long as she continued to be the recipient of Roark's cold looks, as long as he had ignored her, the story held some semblance of credence. The previous night that credence had been pretty much torn to shreds.

She wanted to trust Roark. She wanted to believe that he was not a rake and bounder, yet she was frightened to do so. She hadn't understood before that a woman-hater was not just a man who spurned women, but one who could be with them and still keep his heart intact. Worse, the previous night had awakened her from the dream she had created. She did not know what Julian's kiss would do to her. She hoped, though, that if Julian held her close it might blot out the need she felt for Roark.

Anna drew in a deep breath. "I believe I need to return to the castle." She cast a hesitant glance at Julian. "My coachman will not be here until later. Could you escort me home?"

"I could at that," Julian said, his blue eyes lighting. "It would be my pleasure."

"I shall get my wrap," Lydia said, rising.

"No," Anna said quickly, then flushed. "You have prepared an excellent dinner. Please remain and rest."

"Yes," Julian said. "Besides I shall take her in my phaeton. It would be crowded with three."

"Oh," Lydia said, sinking back into her chair. Then she rose again. "But, dearest, isn't it dangerous and too dark for the phaeton?"

Julian smiled. "There is a full moon tonight, and I know every road and path there is in the area. Remember?"

"Oh, yes," Lydia said, sitting back down, "I remember."

Julian winked at Anna. "My brother and I have visited Aunt Lydia many times over the years. I hope I am not a braggart when I tell you I know the roads as well as any coachman. But wait. I shall hitch the team, since Aunt Lydia refuses to keep a groom or even a carriage, for that matter. But modest is our Aunt Lydia, and modest will she always be." He bolted from the room.

Anna glanced at Lydia, who was wringing her hands, which she often did. "Permit me to help you with the dishes while we wait."

"No, no. I shall do that," Lydia said. "Are you sure that you wish Julian to drive you home?"

"I truly have a headache. And as Julian said, there is a full moon tonight."

"Yes."

Silently, as if in deep meditation, Lydia picked up the dishes and took them to the kitchen. Anna wished to assist her, but since Lydia had turned down her offer, she remained at the table, growing more and more uncomfortable. When Lydia returned to the table and fumbled with the silverware, the tension between them was obvious.

"Mrs. Talboth," Anna said, diffidently, "if you are concerned about us traveling tonight, we can . . ."

"What is Aunt telling you now?" Julian asked, entering the room.

"Nothing," Lydia said, dropping the silverware. "Only I fear for your safety."

Julian laughed. "I know you do not like the phaeton, but I can drive it to within an inch." He wiggled his brows at Anna. "I haven't overturned anyone in years. Aunt Lydia is remembering when I was young."

Lydia smiled, her relief showing. "Yes, I fear I am. But you will be careful?"

"Of course I will," Julian said. "Anna is very precious to me."

"I know," Lydia said, looking down. "Forgive me."

"Perhaps it would be wiser to wait for my coachman," Anna said. "You know the circumstances at the castle. . . ."

"I have thought of that," Julian said, smiling. "If you are worried over a confrontation of any sort, I shall simply take you to the back entrance."

Anna blinked. "There is a back entrance?"

Julian laughed. "I was quite the explorer when I was a child and spent summers here with Aunt Lydia."

"Yes," Lydia said, nodding in her nervous fashion. "Yes, he was."

"I see." Anna refrained from mentioning that the confrontation she feared most had nothing whatsoever to do with the human inhabitants of the castle seeing her. "How fortunate."

After leaving Lydia's cottage, Anna did not relax until they had traveled quite a distance. Julian, true to his word, followed different paths and roads that Anna did not recognize. It was a warm evening, and with the full moon above, the country landscape glinted silver in its glow. Julian continued a light stream of polite conversation. Anna flexed her tightly entwined fingers, deciding to forget her purpose. Julian was a gentleman. For her to try to discover how he kissed, merely because Roark was no gentleman, was unworthy of her.

Only when they drew close to a large house, which she could only define as a dark looming shape, did Anna speak. "Where are we?"

"This is old Anton's place," Julian said. "It is by far the shorter way to the castle."

"The Anton estate?" Anna gasped. A sudden feeling of guilt, of trespassing, filled her. "We shouldn't be here."

Julian's laugh rang loud in the night air. "Never say you have acquired the Seeton superstitions after all?"

"No," Anna said quickly. "I did not think you knew of them."

"Of course I do," Julian said. "Anyone who's grown up in these parts knows of Charles Seeton and Genevieve Anton. When I was a boy and visited in the summers, Aunt Lydia would tell me that ghost story all the time. No doubt she labored under the belief that it would keep me from wandering." He slowed the phaeton. "But an adventurer was I. An absolute pirate."

"Were you?" Anna asked absently. Still she felt like a trespasser, a Seeton stepping beyond the line, which was ridiculous. She was not a Seeton, nor would she ever be one.

"Indeed," Julian said, drawing the horses to a complete halt. He gazed the darkened landscape. "We boys would sneak out at night and skulk through these woods, hoping to see the ghost."

"But Charles is bound to Seeton land," Anna said. "You'd not see him here."

"You *are* falling for those ghost stories," Julian said, his gaze teasing.

"I am not," Anna said. "Only it is what I have always heard about ghosts. They cannot leave from the place where they died. They are held to it."

"Then you are not afraid?" Julian asked, grinning.

"Of course not!" Anna said. She had surpassed fear a long time ago.

"A pity. I'd hoped to scare you into my arms," Julian said, grinning. He promptly slid one arm about Anna's shoulder. "But you are too spirited for such a ploy. I determined that the evening of the ball. Only since then you've behaved so very properly. Was it for Aunt Lydia's sake," Julian asked, lowering his head toward her, "or because you wanted to tease me, to torment me?"

Julian kissed Anna then. Unwillingly she stiffened, almost cringing back against the seat. His hold incited no passion within her; rather she felt confined, imprisoned. His lips stirred no warm desire. They felt cold to Anna and she shivered from their touch.

Stunned, Anna tried to control her emotions. This was Julian, a man whose gaze was always warm upon her, whose admiration was constant. Still, his lips inspired a chill within her. Indeed, a suffocating panic overwhelmed Anna. She lifted her hands to push at Julian's chest. He did not draw back. Instead, his arms tightened about her and his lips pressed harder, even more brutally upon hers.

The shrill neigh of a horse sounded and the phaeton lurched forward. Julian quickly released Anna, grabbing for the reigns. Anna drew in deep, quick breaths, grateful for the moments it took Julian to bring the horses back under control. She desperately needed those moments to bring her own emotions back under control.

When all was still again, Julian turned to her, his gaze hot. "Stupid beasts—they always misbehave at the worse possible moment."

"Don't they?" Anna said, smiling weakly. In truth, she harbored a deep gratitude for those dumb animals. Faith, she would have been beholden to anything and anyone who would have disturbed them at that moment. She forced a laugh. "Perhaps they were just trying to remind us that it is time for us to go home now."

"You do know how to play a man," Julian murmured. "I've never met a woman like you, Anna. You and I should be together always. We are a perfect match."

Anna looked swiftly away. It seemed as if the night itself watched and waited—not as an distant observer, but as a friend, an understanding ally. Anna shivered. Roark had often called her a romantic. But that night she was all too aware her flights of fancy were overly active. "Let us go. I think I am slightly spooked after all."

Julian laughed, his eyes glittering like diamonds in the moonlight. Beth had said diamonds were too hard a stone for Anna. "Spooked? Did you not hear what I said? Anna, I am asking you if you will wed me."

Anna swallowed hard. What had she brought about by attempting that one kiss? "Julian, I do not know what to say."

"Say yes," Julian said.

An overpowering fear filled Anna. The night—and Julian—still awaited her answer. She shook her head to clear it. "I must have time to think."

Julian laughed. "Indeed, you know how to play a man, but I love the game." He leaned over to kiss her once more.

"No!" Anna exclaimed, turning her face from him. "I must think."

"Very well, my maiden of fire and ice," Julian said, drawing back. "Only how long shall you make me wait?"

Anna blinked. "I do not know, but you must give me time."

"Your wish is my command," Julian said. "Only you must tell me soon."

"I shall," Anna said. "I promise you."

She only breathed easy when Julian started up his team.

Anna crept up the stairs, carrying a taper she had discovered in the kitchen in her hand. Julian, once again proving his knowledge, had delivered Anna to the back door. Surprisingly enough the back door was open. Julian had laughed, whispering that the Seetons had always been lackadaisical—or they considered themselves beyond attack. Anna had cast such thoughts from her mind, only too glad to escape and find the stairs to her bedroom.

Her mind whirled; a vortex of emotions churned within her. More than anything, she could not understand the problem with Julian's kiss. It made no sense, and despite what Roark said, Anna believed she still held some grasp upon sanity. Her feelings of panic when Julian had kissed her, though, had been too strong to be considered reasonable and might not be the best testimony to her mastery of reality.

Anna made it to her room and only felt safe when she had entered and closed the door. She stepped with the taper in her hand over to the bedside table and lighted the candle upon the table as well. Irrationally, she desired all the light she could find. It was the child wishing to chase away night fears, she knew. Regardless, she did it acting like a woman who was no greater or less than she had been as a child.

After staring into the candle's flame for a moment, Anna turned and went to the fireplace to kindle a fire. She stoked it high, not for the warmth, but for the blessed light. She needed the light. She needed to see clearly. Only when she glanced around the lit room, did she notice a dark, gaping hole in the side wall.

Anna's eyes narrowed. The door to the secret passage stood open. She knew where the passage led. Both the woman and child in her cried out together. The woman wished to run to the passion which made her feel alive. The child wished to run to the arms that made feel her safe.

Anna fought the two within her. She felt outnumbered. Infuriated, confused, and angry, she tore her gaze away. She knew the devil who was trying to tempt her.

"This is it! Show yourself, Charles. If you still can be the man you once were, you will show yourself."

"Aha," a voice said from behind her. "Then you can

recognize a man after all. I feared for a moment you could not."

Anna spun to find Charles standing behind her, a wicked smile upon his face. She glared fiercely at him. "I can recognize a man—especially a deceitful one."

"Can you?" Charles said, his tone dry.

"Do not play the innocent with me," Anna spat, pointing toward the open passage. "Did you truly expect me to use that? Did you truly expect me to sneak through it to Roark?"

Charles eyes glowed. "Better that than you sneaking into the castle through the kitchen. Are you a serving wench now, milady?"

Anna stiffened. He was a ghost, yes, but surely not omnipotent. "How did you know?"

"I know all that happens between these walls."

Anna sighed in relief, realizing Charles did not know about her kissing Julian. "Well, whatever might pass between them, I shall not, I assure you. And I will thank you not to open secret passages I have no wish to enter."

Charles's eyes glowed. "Do you not, milady? I think thou dost."

"I do not!" Anna said.

Charles crossed his arms. "Then you were not pleasured within Roark's arms last eventide?"

Anna choked and sputtered. How dearly she wanted to tell him he was wrong. She could not. "What does it matter if I was? It does not count one wit. What does it matter what Roark's kisses do, what his touch does, when there is no love?"

"Methinks there is love, lass," Charles said, his tone soft.

"There is no love," Anna said, her head aching as she had declared it did hours before. "Roark cannot love. He hates women. He may use them and he may have liaisons, but he does not love. And I do not know what I feel. Passion is not love. No matter what I feel with Roark, I cannot trust him. That cannot be love." She shook her head numbly and laughed hollowly. *"My love for thee is* not *true. 'Tis* not *pure and undefiled. 'Tis* not *a simple sweet bud."* Anna conceded defeat. Exhausted, she sank to the floor beside the fire *"It shall* not *bloom for only thee."*

Charles stared at her, his eyes far brighter and hotter than the fire. "Are you a witch, woman?"

Anna blinked. "You have called me vixen. Indeed, you have called me many names, but witch? Is that called for?"

"You spake Genevieve's words"—a dry chuckle escaped from him—"or how they should have been."

Anna gaped at him. "I did not."

"You did!"

When the roar of wind pounded at Anna's ears, she clasped her hands to them. "I did not. I only recited some poetry I remembered." The wind increased. "Only I misquoted it."

The wind died an abrupt death. If a spirit already dead could be stricken once again, Charles would have been the picture of such misery. "Misquoted?"

Anna, her heart catching, said softly, *"My love for thee is true. It grew within my heart, a simple sweet bud, pure and undefiled. And only for thee, forever for thee—"*

"No!" Charles cried. "Do not say it."

Anna swallowed hard. *"'Shall it bloom."*

Charles's head lowered. "How did you know she wrote that, witch?"

"I didn't," Anna said. "A poet wrote it. A lady from Devonshire did."

"Genevieve wrote that," Charles said. "She wrote it for me."

"Impossible," Anna said.

Charles's face darkened. "Follow me. See if I do not tell the truth."

Anna, unable to speak, rose. Charles did not speak either, but moved toward the door. When they left the room, the hall grew dark. Anna halted, turning back. "I must have a candle."

A glow exploded about her. "Follow me, witch."

Anna nodded and followed within Charles's beacon of light. He led her through winding halls to a place Anna had never seen. Roark had said the castle covered a vast terrain, yet she and Roark had believed they had covered most all of the territory. However, Charles had led her to a wing she and Roark had not discovered.

The room was dark, almost bare of furniture, and completely free of dust and cobwebs. Within the glow Charles provided, Anna saw one solitary escritoire, or what she would have defined as such. It was of delicate proportions dwarfed by the barren chamber around it. Its front was one solid panel of dark wood carved entirely with tight scrollwork of entwined vines and rose-buds. Each leg was carved as if it were a stem from which branches grew outward to entwine in an open fretwork with branches from a neighboring leg. Charles stood beside the escritoire. "Drop the front. Open the left drawer inside. The last one."

Anna, shaking, obeyed. It was empty. "There is nothing here."

"Pull the drawer farther out," Charles said.

Anna drew the drawer out its entire length. A thin sliver of wood popped out and down. Paper after paper flitted to the floor. Anna slowly picked them up. Silently she read what could only be letters. The archaic spelling and wording were nothing to Anna. The words of love and passion were everything.

"Genevieve liked to write," Charles said, his words

soft. "Though we saw each other every day, she would send these by servant. Else she would give them to me and swear me to an oath that I would not read them until she was gone."

Anna heard Charles, yet she could not stop reading. She gasped when she read the words she had spoken only moments before. "The lady from Devonshire."

"No," Charles said, simply. "Genevieve."

Anna finally looked up. The poetry she had always cherished were love letters written to Charles Seeton. Bemused, she gazed about the barren room. "They have been here all this time?"

"No one enters here," Charles said.

Anna nodded. "You have guarded these letters."

"Yes," Charles said. "God help me, but, yes, I have guarded them."

A sudden, sure knowledge filled Anna. It was bitter and sweet in one stunning moment. "Genevieve is our bond."

"What did you say?" Charles asked.

"It is her poetry, the words that I love, that have drawn you to me." She gazed at him. "They were words that you loved as well."

"No," Charles said, his tone anguished.

"Words you still love," Anna said softly.

"Nay, woman," Charles roared. "I no longer love those words. They are a lie. Genevieve was a lie. She betrayed me."

"I cannot believe she could," Anna said, "not if she wrote this poetry to you."

"She may have given this to me," Charles said, his tone bitter, "but she meant it for another."

"I cannot believe that," Anna said.

"You cannot believe that, mistress? You cannot believe that?" Charles laughed bitterly. "I could not believe it either upon my wedding day. I stood before the altar, moment after moment passing. Waiting, while the guests murmured and whispered. Me the fool, waiting while Genevieve and William Thornton fled Devonshire."

"William Thornton?" Anna asked.

"William Thornton," Charles said it softly. "I have not spoken his name since the day of the wedding. William Thornton, Genevieve's lover."

"You knew she had another lover"—Anna shook her head—"and you were willing to marry her?"

"Nay," Charles said. "She'd sworn he meant naught to her. 'Twas I who held her heart, she claimed. 'Twas I to whom she wished to pledge her life. Yet William was always there. She vowed to me his roses and billets-doux were not sent by her invitation." He chuckled dryly. "Even upon the eve of our wedding, William came between us. We fought. She declared it was my jealousy that came between us, and not William. Ah, the tears she cried. And I, weakling man that I was, gave her my faith once more. I actually went down upon my knee and begged her forgiveness, begged her to marry me upon the morrow."

"But she chose William the next day," Anna murmured. "It makes no sense."

"Sense?" Charles said angrily. "When a woman wishes to betray one man for another, sense is not involved. 'Tis her deceitful heart that leads her."

"Deceitful heart," Anna repeated, shaking her head. *My love for thee is true.* . . . Clutching the letters to her chest, Anna rose. "May I take these and read them again?"

"Yes, milady. It is not as if they are of any use to me," Charles said. "But I pray you divine the depths of your own heart, lady. Let there be no deceit."

Sadness and regret filled the air. Anna now understood Charles's constant interference, his need to arrange Roark and Anna's lives. It had everything to do with Genevieve Anton.

"What happened to Genevieve and William?" Anna asked softly.

"How should I know?" Charles said, shrugging.

Anna blinked, realizing she had never heard that part of the story from any member of the family. "But even after your death, surely you heard what happened to them."

"Nay," Charles said. "The last words spoken between the Antons and the Seetons were said when Genevieve's father arrived to confess their shame. They knew William had visited Genevieve early that morning, but they had chosen to look the other way. They permitted her to see him alone as she requested, believing it would be their final parting." He laughed. "Indeed it *was* Genevieve and William's final parting. They escaped without the family being the wiser. The family had refused to send a missive to us. They allowed all of us to assemble at the chapel because they had hoped to give chase and discover them upon the roads."

"No wonder your families did not speak," Anna murmured.

"They owned up to their disgrace. The bride's party left," Charles said. "My family proceeded to hold the so-called reception to at least feed our guests. I confess I was in no mood to revel. I went to the turret to be alone. Apparently I was not alone. I remember feeling a stunning blow from behind; then I was pushed from the turret's window."

"Dear Lord," Anna whispered.

"It was rather a public suicide," Charles said, his tone dry. "The wedding guests discovered me when they were leaving. That is the story everyone remembered. Genevieve and William's escape was far overshadowed by it. Where they went, what they did, I do not know. I do not care."

Anna clutched the letters to her. No matter what he said, she knew he cared. And so did she.

Anna toyed with her eggs and bacon. She felt groggy. She had read and reread Genevieve's letters to Charles well into the dawn hours. She had compared them to the poems of *A Lady from Devonshire*. They were one and the same. How could a woman write such feelings to one man, and then run away with another? The question plunged to the very depth of Anna's heart.

"Anna?" Aunt Deirdre's voice drifted into Anna's roiling thoughts. "Is anything amiss?"

Anna had been so deep in contemplation she had forgotten she sat at table breaking her fast with four other people.

"Perhaps she remained out too late last night," Roark said, his tone dry.

Anna cast Roark a narrow look. "No, I did not stay out too late. I . . . I . . ."

"Oh, no," Beth wailed. "You saw the ghost again last night, didn't you?"

Anna cast Roark a covert glance. Apparently he had taken her track and had not mentioned Charles's pranks of two nights earlier. "Well . . ."

"You did," Beth said, her tone accusatory. "I can tell by that look in your eyes."

"She has seen him," Terrence said. "Confess it, Anna. It's as plain as daylight that you saw him. What did he have to say?"

"Terrence," Beth said, her voice a plea. "Please don't ask."

"No, I'm glad you asked," Anna said quickly. She suddenly knew what she needed to do. She would never be able to rest until she had discovered Genevieve's story. "Charles and I talked about Genevieve Anton last night."

"Did you?" Roark asked, his brow rising.

"Yes."

"Is that all you talked about?"

"No," Anna said in a cool tone. "I asked him to kindly refrain from playing games with me or attempting to interfere in my life."

"Touché!" Roark said, actually laughing.

"What did Charles have to say about Genevieve Anton, dear?" Aunt Deirdre asked.

"He does not know where Genevieve and her lover went," Anna said, refusing to attack the subject directly. "Do any of you?"

"If Charles does not," Roark said, "then why should we?"

"I don't know, but it is important. Last night I discovered why Charles has been drawn to me. Genevieve's poetry is the tie."

"I thought you said you needed to find his murderer," Aunt Deirdre said, a frown marring her face.

"She did," Roark said, his tone derisive. "Apparently we were off on a wild-goose chase when looking for Charles's murderer."

"No," Anna said, glaring at him. "That is still important. I'm sure that is what still binds him to the earth. His honor must be reclaimed."

"Then what does Genevieve Anton matter?" Roark asked.

"Yes, dear," Aunt Deirdre said, an odd tone in her voice. "And what do you mean by her poetry?"

"Genevieve wrote letters to Charles," Anna said in excitement. She turned her gaze to Beth. "Beth, those letters are the *Poetry of a Lady from Devonshire.*"

"Who?" Aunt Deirdre asked.

Beth frowned. "I don't remember."

"She is one of my favorite poets." Anna almost laughed. "Remember, I spoke of her the very day we arrived here."

"Yes," Beth said, her tone even more frightened. "I remember."

"Good gracious, how could that be?" Aunt Deirdre said.

"It was fate," Roark said, his tone derisive. "Destiny, no doubt."

Anna flushed. "No, I am not such a ninny to believe that. It is coincidence, and even *you* will believe in that. I bought the volume because of the title since we were traveling to Devonshire. But Genevieve's poetry is beautiful. I cannot believe she was as coldhearted or deceitful as everyone believes. I'd like to know what happened to her."

Roark's eyes narrowed. "And how do you propose to do that?"

Anna drew in her breath. "If anyone knows what happened to Genevieve, it would be the Anton family."

"No," Roark said. That one word was a command in itself.

"What would it hurt if I asked them?" Anna said, her ire rising.

An odd silence fell in the room. Anna glanced quickly from Roark to Terrence, then to Aunt Deirdre. Their faces were stony. "It has been so very long ago, surely it would not matter if I went to see them."

"There is only one of them left," Terrence said, looking away.

"One of them?" Anna asked.

"The last of the Anton line," Roark said, his tone cold. "His name is Henry Anton. I assure you he will not welcome your inquisitiveness."

"Why not?" Anna asked. "Since your family and his

have never conversed, how would you know whether he would mind or not? Perhaps he is not so very bound to ancient traditions as you Seetons are."

"He's a recluse," Terrence said, shifting in his chair.

"A recluse?" Anna stared at the family one after another, but met only deadened looks. Unaccountably, anger rose within her. "Do not tell me he was blighted in love and he is now a recluse and woman-hater too." When Aunt Deirdre gasped, Anna flushed in embarrassment. Her remark had been an utterly dreadful thing to say. "I am sorry. That was unforgivable."

"It was," Roark said, his face dark and threatening. "And if you are as sorry as you say, you will stop this discussion. Forget the notion of trying to contact Henry Anton."

"But it is important that I know," Anna said.

"Why?" Roark retorted. "Has Charles asked you go to Henry Anton?"

Anna looked down. "No, he hasn't."

"I wouldn't think so," Roark said. "In fact, he'll not thank you for it. Nor will any of us. Nor will Henry Anton. Do not interfere, Anna. That is an order."

Anna glared at him in defiance. Before she could speak, Aunt Deirdre rose. "If you will excuse me, I have work to do." She hastened from the room.

"Please, Anna," Beth said. "Do not talk anymore about Genevieve and"—her voice became quiet—"that ghost."

Anna bit her tongue. Yes, she had been needlessly ungracious earlier. It would have been pointless to fight. Roark might order her about, but that did not mean she had to listen to him. "Very well. Let us discuss something else."

Beth sighed in relief. Terrence promptly began discussing the day's plans. Roark settled back, clearly confident he had won the battle. His satisfied expression only fueled Anna's determination.

Anna hastened about her room, preparing her reticule. Her mind raced with the questions she would ask Henry Anton. She had asked for the carriage to be brought around. Roark had already disappeared into his study, and Beth and Terrence were sequestered in the library, once again lovingly deferring to each other's opinion concerning their wedding plans.

A knock sounded at her door and Anna halted. "Yes? Who is it?"

"It is me, dear," Aunt Deirdre's voice called. "May I come in?"

"Certainly," Anna said.

Aunt Deirdre fluttered over to a chair and sat. Her blue eyes were solemn. "You are intending to visit Henry Anton, aren't you?"

Anna couldn't bring herself to lie. "Yes, I am."

Aunt Deirdre gazed steadily at her. "Roark *ordered* you not to see Henry. I am *asking* you not to see him, for my sake."

"Why?" Anna asked.

"I knew Henry once."

"But everyone has said that the Seetons have never talked to the Antons."

"I know, dear," Aunt Deirdre said, nodding. "Only I did. When we were young." Her faded blue eyes grew bright. The sweetest smile touched her lips. "He and I met, quite by accident, mind you. I had been out riding—upon our land, of course. I was alone. You cannot imagine it, I am sure, but I was rather rebellious and perhaps somewhat wild as a young girl."

Watching the smile upon Deirdre's lips, Anna could very well believe her. "I understand."

"I took a fall from my horse," Deirdre said, sighing. "Henry had been out hunting in his woods at the time. He came dashing to my rescue." Deirdre paused, her eyes staring off into space. "He was the handsomest man I had ever seen."

"What happened?" Anna asked softly because the emotions crossing Aunt Deirdre's face demanded respect and awe.

"I was quite unharmed," Aunt Deirdre said, a laugh escaping her. "Far more embarrassed than anything else. But then we walked and talked together. We knew we shouldn't, but we couldn't help ourselves."

"Then what?" Anna asked.

"I discovered he was the kindest, most gentle of men," Aunt Deirdre said. Her voice was spellbound with wonder, and Anna was enchanted by her tale. "We met every day then. We would walk and talk. Sometimes we would have picnic lunches." Aunt Deirdre's face changed. "One day, my Henry went down upon bended knee. He asked me to be his wife." She shook her head slightly. "It was spring, and the wildflowers were everywhere, yet the bouquet he held out to me was the only thing I could see. He knew I loved flowers, and he had grown those flowers especially for me. There was every color, every kind, imaginable"—she laughed softly—"or it seemed so to my eyes."

Anna swallowed hard. "You did not wed."

"No," Aunt Deirdre said. "I, foolish girl that I was, took his offering and asked that I might approach my father first. Henry had said that he would rather speak to my father, but I persuaded him to permit me to do so. I thought I would be able to sway my father far better then he."

"You were not able to sway your father," Anna said, sadness filling her.

"No," Aunt Deirdre sighed. "It was Father who made

me see reason. There had been too much tragedy between the two families already; they could never be united after that. Never should they be united."

"I see," Anna whispered.

Genevieve, Genevieve, Anna's heart cried. *Do you know what torment you caused when you denied Charles, what pain you passed on to the following generations when you chose William Thornton? Your words spoke of your love being true. Only look what your betrayal has done, how many lives have been affected.*

Aunt Deirdre smiled sadly. "I cannot remember the many reasons Father gave. They were all worthy. But one stood out from among them. He told me Henry's and my love could never prosper. Indeed, to imagine a Seeton and an Anton once again trying to wed within the chapel was unthinkable, a disgrace to both families. A disgrace to . . . Charles."

"You thought Charles would appear," Anna asked.

Aunt Deirdre appeared shaken from her reverie. "Could you doubt it? It is one thing to say that Charles would have rolled over in the grave if I married Henry, but since we knew he was not in his grave, thinking he would do anything so polite would have been foolish, would it not have?"

Anna grimaced. "You are right."

Aunt Deirdre's smile twisted. "I turned my Henry down. It would have been an ill-fated love. We were young. Surely we were each meant to find happiness with another."

The final, obvious words filled the room: Deirdre had not found happiness with another.

"Did Henry marry?" Anna asked, almost choking.

"No," Aunt Deirdre said. Her smile wavered. "I am sure that had nothing to do with me. I am sure he does not even remember me, but I would ask that you do not go to see him."

Anna looked down. "I have to see him if he will permit it. I need to know what happened to Genevieve."

"I understand"—Aunt Deirdre rose—"or at least I am trying to. Only I wish you would not."

"I must," Anna said softly.

My love for thee is true . . . Where was the truth in these words . . . for Charles . . . for Aunt Deirdre . . . for Anna herself?

Nine

Anna watched from the carriage window as the coachman followed the road she had directed him to take. At last, she was able to view the path she had not been free to see before. It indeed was drenched in flowers as magnificently as she had imagined. Even to the edge of the carriage track, it was lined with every kind of brilliant color possible. Only they did not grow wild; they were well tended and well designed. Groupings of mums and dianthuses in vivid hues of red, orange, and pink danced in a pattern now and then cooled by a background of rich purple iris and the peaceful calm of blue bachelor buttons. Farther back from the path, as if standing guard over that array, were the tall soldiers of the garden: Huge bright yellow sunflowers nodded their heads to their comrades, the resplendent hollyhocks that shot to human height. It was a landscape artists dream. Anna could feel her heart wrench. Aunt Deirdre had said she was sure Henry had forgotten her, but surely here was a magnificent bouquet to her in the woods.

Anna's nerves tightened as she approached the house. The night before, when riding with Julian, she had merely seen the house as a looming shape in the distance. In the light of day, she could see that it was a splendid house, or had been at one time. It was clearly in decline. In complete contrast, the yard was freshly trimmed and mowed. The covered porte cochere spanning out from the front landing was missing tiles here and there, but along the side, spaced between the columns, were huge stone planters filled to overflowing with forget-me-nots thoughtfully protected from the high sun by the roof above them.

Anna alighted from the carriage. She cautiously approached the house and knocked upon the door. She waited a good few minutes and knocked again.

The door was finally opened by an ancient grizzled-haired butler, who peered at her from within. "What do yer want?"

Anna started back. "I am here to see Henry Anton."

"Ye are?" The butler frowned severely. "Then what are ye doing standing here knocking on the door fer?"

Anna blinked. "I don't know. I thought it only proper?"

The butler's face screwed up in suspicion. "Are you really here to see Master Henry?"

"Yes," Anna said quickly. "Yes, I am. Truly."

"He's in the gardens," the butler said, his tone querulous. "If you were here to see him, ye should have known he'd be in the gardens."

"I see," Anna said, biting her lip. "Please forgive my mistake. Could you take me to the gardens then?"

"Very well," the butler said, turning. "Ye should have gone there in the first place."

Anna remained judiciously silent and followed the tottering man through the dark and gloomy house. Dust coated everything, creating a world of dingy gray as they crossed from one room to another. Many rooms, their doors standing open beyond, contained furniture covered with holland covers. The air was stale and musty.

Anna sighed in relief and gulped in the fresh air as

they emerged from the house. The old butler wasn't senile, after all. If she had possessed any foreknowledge, she would have gone to the gardens directly and bypassed the depressing aspects of the house.

"Himself is over there." The butler nodded in a surly manner and raised one gnarled finger to point toward a lattice-covered promenade.

Anna looked toward a stooped figure shaking a large plant from its clay pot. She sincerely hoped Henry Anton had not grown into a volatile recluse. She drew a breath and with determination strolled forward. "Mr. Anton?"

"Hmm, what?"

Anna realized her last thought was totally unworthy. Henry Anton possessed the gentlest, vaguest brown eyes. Of medium build, he had brown hair, with gray liberally weaved through it. His hair shot out from his head in tufts. His skin was tanned from years in the sun.

"Hello."

"Hello." Henry smiled kindly.

"Your butler led me here," Anna said, rather stupidly. Suddenly she did not know how to make her introduction.

"Yes, that would be Creigs," Henry said, nodding. "Did you wish to be led here, or did he not give you a moment's chance to explain your purpose?"

"No," Anna said, finally smiling. "I wished to see you."

"You did? How nice," Henry Anton said. He dusted off one of his hands upon his old faded trousers. "Forgive me and Creigs. We are not used to entertaining young ladies."

"Oh, of course. It is not as if you knew I were coming. Nor am I sure you will be pleased that I have. I am Anna Winston."

"Hello, Anna," Henry said, nodding and smiling gently. "Why would I not be pleased that a pretty young girl has come to visit me?"

"I am staying at the Duke of Whynhavens," Anna said.

His smile remained. "Are you?"

"I have come to—" Anna halted. She was making a mess of it. "I have come to ask you about Genevieve Anton."

He did not start or pretend confusion. His eyes only grew sad. "And why, my dear, would you wish to know about Genevieve Anton?"

"Because I wish to understand. I do not know if you will think me crazy, but I have seen Charles Seeton."

"I would not think you crazy," Henry said. "It is well known his spirit still walks the castle."

"Yes," Anna said. "He is tormented. He acts as if he does not care to know what happened to Genevieve, but I know he cares."

Henry picked up a pair of shears and began to gently prune the myrtle tree before him. "I am afraid I cannot help you. I know nothing about Genevieve Anton."

"But you must," Anna said, frowning.

"Must I?" Henry asked gently.

"Did you know she wrote a volume of poetry?" Anna asked in determination. Henry's shears froze. "It is beautiful, wonderful poetry of love. Those poems where written to Charles Seeton as letters. I have seen them."

"Have you?" Henry murmured.

"Yes," Anna said. "But she ran off with William Thornton instead. Why? Her heart was in her poems. I truly believe so."

Henry Anton stopped. "You are very vehement in your support of Genevieve. Why, my dear?"

"I don't know," Anna said honestly. "I only know it is important to me. Why did she run away? She caused so much tragedy."

"Anna, you are young," Henry said. "You must learn to leave the past in the past."

"But is it in the past? Has it been laid to rest for either family?" Anna asked. "Or has it haunted you, just as Charles Seeton haunts the castle?"

Henry Anton looked off into the distance, and Anna followed his distracted gaze.

"Gracious," Anna breathed. A sea of crimson met her stunned gaze. Only the white-washed structure of a gazebo broke the color, and it too appeared entwined with red. "What are they?"

"Roses, my dear." Henry began walking.

Anna, bemused, followed. The bright colors of blue and pink and yellow flower beds teased the edges of Anna's sight, but her focus was upon the red roses she approached. The closer she drew, the deeper and darker the color of the roses was to her. She could not speak when she finally stood before the gazebo. The mass of blooms was too overpowering.

"They bloom every June," Henry said in a musing tone. "And only in June."

"I have never seen a rose that was such an intense shade of red," Anna whispered.

"Neither have I," Henry said.

"You did not plant these?"

A gentle smile crossed Henry's lips. "Yes, I planted them—or I planted the original rosebush when I was a young man, even younger than yourself." Walking over, he clipped a bloom. "I planted it in memory of a love of mine I had lost. What a silly, heartbroken young man I was." He offered her the rose. "I thought I had planted a bush of white roses. If I remember correctly, it was meant to represent the truth and purity of my love for the lady. The bush did not bloom until late in the month, and when it did, it bloomed red."

"Red roses are my sister's favorite," Anna said, taking

the rose from him. She could not tear her gaze from the flower. "They say red roses are for passion."

"They are at that," Henry nodded.

A thought whispered through Anna's mind, and her fingers trembled, almost dropping the rose. It glowed more like the depths of a ruby stone rather than a flower. "Or of blood. Of tears."

Henry gazed at the flowers. "They grow more and more each year. No other flowers can survive here. The roses and thorns choke them out."

Anna drew in a breath. "You tell me to leave Genevieve's story to the past where it belongs, Mr. Anton. I will do so if you truly believe the past is in the past."

"You may keep the flower, Anna Winston."

"Thank you." Anna turned and walked a few steps, then halted. She had no right. Yet she had stepped onto Anton land, and before she left it for good, she would have her last say. "Aunt Deirdre asked me not to come here."

Pain flashed through Henry's eyes. "She did?"

"She believes the past is past as well. In fact, she was sure you would not remember her."

Henry Anton started. "Not remember her?"

Anna deliberately gazed about the rest of the gardens. She smiled innocently. "Your garden looks like a giant bouquet of flowers. You have every imaginable color, do you not? Aunt Deirdre would love it, I believe."

Anna left Henry Anton standing stock-still. She walked even farther away. Stifling a laugh, she turned again. "If you ever change your mind, Mr. Anton, I invite you to visit me. I cannot guarantee your welcome by anyone else, but I assure you, I will welcome you."

With that last parting shot, Anna picked up her skirts and hastened away. She chose to walk around the old house, enjoying the fresh air.

* * *

Anna entered the castle holding the single rose protectively. She halted as she discovered Roark within the hall. He sat with a negligent air in a chair, leafing through a newspaper. Such behavior was in no way customary for him.

"What are you doing here?"

Roark lowered his paper. "I wished to speak to you."

"Yes?" Her heart suddenly pounding, she approached him.

Roark's gaze fell to the rose. "Julian gave you but one rose this time?"

Anna flushed. "What did you wish to speak to me about?"

"You best beware," Roark said. "His interest must be waning. He used to give you bouquets. Now a mere stem?"

Anna started, then glared at him. "It is not from Julian."

Roark stood abruptly. "Who is it from then?"

"What did you wish to discuss with me?"

"Playing Julian upon the sly as well?" Roark asked.

"I am not playing him upon the sly," Anna gasped. A sudden burst of guilt rose within her. Indeed, she was in a fashion since she knew Julian's kisses could never reach her as Roark's had. Then the last two words Roark had spoken sunk into her conscious. "And what do you mean *as well*? If you are insinuating I played you upon the sly, I have told you it was no such thing. Furthermore, in order to play someone upon the sly, it means you must have some sort of understanding to deceive. We had agreed only to pretend to be engaged. We had no understanding." She laughed bitterly. "And we most certainly have no understanding still." She turned and stalked away.

"Anna!" Roark called. "Anna, stop."

Anna halted. "Why?"

Roark sighed. "I am sorry. I *was* hoping to try for some kind of understanding. Or truce, at least." He smiled wryly. "Who is the rose from if not from Julian?"

"You will not like it."

"Who is it from?" Roark persisted.

"From Henry Anton," Anna said.

"What?" Roark roared.

"I told you you would not like it," Anna said, flaring.

"You went to see him after I told you not to do so?"

"Yes, I did."

"Confound it, woman! You are meddling in things you are not aware of."

"You knew about Aunt Deirdre and Henry."

"Of course I knew," Roark said. "My father told me when I was a child curious as to why Aunt Deirdre had not married."

Anger exploded in Anna. "And of course you accepted that and still accept it."

"I respect Aunt Deirdre's wishes if that is what you mean," Roark said curtly.

"As she supported her father's wishes," Anna said. "As every Seeton before has supported his father's wishes. The rift between the families must be respected above all cost—even at the cost of love."

"I did not make that decision," Roark said angrily. "I was only a child."

"And now you are a man," Anna retorted. She clenched the rose so tightly a thorn pierced her. "Excuse me. I must put this in water."

When a knock sounded at the door, Roark glared toward it. "What now?" He stalked over and jerked the door open. "Yes?"

Anna, curiosity driving her, walked over to stand behind Roark. A messenger held a bouquet of roses. He appeared to cringe back. Any servant faced with the thunderous look in Roark's eyes would naturally have done so. He shoved the roses forward. "I's got a delivery."

Roark snatched the bouquet from the servant. "Thank you."

"Yes, sir . . . I mean, milord,"

"Your Grace," Anna said, her tone sweet. "For he is ever so gracious."

"Aye," the messenger said before he bolted away.

Roark slammed the door shut. He looked rather foolish, for he held the roses away from him as if they were three-day-old fish. "And who are these from?"

Anna reached out and plucked the white filigree card from among the blooms. With a calm aplomb, she studied it. "I await your answer, my maiden of fire and ice." Anna hid her emotions. She looked at the single rose in her hand, then at the bouquet in Roark's. The single bloom showed a depth and distinction in color that made the others appear tawdry.

"As I said, I must put this in water." Anna turned and walked away, saying over her shoulder, "You may put those in water if you please."

Anna sat upon her bed, her knees drawn up, her arms wrapped about them. She stared at the rose she had set across the room upon the bureau. She had first set it on the bedside table, but its scent filled her with a sense of deep sadness. The poetry of Genevieve Anton whispered in her mind as if it were spoken. Knowing she was being fanciful, but unable to stop herself, Anna had risen and moved the rose to the bureau. She had returned to her bed, but she still sat gazing at the rose, its dark red color mesmerizing her.

"Who is the rose from?" Charles's voice asked. Anna blinked as he appeared next to the bureau.

Anna laughed. "The Seeton blood certainly runs true. Roark asked the same of me."

"Ah, then it is from your courtier, Julian," Charles said, reaching out to tweak the petals.

"No," Anna said baldly, "it is from Henry Anton."

Charles's hand jerked back. "What did you say, milady?"

Anna forced a calm. "I called upon Henry Anton today."

"B'gad, woman," Charles roared. "Why would you have done a thing like that! Do you have no loyalty?"

"I have loyalty," Anna said angrily. "I respect you, and I care, indeed I do. That is why I went to Henry Anton. This rift, this silence, between the families does no one good. What happened occurred more than two hundred years ago. However, both families still act as if it happened just yesterday."

"To me it has," Charles said. "Why should it not to them?"

"Why?" Anna asked, shaking. "Because they are of the living and of the present." She sprung for the bed and stalked up to him. "You have taunted me. I do not *live*, you claim. You ask me not to make the mistake that Genevieve did or to betray my heart. But what have you asked your own blood to do? Answer me that. What will you have of them?"

"What do you mean, lady?" Charles said, his face grim.

"Did you know that Aunt Deirdre loved Henry Anton when she was young, but would not marry him because he was an Anton."

"Of course I knew it," Charles said. "What of it? She did what was right. She turned away from the pain of loving an Anton."

"Henry Anton is not Genevieve," Anna said angrily. "Deirdre is not you. You died, remember? And Genevieve—" Anna halted. "I do not know what happened to Genevieve."

"What does it matter?" Charles asked. "Is it not enough to know she betrayed me? Is it not enough to know she chose another lover and left me waiting at the chapel altar, looking like a pitiful fool?"

"No, it is not enough," Anna said. "Not for me. And I think you lie when you say it is enough for you."

Charles turned from her. Almost absently, without thought, he passed his hand through the rose. "Nay, you are wrong there, lady. I need not know what happened to Genevieve after she left. If I have lied, it would be regarding my wrath at my murder." His hand passed through the rose once more. "Whoever killed me may have done me a favor. I think I died the moment I heard Genevieve had betrayed me. Whoever killed me put me out of my misery"—he laughed—"or should have if he had successfully blotted out my existence. Yet here I am. I still think of Genevieve, and if a ghost can dream, I dream of her. I see her eyes, both laughing and crying. I remember her lips and our stolen kisses. And her spirit. I remember her spirit. Yes, she was gentle, but also strong and wild and free. No matter that she betrayed me, sometimes I still feel close to her. And despite all, I welcome that feeling." His hand and the rose seemed to blend. "As I do at this moment. A mere rose grown from the soil of her home has me hearing her voice again, has me feeling the way I did the day I asked her to marry me and she told me she loved me."

"I am sorry," Anna whispered.

Charles drew his hand back. "You wish to know what happened to Genevieve, milady. I shall tell you. She lived. She died. No doubt her body is buried beside her beloved William. She rests in peace while I remain to haunt this castle, to grow maudlin over a simple rose from her garden. A red one at that."

Anna forced a smile. "You do not like red roses?"

"I like them fine," Charles said. " 'Twas Genevieve who did not care for them. She said they saddened her for some reason. She always requested white roses—for true love and purity."

Anna sipped her tea, and nodded absently as Beth chattered on eagerly about the wedding. Terrence sat beside Beth, grinning. Anna covertly glanced at Roark, who sat beside Aunt Deirdre. They were noticeably silent as well. Anna felt a twinge of guilt. Perhaps she had been unthinking when she had visited Henry Anton the previous day—not because she believed she was wrong in what she had done, but because she had stirred up strife when it should be a time of celebration for her sister.

Voices sounded outside the parlor. Salome's voice was clear and excited. There was another voice—male, low, and soothing.

"Aye, I am dreadful sick most every morn," Salome said over her shoulder as she entered. For once Salome did not clutch her rosary beads. Instead, she held a red rose. "I pray and pray, but I am cursed."

"No, it is a very natural thing, my dear," Henry Anton's voice said as he followed behind her. His arms were overflowing with flowers. "Chamomile tea should be helpful."

"Do you think?" Salome actually twirled her rose.

"Henry," Aunt Deirdre whispered. Her cup fell from her fingers.

"Mr. Anton!" Anna exclaimed, springing up.

Salome turned and beamed. "Miss Anna, this fine gentleman has come to visit.

Deirdre rose slowly, as if under a spell. "Hello, Henry."

Henry and Deirdre stood staring at each other. The emotion passing between them was both compelling and infinitely private.

"I brought you these." Henry held out the massive bouquet.

Deirdre stepped forward and took the flowers, gathering them to her heart. Her smile was tremulous. "You remembered."

"I've always remembered," Henry said, his tone soft.

Deirdre suddenly appeared young and shy. "They are beautiful."

"They truly are," Anna agreed.

"Indeed," Beth said, her voice more curious and hesitant.

Only then did Deirdre start. "Oh, dear, permit me to introduce you to everyone. Henry, this is Beth, Anna's sister. She is going to wed my Terrence."

"Hello, Miss Beth," Henry said. "Please forgive me. I should have brought you flowers as well. I do hope you will permit me to rectify my oversight in the future."

"There is no need," Beth said.

"I hope I may rectify many things in the future."

"I hope I can too," Aunt Deirdre said. "It was all my fault, Henry, all my fault. Can you forgive me?"

"The past is past," Henry said gently, "or as I told Miss Winston, it should be past."

Immediately the room was filled with the roar of wind.

"Oh, no, Charles!" Aunt Deirdre exclaimed.

The temperature plummeted while the silver teapot shot up in the air. A duet of shrieks from Beth and Salome rose just as high.

"Charles!" Anna cried. "Don't you dare."

The teapot hovered a moment, then swerved toward Henry. Roark bolted over and grabbed it. "The past objects, I fear."

The cream and the sugar bowl promptly sailed up.

"Roark!" Terrence shouted. "To your right!"

Roark turned and swung the teapot, hitting both the creamer and the sugar bowl in one swipe. Tea and cream rained down, and sugar dusted everyone.

"Jolly good shot," Terrence hooted.

"Charles, stop misbehaving toward our guest," Deirdre said, her tone severe.

The teacups promptly soared into the air. Anna leapt forward and caught one. Roark took one another with the silver teapot. Terrence, shouting out a battle cry, snatched up the empty serving tray and wielded it deftly. Beth screeched and scurried away. Salome darted in the other direction.

Anna had no time to notice, for the biscuits shot forward. Those missiles did successfully hit. The jam splattered in the next volley. Only then did Anna realize that, though all the other objects had come close, none had truly hit anyone. "Charles, you are trying to scare us? Stop it!"

"Yes, stop trying to scare Henry," Aunt Deirdre said. Her hair splattered with jam and her shoulders white with sugar, Deirdre still nursed her bounty of flowers. Her normally kind blue eyes were snapping. Instantly, the flowers in her hands seemed to be pulled forward, but she clung to them. "No, they are mine! I should have fought my father years ago, and if I must fight *you*, I will. These flowers are mine! And Henry stays!"

"She is right," Anna said, coming to stand staunchly beside Deirdre and Henry.

"They are both right," Roark said. He stepped close to Anna and placed a hand upon her shoulder. Anna looked at him in surprise and warm gratitude.

The parlor fell silent. Nothing moved. Then the sound of clapping started.

"Well, I'll be hanged," Terrence breathed.

Charles grew visible across the room. His smile was odd. He proffered Anna a bow. "She's grown a spine, has she not?"

"You were testing them," Anna gasped.

" 'Twas not my intention," Charles said wryly, then shrugged. "If she still loves an Anton and he her, there is naught more to say. If only Genevieve had done as much. Yet the past is past, as I should be. Farewell, mistress, I shall not interfere again. I could say I'd hope to see you at a wedding, but that would be unfortunate, would it not?"

"Charles, wait," Anna said, aghast. As he disappeared, with the saddest look upon his face, regret washed over Anna. "Charles!"

"By the by," Charles's voice said. "The banshee is stuck, and you'll find your sister beneath the table."

"Banshee?" Anna asked, frowning. Then she realized that she hadn't heard Salome's wails during the melee. She looked swiftly around only to discover that Salome had wedged herself firmly between the wall and an ancient grandfather clock. "Oh, dear! Roark, we must help Salome. Are you all right, Salome?"

"I'm hiding, miss," Salome whispered.

"He's gone, Salome," Anna said, her heart wrenching slightly. "Roark will help you."

"Just one moment." Roark stepped forward and inched the clock over.

"Thank you, Your Grace," Salome said in an astonishingly subdued voice. She glanced around, opened her mouth wide, then clamped it shut. Without another word, she tiptoed from the room.

Roark looked at Anna, grinning. "Old Charles finally accomplished the impossible. Salome is soundless."

"Beth?" Terrence exclaimed. "Where is Beth?"

"She's under the table, Terrence." Anna walked over to the table. Its heavy damask cloth was bunched up. Beth's skirts, jam besmirched, peeked out. "Beth, you can come out now. Charles has left now."

"No." Beth's muffled voice was a sob. "He'll never leave!"

"Beth," Terrence said, running to the table, "do come out."

"I can't," Beth cried. "I won't."

"Dearest," Aunt Deirdre said, coming to stand next to the table. "We shall have Cook make us another pot of tea, and she might still have more biscuits and jam."

"No," Beth wailed. "No more. Please, no more. I'm not coming out."

"Perhaps," Henry said, walking up quietly, "it would be best if I leave."

"Must you?" Aunt Deirdre asked.

"I believe you have enjoyed enough of my company for the moment," Henry said, a twinkle appearing. "However, I will gladly return whenever you wish."

"Tomorrow?" Deirdre asked, her heart in her voice. "Will you come tomorrow?"

"I would be pleased to return tomorrow," Henry said.

A frightened squeal came from under the table. "Oh, no."

"Aunt Deirdre, perhaps you would like to escort Henry out." Anna looked to Terrence and Roark as well. "If you do not mind, I would like a private word with Beth."

"But . . ." Terrence began, his face dark with concern.

"Please," Anna said.

"Come, Terrence," Roark said.

Anna patiently waited for the group to depart. She

strove to keep her voice calm." Beth, everyone's left. You may come out now."

"No, I won't! I won't!" Beth's tone was so reminiscent of when she had been a child, Anna smiled despite herself.

"Then you must move over," Anna said, bending down. Without compunction, she squirmed her way under the table. It was extremely cramped. Beth sat quivering, and her tears could be seen even in the dimness. "Beth, I am sorry, but it is all right now."

"No, it isn't," Beth said. She flung herself into Anna's arms, great sobs racking her.

"Shh, now," Anna murmured, rocking her. Time's memories once again filled her. "Hush, Beth. Everything will be all right."

"I'm scared," Beth said, with a sob.

"I know, dear," Anna said. "I know. But Charles didn't mean to hurt anyone. He was angry and hurt himself."

"I hate him," Beth said, her voice shrill. "I hate him."

"Please don't say that," Anna said. "He is difficult, but he has been tormented, Beth."

Beth drew back, her tear-filled eyes flashing in anger. "Why are you saying these things? You were the one who said I shouldn't believe in ghosts. You were the one who said that it would be gloomy and unhealthy to live here. And now you support it. You support him."

Anna looked at Beth helplessly. She *had* said all of that. Was it but a month or so ago? She indeed was the one who hadn't wanted Beth to come there. She remembered her protectiveness toward her sister, her anger that someone would dare to ask her to live with such superstitions. Only they weren't superstitions and it was she who had become so deeply involved with ghosts and the past. Anna shook her head. She had changed so very much. "I know, dearest."

Beth broke into great sobs again. "Why does everything have to be this way?"

"It is life, dear," Anna said. "Not that I thought the dead were supposed to be part of it, but there you have it."

Beth stared at Anna, then threw herself into her sister's arms again. "Can't you make him go away?"

"He might have already," Anna said softly.

"Then he won't be at my wedding?"

"I can't tell you that, dear," Anna said, smoothing her sister's hair.

"Please," Beth pleaded, clinging to Anna. "Make him promise he won't appear. Please make him promise."

Anna had tried to make him promise that exact thing. As she held Beth, Anna realized that she had changed, but Beth hadn't. Beth was still her little girl. Yet Beth was to be married soon. She had to become a woman in her own rights. "I can't make Charles promise that, Beth. He has told me he has no control over his appearances."

"He will ruin everything! He will smash things and destroy things."

"No, you must believe he will not."

"How can I?" Beth sobbed.

Anna gently pushed Beth away. "Because you must. If you do not have faith in your love for Terrence and his for you, why should Charles not appear? Charles has no control over what he does. He is dead. But you are living, Beth. You have control over what happens. You are a woman now and you must make your own decisions." Anna knew she spoke the truth, yet saying the words caused a pain inside her. It was difficult to acknowledge the natural severing that would come to pass. "I cannot do anything, dearest."

"I am so scared," Beth whispered.

"I know," Anna said, tears forming in her eyes. "So am I."

"But you are never scared," Beth exclaimed.

"I'm sorry, Beth," Anna said, the tears falling. "But many times I am."

An odd gurgle of laughter escaped Beth and she hugged Anna. "I love you, Anna."

"I love you too," Anna said. As they clung to each other, Anna gave a shaky laugh. "Look at us, two grown women hiding beneath a table."

Beth giggled. "Silly, isn't it?"

"Yes," Anna said. "Silly."

Only it wasn't. It was two girls. It was two women. It was growing and changing. It was life.

Ten

Henry Anton appeared the next morning just as everyone had sat down to breakfast. Salome escorted him into the room. Considering the events of the previous day, one would have expected her to be cringing and entangled with strands of rosary beads; instead, her arms were once again filled to overflowing with flowers of sunny yellow and azure blue.

"Mr. Henry Anton, Miss Deirdre." Salome actually dipped a curtsy before she departed, hugging the flowers close.

Henry was Burnham Woods in floral form. He entered practically concealed behind what appeared to fall just short of a wall of florals. He walked over and offered Deirdre a bouquet of creamy pale pink English roses and Queen Anne's lace. "For you, Deirdre."

"Thank you, Henry," Deirdre said, beaming at him. "How delightful to have flowers two days in a row. That is very special."

"I would gladly bring them to you every day," Henry said.

"No, you couldn't do that," Terrence said in a jovial tone. "Aunt Deirdre has a belief that, if she has something too often, it will not be special anymore."

"Flowers every day would be special," Aunt Deirdre said, flushing, "if they came from Henry."

"Then you shall have them," Henry said simply. He approached Beth. "These are for you, Miss Winston."

Beth smiled and took the bouquet he offered. "Roses and daisies. They are lovely."

"Please accept my apologies for the, shall we say, stir, my visit caused yesterday," Henry said solemnly. A self-deprecating twinkle entered his eyes. "I assure you, in general, I am not a man to cause any sort of commotion when I enter a room. Indeed, I am rather the type who blends well with the furnishings."

"Henry, that is not true," Aunt Deirdre said.

"I would not believe him either if I were you, Beth," Anna said, laughing.

Henry definitely had charm, which was all the more compelling since it came from his gentleness and understanding of people. He seemed to make people bloom like his flowers.

"No, I do not," Beth said. "And it was not your fault, Mr. Anton. It was . . . *his* fault."

"No, my dear," Henry said, shaking his head. "You must remember that an Anton has not stepped foot in this castle since that fateful day. He had his right. But I could no longer stay away. I could no longer respect his right, not once I learned Deirdre still remembered me. Then I could only think of my right—of *our* right. This should be a time of happiness for you, Miss Winston. I know it is quite forward of me, but please accept any assistance I might be able to offer in your wedding preparations."

"Thank you." A smile crossed Beth's face. "I have always loved red roses."

"I cannot take too much credit there," Henry said, laughing. "Your sister had already told me as much."

Beth gazed at the roses. "They are the deepest shade of red I have ever seen."

"Yes." Henry nodded. "I myself have never seen any

to match them. They grow abundantly this time of year. They bring back memories."

Excitement transformed Beth's face. "Do you think I could have these at my wedding?"

Anna held her breath for some reason. Beautiful though they were, they were more haunting than Charles. She forced that notion away.

Henry hesitated a second. "I believe they were always meant for a June wedding. I would be honored if you chose to have them at your wedding."

"Thank you," Beth said, clearly delighted.

"My dear," Henry said to Anna, "I did not bring you any flowers today. I have something in my carriage I thought you might appreciate just as much."

"What is it?" Anna asked, intrigued.

"I have brought you all the family records and history I have."

"And it took you only two days to locate them?" Roark asked, chuckling. "We are still searching the reaches of the castle for ours. You have put us in the shade."

Anna ignored Roark's teasing, her eagerness overtaking her. "Have you?"

"I fear I did not discover much about Genevieve," Henry said. "But I brought you everything I've found in case you might learn something I overlooked."

"What have you discovered?" Anna asked, leaning forward, peeking at Beth. "Forgive me. We should discuss this later. Do join us for breakfast."

"Yes, do, Henry," Deirdre said. "What would you like?"

"I need nothing, thank you. I have already breakfasted," Henry said, taking up a chair close to Deirdre. "To enjoy your company will be enough."

"Mr. Anton," Beth said, her face rather pale, but determined. "Please do tell us about Genevieve."

"Yes, Henry," Aunt Deirdre said, nodding, "I think it is a story we should all know."

"I am afraid there is not much," Henry said. "We all know Genevieve ran away with William Thornton on her wedding day."

"That is in the records?" Anna asked.

Henry crooked his head. "Did you think something else?"

"No, not at all," Anna said, sighing.

"Genevieve's mother wrote in her journal of her grief and regret at permitting William to see Genevieve that morning. She blamed herself for not realizing their relationship had become so strong. The family disowned her from that day forward."

"And Genevieve's poetry?" Anna asked.

"It appears the family did not know of her intent to publish her poetry. They only discovered her works had been published that very June, in fact, when a letter arrived much later, offering the monies for the printing. The family never accepted the compensation, nor apparently did Genevieve."

"What do you mean?" Anna asked, confused.

"For over a year, a series of letters from the printer followed, still offering the funds. Since they came to the family, it is clear Genevieve never chose to claim them either."

"No, she wouldn't have," Anna said softly. "She wrote those poems for Charles."

"My dear," Henry said, his brown eyes sympathetic, "the sums were paltry, and William Thornton was not a pauper himself. He held no title, but from all accounts, he was well situated for a man of his times. The family might have disowned Genevieve, but they became aware of the fact that within a month William Thornton's estates were sold and settled. Whether this fact was discovered even though discharged in such haste and secrecy or if it were a lucky boon in spite of Genevieve's parents refusal to try to discover the where-abouts of Genevieve and William can only be speculated upon. Because William sold off these properties, Genevieve would not have gone wanting while married to him. As a result, however, we do not know where William and Genevieve settled thereafter. It might not even have been in England."

"What do you mean you do not know where they settled?" Anna asked. "Do you mean the family never learned where she went?"

"There is no record of Genevieve ever contacting them," Henry said. "Nor is there a record from anyone in the family acknowledging they knew where she and William finally settled."

"None?" Anna whispered.

"Anna," Henry said, "Genevieve and William must have plotted to escape as they did. Genevieve's mother relates that they sought Genevieve at William Thorn-ton's that day. They were not to be found. His servants admitted that William had prepared for a journey. They also admitted to packing a woman's wardrobe. They all swore, however, that he had refused to tell them his destination."

"I see," Anna whispered.

"Genevieve had prepared," Henry said. "She must have known that, when she left, there would be no for-giveness for her."

"Oh, dear," Aunt Deirdre said, her eyes tearing up. "How very dreadful."

Henry reached out his hand to her. "There have been enough tears."

Deirdre clasped his hand, nodding. "Yes."

"Then let there be no more." A sweet smile crossed Henry's lips. "My servant Creigs tells me there is a trav-eling fair nearby today."

Anna choked slightly. "Creigs told you?"

"Yes," Henry said. Then he winked at her swiftly. "He is always telling me I must get out more often."

"A fair!" Aunt Deirdre exclaimed. "How delightful!"

Henry's eyes sparkled. "It should only be an hour's ride from here if I—if Creigs is not mistaken."

"A fair?" Beth asked, her eyes lighting. "May we go?"

"By Jove, yes," Terrence said. "Anything would be better than doing more wedding stuff—er, I think such an outing would be jolly."

"And you, Anna?" Henry asked. "Will you join us?"

Anna hesitated. She wished to study Genevieve's records. Surely there was more in them than what Henry had discovered. There simply had to be.

"Come, Anna," Roark said.

Anna slowly nodded, her heartbeat suddenly racing. "Yes. I will."

"I must change my dress immediately," Beth squealed, springing up.

"So must I," Deirdre said, her hands fluttering.

Anna blinked. "I suppose I should do so as well."

"We can wait," Roark said, laughing. "But do not take all day, or we'll miss the fair."

The ladies, in a concerted movement, rushed off to prepare. They indeed set a record, for every lady, including Beth, was congregated in the great hall within the hour. There was much laughter as they prepared to depart. Just as a child can forget a cloudy day when promised a treat, everyone forgot past sadness for the fair.

Roark led the entourage forward, swinging wide the castle doors. Everyone halted in unison, else they would have run over the servant upon the doorstep. The servant appeared a statue. He had a bouquet of red roses in one hand; his other hand was raised in a balled fist preparatory to knocking. His stunned expression grew more frightened as he took in all the people staring at him.

"What do you want?" Roark asked.

The messenger flinched and quivered. "Oi've come . . . er . . ."

"Oh, never mind." Roark reached out and took the bouquet. "Thank you for the roses. You may go now."

The messenger stared rather stupidly at his hand, where the bouquet had once been; then he jerked a nod. He whipped about and ran off.

"Very swift fellow." Roark pulled the card from the roses and held it out to Anna.

Anna read the card quickly, knowing everyone watched her:

> *When can I see you? When will you say you will be mine?*
> *Do not torment me with this waiting. Yours forever, Julian.*

Anna, castigating herself as a wretch of the worst sort, immediately pocketed the note, just as she did the thought of Julian. It was definitely neither the time nor the place for thoughts of what she should, or must, do. She looked up, hoping her expression was unreadable.

Roark raised a brow, his gaze intent. "Should I take care of these for you?"

"Please do," Anna said, flustered. "But do hurry. We have a fair to attend."

"Huzza!" Terrence exclaimed.

"Oh, good," Beth said, clapping her hands together.

Roark, the most vindictive smile upon his face, raised the flowers almost in a salute, then tossed them over his shoulder. Anna studiously ignored the flowers sprawling across the flagstone floor.

"Hmmm," Henry said, musingly. "An odd manner of taking care of flowers."

Deirdre sighed and took Henry's arm. "We would

never do that to *your* flowers, I assure you. Your flowers are a pleasure to receive."

"I am glad to hear that." Henry leaned close to Deirdre and whispered in far too loud a voice, "I have never cared for Julian Rotham. I believe he is far less than he presents himself to be."

Anna gasped. "How did you know?"

Henry's face was bland. "I may live quietly, but I do hear the gossip every once in a while."

"Every once in a while?" Anna asked, her eyes narrowed.

Henry had the grace to look embarrassed. "Very well, I have always paid rather close attention to anything and anyone involving the Whynhavens."

"Henry," Aunt Deirdre exclaimed, "have you, indeed?"

Anna realized Henry's difficult position as all eyes turned to him in speculation. Since she was, in a manner of speaking, sitting very close beside him in the same rocking boat, she took mercy on him. "Did you say the fair is an hour away? We certainly have no time to waste."

She strove to keep her steps controlled as she walked toward the door. After all, she didn't wish it to appear as if she were fleeing the scene.

Roark strolled beside Anna in the midafternoon sun. The crowd was still thick and quite boisterous. Considering the simple attractions of the traveling fair, a more urbane crowd would have departed long before, searching for better entertainment. However, the inhabitants of those parts showed their good nature, offering up their full enthusiasm. Roark looked down at Anna, gauging her reaction. She walked beside him with a relaxed gait, her gaze roving about in pure enjoyment.

She suddenly gurgled a laugh and pointed. "Only look. Terrence and Beth are just now going into the tent where the world-renowned, one-and-only two-headed pig in captivity can be seen."

Roark smiled. "That was rather a letdown, wouldn't you say?"

Anna's hazel eyes twinkled. "Do you refer to the fact that the one head dangled rather sadly from that poor, cantankerous sow and that sawdust was seeping out of its ear . . . of the fake head, that is. No, indeed not. I cannot help but think of your ancestor Matilda."

"Matilda?" Roark asked frowning.

"Yes," Anna said, chuckling. "She was the one who took her pig butchering so seriously. Only think what pleasure she would have derived if she had possessed a stock of two-headed pigs. It would have been twofold."

"No doubt," Roark murmured, far more pleased by Anna's enthusiasm than whatever she thought his ancestor's idiosyncrasy would have favored.

Anna peeked up at him. Some other emotion flickered within her good humor. She looked away swiftly, then pointed to the left. "There are Aunt Deirdre and Henry."

Roark's aunt and Henry Anton stood close to each other, watching what Roark knew was the worst Punch-and-Judy show he'd ever seen. "I hope this time when Punch's head flies off, the puppeteers will not chase through the crowds for it."

"That was just an unfortunate accident. Surely it could not happen two performances in a row." Anna tilted her head slightly, her gaze still upon Roark's aunt and Henry. "I know you will call me a nonsensical romantic again, but it seems as if they have always been together."

"No," Roark said softly. "This time I will not tell you that."

Anna drew in a deep breath of air. "This is the way it should be, don't you think?"

Roark stilled at her words. The deepest part of him agreed since she was by his side. "How what should be?"

Anna smiled and waved her hand expansively. "Everyone is happy."

"Then you are happy?" Roark asked, a tension coiling within him.

The merest cloud of distress passed through Anna's eyes. "I am having a grand time."

"What of Julian?" Roark asked point-blank.

"I would prefer not to discuss him."

They continued to walk, and Anna did not say more. Roark knew it was unworthy of him, but he desired to know the answer and he would seek it in any manner open to him.

"I thought we had agreed to be friends. You can talk to me about Julian."

"Friends?" Anna's brow arched elegantly. "I would say that agreement was made under duress."

"No," Roark said, frowning. Her obvious disbelief piqued him. "We agreed to be friends."

With a quicksilver change, a smile flashed across her face. "Then, as one friend to another, I do not wish to discuss Julian."

Roark stared at her. It was a clear about-face that deftly put him at bay. Roark conceded his defeat with a wry smile. "Forgive me."

"I only want to enjoy today," Anna said, her voice rather apologetic.

Roark studied Anna, debating what tack to follow. Suddenly a lone fiddle arose over the other noises. A definite disturbance rippled through the crowd. Roark laughed, knowing himself to be a fool. "Then let us enjoy the day."

He grabbed up Anna's hand, ignoring the sensations his action caused, and led her toward the fiddle's sound. By the time they had wended their way though the crowd, a space had been cleared and people were already swinging into a country dance.

"This time we *will* dance with each other," Roark said, tugging upon Anna's hand.

"Oh, no. I could not," Anna said.

"Enjoy the day, remember?" Roark teased.

She laughed and offered him no further resistance, following him into the dancing throng. The pace of the country dance was fast and furious, unrestrained and exuberant. Anna became part of it all. She was laughter, sun, and flashing movement as she twirled from one step into the next.

"I must rest," Anna called out breathlessly.

Roark nodded and placing an arm about her shoulders, steered her through the maze of dancers. He withdrew his arm in regret once they were safely to the sidelines.

Anna laughed, fanning her face with her hand. "Gracious, but I am winded."

Roark found himself unable to tear his gaze away from her. Her cheeks wore a high flush, and she glowed from the exertion. An errant tendril of soft brown hair had slipped free and clung to her temple. Roark clenched his hand tightly. He wished nothing more than to be able to reach out and smooth it back, to touch her.

"What is the matter?" Anna asked.

"Nothing," Roark said softly. "You are very beautiful."

Astonishment flashed across her face. "I doubt that. I must look a positive fright."

"No," Roark said, shaking his head. "You look beautiful."

"Now is when you think I look beautiful?"

"I do," Roark said, chuckling. A sudden desire to be honest with Anna overcame him. "You were beautiful at the ball that night, Anna. Truly you were."

"Was I?"

"Yes," Roark said, nodding. "But you did not look like yourself. You looked like every society lady I know. You looked like Clarise."

Anna grimaced. "I was hoping to do so. She is very beautiful."

Roark knew he had to explain more. "You looked like Tiffany—not in coloring or in any feature. But Tiffany's appeal was all in her dress and outward style. It was only surface, beneath she had no beauty or honesty. When I saw you dressed as you were that evening, I thought of Tiffany. And when Julian spoke to you as he did, I thought of Tiffany and her ploys and wiles."

"I see," Anna stammered.

"I know I have been unkind," Roark said with regret. "I know we've had our differences."

"Yes, we have," Anna said, softly.

"But cannot we try to be friends?"

"Friends?" Anna asked.

"Yes," Roark said, forcing a laugh. "I'll even promise not to tax you upon Julian if that is what you wish."

"You won't?"

"I won't," Roark said, suddenly determined to make good his word. "I promise."

"I see," Anna said, nodding.

"Then it will be friends between us?" Roark asked.

"Yes, friends," Anna said, appearing bemused.

"And not under duress?" Roark persisted for some perverse reason.

"Right," Anna slowly nodded. "Not under duress."

"Very well, let us—" Roark halted.

"Let us what?" Anna asked, her voice breathless.

"Shake hands on it," Roark said quickly, sticking his hand out.

"Oh, yes." Anna placed her hand in his.

Roark tightened his grip, then cursed himself for being a blamed fool. Just before, Anna had said everything was the way it should have been. It had been. Suddenly it wasn't. Charles had had the right of it. If one must say they were friends, then their agreement should be sealed with a kiss, most definitely with a kiss.

"I cannot wait for them to come. They surely must approve," Aunt Deirdre said. She gazed solemnly about the chapel. "I think it is perfect."

Henry smiled. "We did it together."

"We did," Deirdre said, returning his smile.

"Hello," Terrence's voice called.

He and Beth entered the chapel, then halted. He blinked and Beth gasped. The late afternoon sun slanted in through the stone windows of the chapel, softly touching nestled beds of crimson roses and pristine white daisies. The gray stone pews were festooned with the flowers. At the altar, a white trellised arch stood. It too was entwined with the crimson roses. A prayer rail wrapped in tulle was centered just beyond the arch. Fanning out to each side of the rail was a solid bed of white daisies stretched across the three steps rising to the altar. In the middle of those two flower beds picked out in more of the deep red roses were the monograms of each family.

"Do you like it, my dears?" Aunt Deirdre asked, hastening to them.

"It is beautiful," Beth said, gazing about. "But why did you do this? The wedding is still a week away."

"It was my notion," Henry said. "I wished for you to

see how it would look so you could approve it. If it does not please you, we can do something different."

"I see." Beth clutched to Terrence's hand. "I think it beautiful, but these flowers will not last."

Henry smiled. "There are plenty more of the blooms."

"You do like it?" Aunt Deirdre asked, clasping her hands together. "I am so pleased."

"This is how it will look on our wedding day," Terrence said, grinning.

"Yes," Beth said, her tone soft.

"Imagine," Terrence said.

"Yes," Beth said, her voice weaker yet.

Terrence's eyes grew dark. "What is the matter?"

"Deirdre and I will leave you now," Henry said, gently. "Please consider the arrangements. If you wish anything changed, we can do it."

"Yes. Yes, indeed," Aunt Deirdre said, her brows puckering.

"Come, dear." Henry took Deidre's arm and led her from the chapel.

"He is right, Beth," Terrence said, his tone hesitant. "We can change it if you do not like it."

"No," Beth said. "We can't change what I want changed."

Terrence stilled. "What do you want changed?"

Beth walked down the aisle looking about. "It is so very beautiful." Tears shimmered in her eyes. "But all I can think about is that ghost."

"He won't appear, darling," Terrence said, striding quickly to her. He took up her hands and kissed them. "Our love is true."

"It is," Beth said, her voice choking. "I love you. I love you with all my heart. But I don't want to be married here. Even if he doesn't appear, I will know he is here." She looked about, a frightened look in her eyes. "Can't you feel it?"

"You mean him?" Terrence shook his head.

"No, I mean it," Beth said, shaking her head vehemently. "I can't explain, but I feel sadness here. And I don't want to live with it. I don't want to live with ghosts and the past—their past. I want us to have our own lives, our own love." She burst into tears. "I'm sorry, Terrence. I'm so sorry, but that is how I feel."

Terrence held her close. "No, please don't cry. We don't have to be married here if you don't want to."

"We don't?"

Terrence smiled. "We don't."

"You would do that for me?"

"No," Terrence said, a rather surprised look on his face. "I would do that for us. Your happiness is my happiness."

"But your family's tradition," Beth said. "I know how important it is to you."

"That is what I thought was important to me." Terrence's face showed confusion. "But it ain't. It's the family that is important to me, not the traditions. And it's you who are important to me. The rest of it be hanged. Devil a bit, we'll start our own family tradition."

Beth giggled. "We will?"

Terrence's eyes glowed. "This time *both* the bride and groom are going to run off together."

"Terrence, we can't," Beth gasped.

"Yes, we can," Terrence said, grinning. "I want to marry you, Beth. I want you to marry me now. I don't want to make any more lists of people, no more seating arrangements and infernal silver forks and how many removes. I want it to be just you and me."

Beth's eyes glowed. "Oh, yes."

"Then you'll go to Gretna with me?" Terrence asked.

"Gretna?" Beth gasped. "Oh, dear."

Terrence's eyes sparkled. "If we are going to break with tradition, we might as well do it all the way."

"But what will the family say?" Beth exclaimed.

"That's what I'm thinking about," Terrence said. "Do you really want to go back and tell Aunt Deirdre that all her work was for nothing and that we want to get married somewhere else now? First, there will be the discussion of where we are going to be married. Then a discussion of when. Then the question of who. To be followed by—"

"I hadn't thought of that," Beth said, her face alarmed.

"Well, I just did," Terrence said. "We'd be back where we started. I'd rather we were married before we told Aunt Deirdre that the ceremony is off. That way there won't be any discussion."

"You are right," Beth said, giggling. "It will be just you and me. It would be wicked."

"No," Terrence said with a grin. "We won't *really* be wicked, not until we are made husband and wife."

"Terrence, I love you so much," Beth said, her heart in her eyes.

"Then we'll go tonight," Terrence declared. He took her hand and drew her toward the door. Beth's excited laugh was the last sound in the chapel.

After they left, Charles slowly materialized, with a smile touching his lips. "B'gad, but this generation has gumption, Genevieve." The oddest look crossed his face. He walked up the aisle and stood at the rose-decked arch. He passed his hand through a rose. "Why can't I forget you? Why? An Anton courts a Seeton. Two young children will defy my family's tradition. Ha. They would rather run off to Gretna than be married here, where I might appear. They want none of the sadness, and why should they? The past should be forgotten. You should be forgotten. Why must you haunt me?"

Eleven

Henry had again arrived for morning breakfast. His reason that time was to plan the floral arrangements for the tables and the great hall at the wedding banquet. Neither Beth nor Terrence had come down to break their fast as of yet, but Henry and Deirdre were already deep in discussion upon the matter of which posy was to go where.

Anna smiled at their chatter. Their pleasure in their conversation and themselves was patently obvious. She caught Roark's gaze. He winked at her, the glint in his eyes alerting her that he knew exactly what she was thinking. She warmed, in spite of herself. She told herself firmly it came from the knowledge that she and Roark had finally settled their differences. They were friends.

Anna shoved the fact that she felt as physically warmed as she did spiritually merely from the grace of Roark's smile to the attic of her mind—just as she had tossed in her confusion about Julian and her sudden, inexplicable resistance to seeing him. Already resting there was the harrowing thought that Charles might have disappeared for good. Add to it the concern that she might have caused his absence by her inviting an Anton into the castle. No doubt, the attic was stuffed full. She would have to start another level down. If the wedding did not come about soon, she would be prime fodder for Bedlam.

She shook herself, mentally applying all her weight to the door of that overstuffed room and slamming it shut on all those misgivings. It was a lovely day. She was simply going to enjoy herself and ignore the questions to which she had of yet no answers. Her sister would be married within six days and she had a right to attend to that. She had a right to enjoy the company of the family. Her gaze unwittingly strayed toward Roark again. He raised his brow. Clearly, he had still been watching her.

A keening wail drifted through the walls to the occupants of the breakfast room.

Deirdre interrupted her conversation a moment to listen. She sighed. "Salome."

"Yes," Henry said, nodding. "She's still a distance off."

Deirdre smiled and immediately continued talking to Henry.

Anna looked to Roark, choking back her laughter.

"Shall we time it?" Roark asked, grinning. He drew out his watch fob and pretended to study it.

"Coldhearted wretch," Anna said, chuckling. Then her heart skipped a beat. "Do you think it might be Charles?"

"We must wait and see," Roark said. "She'll be coming in right about . . . now!"

Salome burst into the breakfast room. She waved about madly what looked to be a letter. "Miss Anna! Miss Anna!"

"Yes?" Anna asked, startled. Previously, Salome's pattern had always been to attack Aunt Deirdre first, no matter the occurrence. "What is it, Salome?"

Salome waddled forward, tears raining copiously down her cheeks. She waved the letter so violently about that it slapped Anna in the face. "This was on Miss Beth's bed, Miss Anna!"

Anna quickly snatched the letter before the next blow. She smoothed the creases from the missive and frowned as she discovered the seal broken. "Salome, did you read this?"

"Yes, mum," Salome nodded her head up and down eagerly. "I ciphered all of it."

"Why, Salome," Aunt Deirdre exclaimed. "I'm so proud of you. You have been practicing what I have been teaching you."

Anna blinked a moment, then lowered her gaze to the letter in trepidation.

Dear Anna,

Please forgive me. I do not want to be married within the chapel. Instead Terrence and I are going to Gretna Green to be wed. I do not know if you can ever understand or forgive me, but I pray that you do. You said I must make my own decisions and I have decided I will not have any ghost ruin my wedding. I do not wish to live under those conditions or any family traditions. My beloved has agreed with me.

Love your sister,
Beth

P.S.: Could you please inform the family for me? Please ask Aunt Deirdre to forgive us. Please tell Mr. Anton that his flowers were beautiful in the chapel and we are sorry that we cannot use them.
P.P.S.: Terrence bids you to do the same.

"What is it, dear?" Aunt Deirdre demanded.

Anna looked up, dazed. Beth might have made her own decisions, but she had certainly left Anna with the difficult part. "I do not know how to tell you this. . . ."

"Miss Beth has run off to Gretna Green!" Salome wailed loudly. "Miss Beth has run off to Gretna Green with Master Terrence!"

Aunt Deirdre turned pale. "What? What do you mean?"

"Gretna Green," Salome shrieked again. "Ladies ain't supposed to go there. It is shame, shame, shame. A wickedness."

"But why would she have done that?" Aunt Deirdre murmured, her voice hurt.

"I'm sorry," Anna said sincerely. "She and Terrence—"

"Shame and doom," Salome cried.

"Woman, if you do not cease this instant," Roark roared. "You will find out what doom is."

"Say your rosary, quick, Salome," Anna ordered. "Now!"

Salome cowered back, but her hand went dutifully to her rosary beads and she began her Hail Marys. Fortunately, she did not do so at full lung capacity.

Satisfied, Anna turned her attention to Aunt Deirdre. "Beth didn't want to be married in the chapel. You knew from the first she was afraid of Charles appearing and destroying the wedding. She and Terrence have gone to Gretna Green. She begs you to forgive her."

"But we have everything prepared," Aunt Deirdre said. "And Henry has decorated the chapel so splendidly."

"Yes," Anna said gently. "Beth wrote to thank him for that."

"It is all right, dear," Henry said, rising to stand beside Deirdre and pat her shoulder. "The young ones must do what they think they need to do."

"And all the guests," Aunt Deirdre gasped. "What

shall we do with them? They are coming to a wedding. It will be quite flat without the bride and groom."

"We shall cancel the wedding, Aunt Deirdre," Roark said in a soothing tone. "They will understand."

"No, they won't," Aunt Deirdre said, sniffing. "Everyone invited is looking forward to it. They have all told me so. And we have done so very much work. It would have been quite lovely. Those precious petits fours with the double wedding rings of marzipan atop them were going to be so special. I'm sure Charles would have behaved himself. Indeed, we haven't seen him for days."

"Please, Aunt Deirdre," Anna said. "Do not cry. I know it is a dreadful shock, but do not let it overset you so."

"I'm sorry," Aunt Deirdre said, brushing at her eyes. "You are right, I am just shocked. It would have been such a delightful wedding. All the special things planned and now it shall go to waste. It is such a shame." She halted abruptly, appearing thunderstruck. Indeed, her gaze became unfocused for a moment. When it cleared, her face was fully transformed into one of sheer excitement. "Heavens, what am I thinking? I *am* overset. It doesn't need to go to waste. It can be a wedding for you and Roark now."

"What?" Anna gasped.

"Please don't say you and Roark wish to run off to Gretna Green as well. My heart might break"

"No, of course we don't," Anna said, flushing.

"I didn't think so." Aunt Deirdre beamed. "You're not afraid of Charles."

"No, I meant that Roark and I aren't going to be married."

Aunt Deirdre turned a reproachful eye to Roark. "You haven't settled that yet? I had thought in these past few days that you had."

"No, Aunt Deirdre," Roark said, frowning severely. "We haven't settled anything yet."

"We have decided to be friends," Anna said, then flushed immediately, for everyone looked at her in silent astonishment.

"Friends?" Henry finally asked, his tone brimming with amusement.

"Yes, friends." Anna turned her gaze to Roark for support, but she received none, for he was intently studying the carpet.

"Well, of course you are friends," Aunt Deirdre finally said, her voice staunch. "Every good and loving man and woman are friends. It is very important to a happy marriage."

Anna shook her head in frustration. "Roark, tell them?"

"Aunt Deirdre, do desist. Anna and I are not going to marry simply because you are missing a bride and groom for your wedding."

"No, of course not. You are going to marry because you love each other and you are good friends. But you must admit this would be a perfect opportunity. Everything is already prepared."

The only perfect opportunity Anna could divine was the one Aunt Deirdre was so ruthlessly taking advantage of at the moment. "Aunt Deirdre, please. This doesn't need to be discussed."

"Don't say that you have accepted Julian Rothman instead. Roark will make a much better friend than him."

"No," Anna stammered. She rather felt as if dear, sweet Aunt Deirdre were leveling a pistol upon her.

"Thank heavens," Aunt Deirdre sighed.

"I agree," Henry said, nodding his head. "I have tried to refrain from comment, but Mr. Rothman is not the man for you, Anna. In truth, I don't think he is a man for any lady."

When Roark chuckled at that remark, Anna glared at him. He could laugh, since it was not he under the line of fire. Fuming, she stood. "If you will excuse me, I have pressing work to do. Roark, why do you not remain and continue this discussion with your aunt?"

Astonished, Roark widened his eyes in alarm. Anna nodded her head in malicious satisfaction, then hastened from the room in strategic retreat before there could be any retaliation.

"Oh, dear," Aunt Deirdre said, worrying her lip. "I do so hope she is not in love with Julian."

"No, no," Henry said. "Anna is a bright girl. I am sure she could not be so foolish."

"Of course she couldn't," Roark said, though jealousy shot through him. "Couldn't you see that you embarrassed her."

"Is that what was the matter?" Aunt Deirdre sighed in obvious relief. "Thank heavens. I thought she was offended that we did not approve of Julian."

"I see it does not matter that you embarrassed her"— Roark frowned severely—"or me, for that matter."

"I'd much rather have her embarrassed," Aunt Deirdre said, frowning, "than have her fall in love with Julian Rothman. I know it is dreadfully selfish of me, but I simply cannot help myself."

"Selfish?" Roark asked, confused.

"Yes. I like Anna living here. She's brought a new spirit into this house. And I do not mean her ability to communicate with Charles. It is just that things happen when Anna is about. Why, I have seen you, Roark, more often since she has arrived than I have in years. You are not always hidden away in that turret. And without Anna's help, Henry and I would not be together again."

Henry nodded solemnly. "It is true."

"It is obvious Beth and Terrence will choose not to live here," Aunt Deirdre said, her voice sad. "They will return to London and Anna will go with them, of course. What reason would she have to remain here?"

What other reason indeed? Roark wondered.

"And if Anna marries Julian," Aunt Deirdre sighed, "she will be living with him. I'm sure that could not be avoided."

"Don't talk such nonsense," Roark growled. The thought of Anna living with Julian Rothman actually turned his stomach.

"Well," Aunt Deirdre said, "she would, wouldn't she? I doubt he would let her remain here. And I, as much as I love Anna, would never invite Julian Rothman to live with us."

Roark shot out of his chair, his fingers clenching into fists. His stomach not only roiled, but bloodlust clouded his eyes. It would be a cold day in hell before Rothman ever lived under this roof. Charles might have disappeared, but Roark had not. "You had best never even think that again. Now if you will excuse me, I have studies to perform in the turret."

"Oh, dear, it is already happening, Henry," Aunt Deirdre's voice whispered from behind. "Roark will disappear from life again."

Roark came to a stand, as if shot.

"Give the boy time, dear," Henry's voice returned, soothing and gentle. "Give him time."

"But time is what he doesn't have," Aunt Deirdre said. "That Julian Rothman is always making up to Anna, while Roark just wants to be friends. And now he'll be in the turret!"

Stifling a curse, Roark forced himself to leave before he turned back and said something he might regret. He purposely did not go to the turret, but went to the stables instead and took his horse Comet for a long, hard gallop.

Roark strolled into the parlor at teatime, his mind much more relaxed—or so he told himself. It was his life and he would not allow anyone or anything to push him into marriage.

Deirdre and Henry were cozily settled upon the sofa, a large sheet of yellowed parchment lying across their legs. The teapot was steaming and Deirdre's special scones were heaped upon a platter.

Roark decided to ask the easiest question first. "We have special scones?"

"Yes, I ordered Cook to make them up in celebration of Beth and Terrence's marriage," Aunt Deirdre said, her voice enthusiastic. "We've been wondering how long it will take them to reach Gretna Green. We've been looking at a map we found, but cannot seem to find it."

The second question was answered. Roark cast a discerning look at the aged parchment as he went and lowered himself into a chair. Most likely there were sea monsters drawn in where Gretna Green should be. "Maps can be confusing sometimes."

"My heavens, yes," Aunt Deirdre said. "Have you thought about your proposal to Anna?"

"Deirdre!" Henry said, shaking his head gently as he set the map aside.

"Oh, dear, I forgot," Aunt Deirdre said, looking repentant. "I was not going to press you. You still have"—she floundered a moment—"plenty of time."

"Indeed," Henry said, his face solemn. "One must consider marriage most carefully. One must be certain of one's feelings and let no one else sway one."

Roark studied Henry suspiciously. It was exactly what

he felt himself, but Henry's tone made it sound different. At that moment, Salome entered the parlor. Roark stiffened as he noticed who followed her.

"Miss Deirdre, I've brought Mr. Rothman here," Salome said. "He's wishin' to see Miss Anna, but I don't know where she is."

Roark glared at Deirdre and Henry. Julian Rothman's prompt arrival upon the heels of their discussion smacked of contrivance. However, the alarm upon Aunt Deirdre's face and the frown of disapproval upon Henry's swiftly disabused him of such a notion.

Julian, holding a large bouquet of red roses, gave a bold smile to the group at large and bowed. "Forgive me if I have interrupted your tea."

"No, not at all," Aunt Deirdre said, though her voice did not match her words.

"I am aware I should not be here." Julian's eyes became dark and sincere as he gazed at Aunt Deirdre. It was no doubt the kind of look meant to melt women's hearts and resolve. "Anna has explained that my presence might cause difficulties."

Aunt Deirdre's gaze roved about the room with a rather hopeful expression. After a moment, she sighed. "No, no, it has been very quiet of late. It is all right."

"I simply must see her." Julian's gaze flicked to Roark in an insulting manner. "I must know that she is all right. I have not heard from her in almost a week."

"Yes, I know. That is because she has been dreadfully sick."

"Has she?" Julian frowned.

"Yes," Aunt Deirdre said. "Salome, Miss Anna is sick. She cannot receive anyone at this time."

"She can't?" Salome asked, blinking.

"No, she can't." Aunt Deirdre cast Henry an appealing look. "Isn't that so, Henry?"

"Yes," Henry said, nodding. He rose and walked over

to Julian. "If you will give me your flowers, I will gladly take care of them for Anna." He pointed at the various floral arrangements in the parlor, all of which were his handiwork. "As you can see, many have sent their well wishes."

"She is that ill?" Julian appeared stunned as he gazed at all the flowers. "Why did my poor darling not send me word?"

Roark stiffened. "Because your *poor darling* was too vilely ill to think of such matters."

Julian's eyes sparked. "I should have been here to comfort her."

"And catch what sickness she has?" Roark snorted. He doubted Julian would lay himself open to even a trifling cold for another person.

"Indeed," Aunt Deirdre said in an enthusiastic voice. "The doctor said she was to receive no company. Her illness is quite contagious."

"I would brave anything for her," Julian said dramatically.

"Lawks." Salome made the sign of the cross, then clapped her hand over her mouth as if she did not wish to breathe the air.

"Yes," Roark said coolly. "But I fear you will have to brave it another day. Salome, please show Mr. Rothman out."

"Yes, dear," Aunt Deirdre said. "And do be swift about it. We would not wish him to catch any of the contagion in the air."

"Yes, Miss Deirdre," Salome said, her voice muffled beneath her hand. "If you come this way."

"Good afternoon." Julian turned a compelling gaze upon Aunt Deirdre. "Would you be so kind as to send word to me the moment Anna is able to receive company? And tell her that I—"

"Yes, I shall tell her," Aunt Deirdre said hurriedly. "Only do leave now."

Julian frowned, but turned and followed Salome, who waved one hand about as if she could swat any threatening contagion away while she wheezed air through the other that covered her nose.

"Roark," Aunt Deirdre said, her tone nervous. "I know you have plenty of time, and it must be your decision, but could you perhaps make it hastily? I do not like that man. I do not want Anna to live with him instead of us."

"I fear I agree," Henry said as he went to the table, lifted its damask cloth, and tossed Julian's flowers beneath it.

Roark frowned a moment. Then he smiled, all his tension draining away from him. He'd been fooling no one but himself. He'd been so determined to make sure that nobody forced him into marriage that he had overlooked the fact that he wanted that very marriage. He wanted Anna living with him and nobody else. He wanted Anna loving him and nobody else. "I agree as well. With all my heart, in fact."

"Good boy," Henry said with approval as he went to sit beside Deirdre.

"Oh, thank you, dear," Aunt Deirdre said in a relieved tone. "Thank you."

"Hello," Anna said, her tone hesitant as she entered the room. Roark's heart leapt until he noticed that she studiously kept her gaze from him as she took up a chair even farther from him. "I am sorry I am late. I became involved with some of the histories of your ancestors, Henry."

"Anna," Aunt Deirdre exclaimed all but bouncing up and down upon the sofa. "Roark has something very important to say to you."

Anna cast only the quickest glance at Roark. "What is it?"

Roark frowned, even as remorse filled himself. If it had been physically possible, he would have booted himself firmly in the pants. He hadn't been fooling anyone but himself . . . and Anna. "I wondered if we could perhaps have a private discussion afterward. We could go for a walk or perhaps a ride."

"I'm sorry, but I truly do wish to go back to my studies," Anna said in a dignified tone. "Perhaps another time."

"Oh, no, dearest," Aunt Deirdre exclaimed. "You do not understand. Roark wants to—"

"Deirdre," Henry murmured, his tone gently warning.

"Oh, yes." Deirdre leaned forward. "But truly, Anna—"

"No," Roark said swiftly. "Another time will be fine."

Aunt Deirdre looked bewildered. "But . . ."

"Thank you," Anna said, the first true emotion crossing her face. It was clearly one of relief. "I am just very involved with my studies at this moment. I hope to discover something." She forced a laugh. "In fact, I hope you will understand if I take my dinner in my room."

"What?" Aunt Deirdre exclaimed. "But—"

"We understand," Roark said, calmly.

If Anna wished to avoid him and the pressure of the situation, he had no one to blame but himself. However, he would have his private discussion with her. It was amazing how love suddenly made time become something very important and utterly valuable.

Anna wandered about her bedroom aimlessly, the candle on the bedside table guttering low against the night shadows. She'd already exhausted herself with her pacing earlier. She grimaced. If she were restless and growing to hate her bedroom walls, she had no one else to blame but herself. After all, it was she who had sequestered herself away from every one all day and all evening.

The problem was, she simply couldn't face the others—just as she couldn't face all the overwhelming emotions she was experiencing. She had certainly wrangled with these feelings long enough, but still she could not subdue them.

"Charles, are you there?" Anna waited. Of course, there was no answer. How she wished she could talk to him again. After all, it was he, in a manner of speaking, who had brought her to this impasse. It was he who had thrown Roark and her together in a compromising situation that very first night . . . he who had demanded she face love and the desires of her heart . . . he who persisted when all she wanted to do was turn tail and run.

She wondered how Roark's and her relationship would have progressed without Charles pulling his pranks. No doubt they would have been polite to each other as brother-in-law and sister-in-law. Or perhaps they would have been polite enemies. But he and she would have rubbed along as in-laws, perhaps seeing each other at holidays and whatnot, but they certainly would not be involved with each other outside of their dealings with Beth and Terrence.

Just what clanker was she trying to tell herself? Gone were all the confusing questions or any doubts she had harbored. She loved Roark Seeton. She had loved him from the moment they'd met, though she hadn't realized it. Indeed, the story might have changed without Charles, but sure as a star's course, Anna knew she would have loved Roark anyway. She had thought Aunt Deirdre insane with her talk about love and predestination. Unfortunately, Aunt Deirdre hadn't been insane—Anna had been naive.

Much good that enlightenment did her. Indeed, it only drove the spike deeper into her heart. She was in love with a man who wanted to be her friend. Aunt Deirdre definitely was in there conniving and contriving for Anna's sake, but Anna didn't want that either. She would not want to force Roark to marry her or even to finagle a proposal from him. If his love could not be hers, she did not want less. Being destined to love a man was one thing; arranging matters to gain his hand, but not his heart, was another.

Only after that morning, it was so infernally difficult to resist. Anna feared Roark have been able to read her desire and wishes in her eyes—just as everyone else had apparently done when she had attempted to tell them Roark and she were merely friends. It was all too mortifying.

Anna took another meandering turn about her bed, then stopped. Her heart began to race. The wall was opening up. Relief welled within her. "Charles! It is about time."

"It's not Charles." Roark stepped from out of the passage way, with that special smile Anna loved upon his face. "But I agree. It is about time."

Anna stood very still. "What are you doing here?"

Roark dusted off what appeared to be mortar and stone shavings. "I've finally found the secret to the passage. It is amazing how one can finally see the truth if one really wishes to find it."

"But why would you wish to find it?" Anna asked, flushing.

"I wish to speak to you in private. You told me I could at another time."

"But not at this time," Anna stammered, crossing her

arms about her in embarrassment. "This certainly isn't a good time."

"I think it is," Roark said, walking slowly up to her. "I'm taking a leaf from old Charles's book. The bedroom seems to be the place where you and I settle our differences."

"Roark," Anna gasped.

"Only I hope this time there won't be any differences." With the faintest smile, Roark actually knelt down. "Anna Winston, will you marry me?"

Anna stood frozen. "But you said you wanted to be friends."

"Friends and lovers." Roark nodded slowly. "Husband and wife. Will you marry me?"

Still Anna couldn't move. Despite all her thoughts before, hearing the words come from Roark stunned her.

Roark chuckled hoarsely. "Anna, please answer—or at least breathe."

"*You* want me to marry *you*?" Anna persisted.

"Yes, *I* want *you* to marry *me*." Roark muttered a frustrated expletive and stood abruptly. "Whoever decided kneeling was a good way to propose must have been cracked in the head." He reached out and hauled Anna into his arms. "Marry me, Anna. I love you." He captured her lips, kissing her deeply, desperately. He drew back just as Anna melted in his arms. "Will you marry me?"

"Yes." Anna nodded, dazedly. "I love you."

Roark shouted a laugh, all but cracking Anna's ribs as he hugged her tight. "Did you hear that, Charles? She will marry me. I hope you are satisfied, you old devil. I know I am."

When he kissed her swiftly one more time, she asked, "Why only one?"

"You are my future wife. We'll not be marrying because I've compromised you. We've avoided that to date, though it's been damn hard, and we can avoid it for a few more days."

Anna caught her breath. "Then you do want to marry me at the ceremony."

"We don't need to do so," Roark said, his gaze sincere. "We will wait if you wish. But I am ready to marry you now."

"You just want to avoid what Terrence had to suffer," Anna teased.

"Don't you?" Roark asked, his eyes twinkling.

"Of course." Anna laughed. "Especially since I already know you'd leave all the preparations to me."

Roark frowned slightly. "I would not."

"Yes, you would," Anna said. "I remember. You said no matter how besotted you had been with Tiffany you still refused to enter into the wedding preparations."

"I did, didn't I?" Roark said, rather astonished. "I guess I'm even more besotted than I knew. I'll go through all that with you if you wish. In fact, I damn well intend to be there at the dressmakers this time. I had better be the first to know the color of your next corset!"

Anna flushed. "I think we'd best just get married as swiftly as we can and forgo the planning."

"Hmm, yes," Roark murmured, releasing her and stepping back quickly. "Good night, Anna. I will see you tomorrow."

He strode to the passageway and stepped into it. "What color is that French corset anyway?"

Anna gurgled a laugh. "You'll have to wait to find that out, sir!"

"I assure you, I do wait," Roark said, his voice fading away.

* * *

Anna floated through the next morning in a combination of bliss and excitement. Aunt Deirdre's and Henry's congratulations and exclamations of delight warmed Anna's heart. She had grown to love them dearly.

She remembered the serious look in Roark's eyes the night before when he said they could wait if she wished, but that he was ready to marry her. She smiled. It seemed everyone in the entire family could not wait. She knew she couldn't.

A sudden giggle escaped her. Heavens, she was marrying the Ogre, that renowned woman-hater and recluse. How Roark had changed. He had gone into the village to perform some errands. The teasing look in his eyes had piqued Anna's curiosity, but he had told her she must be patient.

Aunt Deirdre and Henry had been swift to go with him. Anna never doubted that the lowliest villager would know the change in bride and groom by eventide. As excited as Aunt Deirdre was, perhaps even the local livestock would be well informed.

The prospect of her future life unfurled in Anna's imagination. It was everything she wanted. Yet before she could devote herself to that happiness, she knew she had one duty to perform, no matter her reluctance. She shook her head musingly. How had she ever had any confusion in regard to her feelings for Roark versus her feelings for Julian? No, she had to be honest with herself. She had merely tried to pretend there was a confusion because she had been frightened by love. Either way, she owed Julian an explanation.

She waited patiently in the parlor. She had sent a missive asking him to visit her immediately if he could. She didn't want him to hear the news from anyone else but her. She started to worry. What if he was unavailable or out of town at the moment? She grimaced. She could only do what she could. She mustn't worry.

She sighed in relief, therefore, when Salome stepped into the parlors doorway. She would not enter, and she wore what appeared a linen mask over her nose and mouth. "Mr. Rothman's here to see you, Miss Anna."

Anna stared at Salome, but the maid departed immediately. She shook her head. Salome's peculiarities were growing odder by the day.

"My dear Anna," Julian said, advancing with his signature bouquet of red roses. "You have recovered enough to see me, thank God."

"Recovered?" Anna asked, frowning.

"Yes," he said, sitting down and offering her the flowers. "Seeton said you were sick when I came to visit you yesterday."

"You came to visit me?" Anna asked, surprised.

"Yes," Julian said, "but Seeton said that you were very contagious and that I could not see you."

"I see," Anna said slowly. At least one of Salome's oddities was explained. It unsettled Anna that Roark had used such diversionary tactics upon Julian, but since she had not been prepared to see Julian the previous day, she rather accepted his ruse. She focused her attention upon Julian. He at least deserved that much from her. "I am much better now, thank you."

Julian grabbed her hand. "Are you truly, or do you just say that? Are they keeping you from me? Is that is what has happened?"

"No, heavens, no," Anna said, jerking her hand away. Julian gazed at her so intensely that Anna sprang up. She discovered herself wringing her hands. "No one has kept me away from you. I told you I needed time to think. And I have thought."

"Yes?" Julian asked, his eyes almost narrowed.

"Julian, I am sorry," Anna said in a rush. "I cannot marry you. I love Roark."

"No," Julian said, his tone fierce. "You cannot mean it."

"I do." Anna drew in a steadying breath. "I am going to marry him."

"Marry him?" Julian sprang up, his blue eyes blazing. "How can you marry him, after all these weeks. You led me on." He paced toward her so threateningly that Anna cringed back. Only then did Julian halt. He spun quickly away from her. His back was rigid and tense. "You led me to believe that you loved me."

"I did not mean to lead you on that way," Anna stammered.

He turned back. His expression was pleading. "I thought you loved me as I love you."

"I'm sorry, Julian," Anna said helplessly. "I truly did enjoy your company. I truly do admire you, but I do not love you."

"Please give me a chance," Julian begged. "Let me prove that you love me."

"No, Julian," Anna said, her tone soft, her eyes sincere. "I am marrying Roark within the week."

"So soon?" Julian cried out. "You cannot!"

"But I am," Anna said more firmly.

"No, you should marry me," Julian said, his voice desperate. "You must marry me!"

Before Anna could move, Julian descended upon her, jerking her forward and kissing her hard. Anna gagged, the feelings of suffocation rising within her.

"My, what a surprise," Roark's voice cracked through the room.

Relief washed through Anna. She mustered her strength and pushed at Julian. He only held her more tightly to him. Clenching her teeth, Anna turned her head away from Julian's. "Let me go." Furious, she lifted her foot and kicked Julian sharply in the shins. He yelped, his hold loosening. Anna tore from his grasp, glaring at him. "Don't ever do that again."

She heard a low chuckle from Roark. Offended and hurt, she turned equal fury upon him. "And why didn't you help me?"

Only then did she start back. Roark stood not far from her, his eyes blazing with an equal force. "There is no reason to pretend such outrage, for my sake, Anna."

Anna's eyes widened in astonishment. The import of his words snaked its way into her numbed conscience. "You can't think I wanted Julian to kiss me on purpose."

"Dearest, we have been caught out," Julian said, his tone almost exuberant.

Anna gasped. "We have not been caught out! I did not ask you to kiss me."

"But I knew you wanted me to kiss you," Julian said, smiling rather smugly.

Anna shook with rage. "Leave now, Julian. This instant."

"Yes, my love." Julian cast Roark a taunting smile. Without another word, he turned and left with a jaunty step.

Anna stared after him for a moment. His behavior had been far too unexpected and confusing. She shook that part off, however, turning her attention back to Roark. He stood there quietly, his arms crossed. She swallowed hard. "Why didn't you do anything? Couldn't you see I was trying to escape him?"

"No," Roark said, his tone cool, his eyes devoid of emotion. "I didn't. But as I said, there is no reason to pretend such outrage. I have grown since those years ago. I understand and can accept it much better now."

"Accept what?" Anna asked slowly.

"That women are unfaithful creatures," Roark said with a shrug. "I suppose you simply cannot help yourself."

Anna paled. "I thought you said you loved me."

Roark's eyes flared. "I do."

Hurt knifed through Anna. "But you don't trust me?"

"It is rather difficult to do so," Roark said, "considering what I just saw."

"No," Anna said, shaking her head vehemently. "If you trusted me, you would have seen it differently. You told me when I saw you with Clarise that it was she who had chosen to kiss you, that you were not a willing participant. That is something I can accept as truth because I have grown to love and trust you. Why can you not do the same for me now?"

"Because this is different," Roark said, his voice sharp.

"It is not," Anna said. Yet her heart told her that it was different for him. Roark had suffered too much hurt in the past. He had not healed. He might have grown to love her, but he had not grown to trust her. She drew in a ragged breath. "You said you were ready to marry me."

"And I am," Roark said.

"No, you are not," Anna said softly. "You may want to marry me, but you are not ready to marry me—not if you cannot trust me. I love you, Roark. You have my heart and soul, but I shall not marry you until you can give me your trust as well. I will not—cannot—settle for love without trust."

"Then, madam, we cannot marry," Roark said. "For I cannot say I'll play the blind fool and ignore what I just saw."

Tears filled Anna's eyes and she moved hastily past him. So blurred was her vision that she rocketed into Aunt Deirdre.

"Gracious," Aunt Deirdre said. "There you are. Henry and I wanted to ask you about the bride's bouquet for the wedding. I feel it should be a long one trailing to the floor with ivy."

"There will be no wedding," Anna said.

"Oh, dear," Aunt Deirdre sighed. "Not again."

Anna dashed past Aunt Deirdre, with *Not again* ringing in her ears.

Twelve

Henry and Deirdre sat companionably in the drawing room at an immense walnut table protected by the green baize felt cover hastily thrown over it. Across the table's vast surface, sheets of paper with long lists scribbled upon them were strewn everywhere. An assortment of floral arrangements rested next to sample decorations, which rested next to bolts of fabric.

"Perhaps we should order up more champagne," Aunt Deirdre said, frowning as she dropped one sheet of paper and rummaged about for another. "What do you think, dear?"

"It might be wise," Henry said. "All things considered."

"Oh, dear." Aunt Deirdre's face grew alarmed. "We must consider alternate toasts for the occasion, just in case the wedding does not go off as a wedding."

"I don't know," Henry murmured, looking studiously at a list. "We could always toast to our engagement if necessary."

"No," Aunt Deirdre said, frowning. "That might be considered inappropriate. . . . Gracious, what am I saying? Did you just propose to me, Henry Anton?"

"I had meant to wait," Henry said. "But with all these bridal preparations, it makes it difficult to refrain."

"Do you . . . ?" Aunt Deirdre's face was a mixture of hope and fear. "Do you really think we could marry?"

"I don't see why not. We certainly can't leave everything to the young." He leaned over and kissed Deirdre gently, but firmly. "It would be a shame if we did."

"Yes, a shame." Aunt Deirdre flushed a charming rose to match the rose moire of her morning dress. Upon her head was jauntily perched a lace cap with deep rose satin ribbons tied behind one ear. Stuck in the bow of ribbons was one single Anton rose blossom. "Oh, dear, would it be terribly wrong of us to marry?"

"No," Henry said softly, "it would be terribly right."

"After all these years. Oh, Henry, I would so love to marry you."

"Thank you, dear," Henry said, softly. "For I would love to marry you."

"But we must not be selfish," Aunt Deirdre said, drawing a breath. "We must wait until . . ."

"I know—until the children are settled."

Aunt Deirdre sighed. "You are such a dear to understand. Thank you."

"I have waited all these years. I can wait a while longer," Henry said, laughing. "And who knows? Tomorrow may transpire as we have planned."

"I pray it does," Aunt Deirdre said, sighing. "You know, though, that it is—"

"Betting against the odds. But if *we* can be together after all these years, anything is possible."

"Hello?" Terrence called from the doorway, a look of diffidence upon his face. Beth hid behind him, her expression equally hesitant.

"Oh, my dear children!" Aunt Deirdre sprang up, scattering lists right and left as she hastily ran to them. "You are finally home! How wonderful!"

Terrence received Aunt Deirdre's welcoming hug

first. Laughing, he lifted her from the ground in an enthusiastic whirl. "Ha! I knew you wouldn't be angry. I told Beth so."

"Of course not," Deirdre said breathlessly as he set her down. She turned to Beth, opening her arms wide. "My dear."

Beth's face blossomed into a radiant smile and she flew into the tiny woman's arms. "Aunt Deirdre."

Deirdre hugged her close, then stepped back, her smile benign. "You two are married then. It is quite plain to see."

"Of course we are married," Terrence said, his voice as proud as if he had just created the universe single-handedly. "Why wouldn't we be?"

"Oh, nothing," Aunt Deirdre murmured.

"It was so beautiful, Aunt Deirdre!" Beth exclaimed. "We were married in the cutest little cottage—just Terrence and I!"

"And two witnesses," Terrence added quickly. "Oh, and a preacher. It was all done proper, I assure you. We've tied the knot up, right and tight."

"Oh, my darlings, I couldn't be more pleased," Aunt Deirdre sighed.

"Auntie, it is *so* marvelous to be married," Beth said, her eyes full of stars. "I think everyone should be married."

"I quite agree."

"Yes," Terrence cleared his throat. "I couldn't help but notice all the servants running about the hall. What is happening?"

"We don't really know yet," Aunt Deirdre said.

"What?" Terrence asked.

"What Deirdre means to say," Henry explained, "is we do not know if there is to be another wedding to-morrow or not." He held out his hand. "Congratulations on your marriage."

"Thank you." Terrence frowned. "Whose wedding?"

"Congratulations, my dear," Henry said, smiling to Beth.

"Oh, thank you. "Whose wedding?"

"Roark and Anna's, of course," Deirdre said.

Terrence grinned. "By Jove, they are finally doing it. That's grand!"

"You said you are not sure," Beth said.

"Do let us sit down." Henry led the way to the table. Everyone joined in and shifted papers to uncover chairs.

"Why are you unsure?" Beth asked as she lifted her skirts to clear a stack of fabric bolts to take a seat.

"Because neither Roark or Anna will give us a straight answer," Deirdre said.

"I don't understand," Terrence said, shaking his head. He shoved aside a monstrous candelabra covered in ivy and roses to better see across the table.

"Roark proposed to Anna after you two left for Gretna Green," Henry said. "They will marry in the chapel instead of you."

"Yes," Deirdre said. "It was quite perfect. After all, the preparations were already made, and this way they will not have gone to waste, nor will the guests be disappointed."

"You are going to pass on our wedding?" Terrence asked, blinking.

"In a manner of speaking," Henry said.

"B'gads, that *is* economy," Terrence hooted.

"We did not think you would mind," Aunt Deirdre said.

"No, 'course not," Terrence said. "After all that blasted work, it would be nice to know that it was to a purpose."

"Oh, yes," Beth said, "especially if it means Anna will marry Roark."

"Indeed, that is what we thought," Aunt Deirdre said. "Only that awful Julian Rothman has ruined everything."

Beth gasped. "Never say that he and Anna are . . ."

"No, no," Aunt Deirdre said quickly. "At least, we hope not."

"Roark and Anna had a fight over Julian," Henry said. "Roark discovered Julian kissing Anna. Anna declares that she did not want Julian to kiss her and that Roark should have understood that. Roark says she must have wanted Julian to kiss her."

"Anna must be right," Beth said, wrinkling her nose. "What woman would want Julian Rothman to kiss her?"

"Hmm, I don't know the answer to that," Terrence said. "But I do know that no man wants to find his fiancée kissing *anyone.*"

"There you have it in a nutshell," Henry said. "We are at an impasse."

"Then the wedding is off?" Terrence said.

"Not exactly," Henry said slowly.

"So it might be on?" Beth asked.

"Perhaps," Aunt Deirdre said cautiously.

"Faith, it's confusing." Terrence frowned.

"And very exhausting," Aunt Deirdre said. "I have all but run my legs off between the two. For if Roark is in the turret, that assures me Anna must be in the cellars."

"And if Roark is in the west wing . . ." Henry said, his tone wry.

"Anna is in the east wing," Aunt Deirdre finished.

Terrence shook his head. "It doesn't look to me as if there will be a wedding."

"True, that is how it appears," Henry said. "However, when we ask if they are positive they wish for us to cancel the wedding, neither will give us a direct answer. Roark tells us it is not his decision to make and to apply to Anna for the answer."

"And Anna tells us it is Roark's decision to make and to ask him," Aunt Deirdre said.

Terrence whistled. "That's a tangle."

"To make matters worse," Aunt Deirdre said, "that dratted Julian Rothman is still sending flowers and cards. He even sent Anna a ring!"

"Oh, no!" Beth exclaimed.

"Yes," Deirdre said. "That is why Henry and I are proceeding with all the preparations regardless. This wedding shall be Roark and Anna's if only they will realize it before it is too late."

"And what if they don't?" Beth asked, frowning.

"Why, then the wedding will be decidedly flat tomorrow," Aunt Deirdre said. "But I am ordering up more champagne for that purpose."

Anna sat quietly upon her bed. Laid out beside her was a wedding dress. Even if Anna had commissioned it herself, it could have not been more to her taste. Aunt Deirdre and Mrs. Baxter had in some way divined the exact dress Anna would have dreamed of wearing. The heavy, figured brocade was a subtle white-on-ivory pattern and draped full skirted to a demitrain. The style was romantic yet it bore subtle historical touches. The dress was perfect for a wedding held in a centuries-old chapel. Its puffed sleeves were slashed and laced with white satin ribbon reminiscent of that of an Elizabethan lady.

In her hand, Anna held a ring and a letter, both from Julian. The letter begged her to meet him at midnight at the back entrance. He would have a coach prepared for travel. If she would consent to marry him, they could flee together. If she would not, he begged her to see him at least one last time in farewell.

What an awful position in which to find herself. This could very well be the night before her wedding. She even had the choice of two men—or it appeared she had two choices. Her heart knew she only had one.

When a knock sounded upon the door, Anna's pulse jumped. If only it were Roark. "Yes? Who is it?"

"It is me," Beth called. "May I come in?"

"Yes, certainly," Anna said, stifling a sigh. How foolish she was. Beth entered, quietly closing the door behind her. Anna forced a smile and moved the wedding dress farther aside. "You must come and tell me all about your wedding. We were not able to discuss it much this evening."

"I'd rather talk about *your* wedding," Beth said, walking over to sit on the bed next to Anna.

"I'm not sure I will have one."

"Not if you will not talk to Roark or he to you," Beth said. "I am pleased you both came to dinner, and it was very nice of you to try to celebrate with us, but it was very painful to watch."

"I'm sorry," Anna said, flushing.

"Roark loves you, Anna," Beth said softly. "And you love him. Why will you not marry him?"

"He does not trust me," Anna said, the hurt welling within her. "He may love me, but he does not trust me."

"He was deeply wounded by Tiffany's betrayal. You must give him time."

"I will give him time. I love him, but I will not marry him if he does not trust me."

"Is that so very important to you?"

"Yes. I don't think love can grow without trust."

"But couldn't it be the other way?" Beth asked. "Trust will grow with love."

"No, I don't think trust can grow, even with love, if it is not given first." Anna rose, clasping her hands tightly together. "I have thought and thought about this. You did not see Roark's face when he told me that we women were unfaithful creatures and he supposed we could not help ourselves, but he was still prepared to marry me. I could not live with him every day, Beth, knowing that is how he felt, knowing that is what he thought of me."

"He must have said that because he was hurt."

"I know. But if he will not give up his hurt and bitterness for me, what hope do we have for a happy marriage?"

Beth shook her head. "I don't know. I fear you and Roark make love so very complicated. You are demanding everything."

"Yes," Anna said. "But that is love. It does demand everything."

When the candle flame suddenly flared high, Anna started and quickly gazed about the room.

"Is it the ghost?" Beth asked.

Anna waited a moment. "No, it isn't."

Beth sat still a moment before a slow smile crossed her face. "Do you know, I'm not afraid of him anymore."

"You aren't?" Anna asked in surprise.

"No, I'm not," Beth said, her own voice sounding just as surprised. "Perhaps you doing the right thing, Anna. I was afraid of the ghost because I thought he might be able to stop our wedding. Now I know Terrence wouldn't have let that happen. And I know I wouldn't have let it happen. I didn't realize it before, but it is because I trust both of us. I have complete faith in our love." She rose and walked over to Anna and hugged her. "I want you to marry Roark. You two belong together. Yet I want you to do what you feel you must. You have always seen things more clearly than I."

Anna laughed. "Not anymore, I think."

"I do love being married. It is so very nice." Beth walked to the door. "I will leave you now. And do not worry about tomorrow. Aunt Deirdre has ordered up more champagne in case you and Roark do not appear at the ceremony. She and Henry are still at work devising different toasts they can make in event of that happening."

Anna, a candle in her hand, and Julian's ring in her pocket, walked slowly through the castle. She did not look forward to seeing Julian again. Part of her was still angry at his behavior the last time she had seen him, and part of her felt guilty that she had ever permitted the relationship to go so far. It was the guilty part that demanded she talk to Julian one more time before he left. She could not right what pain and disappointment she had caused him, but she could at least return his ring and say good-bye.

She opened the kitchen door and slipped out.

"You have come, my love," Julian whispered. "I knew you would."

Anna gasped and spun when Julian seemed to step from nowhere. It was nearly a moonless night, with threatening clouds blacking out the stars. Anna's weak candle did little to chase the darkness away, only casting odd shadows upon Julian's face. His eyes glittered within its meager glow. He smiled and, leaning down, blew the candle out. "No need for that. It might draw attention."

Anna blinked. "Julian, I—"

He grabbed her elbow. "Let us go to the coach."

"But I—"

"I have everything prepared for us. You will want for nothing," Julian said, his voice confident.

As he drew Anna along, his grip almost hurting, she slowed her steps. "Julian, I am sorry. I came only to talk."

"We can talk in the coach." Julian dragged her forward.

The waiting coach loomed out of the darkness. A sliver of moonlight broke through the clouds for a moment. Anna saw the coachman, who sat atop the box, glance at her. He then looked away. Something in that glance made Anna shiver.

"Julian, no," Anna cried, resisting in earnest. "You must understand. I am not going with you."

"Anna, please," Julian said, his voice desperate. "You said you would talk—just give me a moment of your time."

"We can talk here," Anna said desperately.

Julian opened the coach door. A lantern's light glowed within. "Please. We will only talk. If you are rejecting me, give me a moment. Let me see you when you tell me it is over. I will not believe you otherwise."

"Very well."

Anna entered the coach, and Julian followed directly behind. As he began to close the door, a specter appeared beyond the carriage. Inexplicably, Anna's heart burst with fear. It was a vision of Charles, yet Anna lunged for the door.

"Roark!" she cried.

Suddenly, Anna felt a stunning blow to her jaw. The force of it drove her back against the seat. Through a miasma of pain and shock, she watched Julian swing the door shut; then the coach jumped forward. She raised her hand to her cheek. "Why did you do that?"

"We are going to be married," Julian said, his tone cool as he settled back upon the seat.

"Are you insane?"

"No." Julian smiled. "Only perilously close to debt-ors' prison."

Anna winced through the pain. "You *are* a fortune hunter."

"Yes, I need a fortune. But I do want you, Anna. You are like no other woman I have met. Indeed, you are the first one I am willing to marry."

"I suppose I must count myself blessed," Anna said, shaking off the pain and drawing herself up into a sit-ting position.

"You should," Julian said, his tone sharp. "All the others I have abducted, I've merely ransomed in ex-change for silence. They could never have held my in-terest for long."

"I see," Anna said. "And you still need another for-tune?"

A faraway look entered Julian's eyes. "There was one I would have married—my first love. I was very young then."

"What happened?" Anna asked, attempting to keep her voice calm and neutral.

"She refused to marry me." Julian's face darkened with rage. In another second the fierce emotion disap-peared, and Julian turned upon Anna the most inno-cent of smiles. "She committed suicide with my help. She couldn't live without me, you see."

Anna sat frozen. How could she have missed the in-sanity in the man? Her stomach lurched. She had not seen it, but she *had* felt it. That had been the problem with his kiss. She shivered. Heaven help her, she had thought her reaction at the time was fanciful and fool-ish. Anna strove for an unattainable sangfroid. "You are just saying that to frighten me."

"No," Julian said, his smile appearing loving. "You are never afraid of anything. That is what I admire in you most. I can be myself with you. I can tell you what I have told no other woman."

Shock numbed Anna so deeply that she did not consider what she said, though her words were filled with regret. "Charles was right. I should have told you to bugger off."

Roark gazed out the turret enclosure. The moon was well nigh nonexistent; the stars were blotted out by dark clouds. How appropriate. He had sought the study of the stars after Tiffany's betrayal. They had comforted him. But, on that night, when he fought his tortured emotions for Anna, they would not even show themselves to offer solace.

When the temperature suddenly dropped, Roark stiffened. "Charles?"

"Love demands everything."

Slowly a nimbus of light appeared followed by a vision of a man within it. Roark blinked, amazed at his ancestors features. If the apparition didn't have a beard and ancient garb, Roark could have very well been looking in a mirror. "Charles. I'd recognize you anywhere."

"You can see me?" Charles asked.

"Yes," Roark said, "I can see you."

"Blast and damn! You would have to be camped out here. 'Tis not my favorite place."

"Why *are* you here?" Roark's heart hardened. "No doubt you've appeared to tell me my love is unfaithful. This time, you need not do so. I know."

"Nay, I've come to tell you that you must save Anna," Charles said, his eyes shooting sparks. "That spawn from hell, Rothman, has abducted her."

"Has he?" Roark asked dryly. "Or did she go with him willingly?"

"Forsooth, man!" Charles cried. "She went to tell him farewell. She loves you, you blind, jealous fool."

"No," Roark retorted. "I was the fool before."

"Anna is not of the same cloth as that jade you tried to marry afore," Charles said. "And if I am appearing to you now, 'tis because it is *your* love that is unfaithful, not Anna's. She is willing to give you everything, including her faith and trust. But you will betray her with your jealousy."

Roark glared at Charles. "I have the right."

"Fiend seize it! Do not whine to me of jealousy's rights," Charles roared. "Rothman is taking Anna away. She tried to leave the coach and the bastard struck her down."

"What!" Roark growled.

"Then his whoreson of a coachman cut the whip forthwith and his cattle took off," Charles said. "I do not know my powers outside these walls, nor do I know how far I can follow. I would have killed the man if I could have, but as a spirit—"

"I'm no spirit," Roark said. "Permit me."

"They left from the back. At the kitchen garden. Meet me there. I know the road they must take."

Roark, rage driving him, strode through the castle. Julian had struck Anna. The man would pay for that. And he would pay for trying to take Anna anywhere against her will.

Roark strode out the kitchen door and into the darkened night. His rage turned to fear. How could he have even wasted a moment in debate with Charles? Faith, if anything happened to Anna, it *would* be he who had betrayed her.

Charles appeared leading Comet, who was already saddled. "The beasts always accept us willingly. They do not question what they see."

"Thank you." Roark swung into the saddle.

"You go by horse," Charles said. "We should be able to overcome their coach. Follow me."

Roark nodded. He dug in his heels, driving Comet forward. Charles wafted ahead, a luminary figure. Roark might have mistaken the ghost for an angel if he hadn't already experienced the pranks of his personality—or for that matter, the bite of his tongue. Such surely was not the makeup of an angel.

It was a nightmarish ride. Roark trained his focus upon the spirit before him while fear and desperation gnawed at his soul. Charles would disappear every now and again. He'd then reappear beside Roark to report that the coach was still ahead, and couldn't he push his infernal hack any faster than that? Roark never responded. In truth, he felt the same, though Comet, a swift stallion, was giving Roark his best.

Roark knew his estate well, and it became clear which road Julian was making for. It was the shortest path to the main roads and it would soon cross onto Anton land. He spurred Comet hard. Once upon Henry's land he would be unsure of the road or its condition. He would be entering woods and he would not know the turns or bends. And in all probability, he would not have the light emanating from Charles to assist him.

Clearly, Charles knew the same. He appeared beside Roark, his light ebbing. "We are coming to the boundaries, lad."

"I know," Roark gritted. "I know."

"I wish to God I could follow," Charles said, his voice frustrated. "Save her, dammit. You must save her."

"I will," Roark vowed as he approached the woods. From the corner of his eye, he saw Charles fall back. "I promise you."

"My God," Charles's voice suddenly cried out from behind. "Genevieve! My Genevieve!" The raw pain in that cry wrenched at Roark, but he dared not look back. The woods loomed before him.

"My Charles," a woman's said, seeming to fill the night. "I vow thee, I will not permit it to happen. Not again."

Roark stared straight ahead as he crossed into the Antons' woods. He refused to think. He had to stay focused. He could not afford to lose his sanity. He had to hasten to save Anna.

The canopy of trees darkened the starless night and Roark was forced to slow his pace. He could barely see the curve in the road before him. Suddenly an inhuman screech split through the woods, echoing into silence.

Roark's heart drummed fear and heated blood into his veins. Comet shrieked his own terror, but Roark spurred him forward. They turned the sharp curve, and Roark, cursing, sawed on the reigns. The coach he sought was halted directly in his path.

Roark bolted from Comet's back even before the horse had completely stopped. He ran forward, fear overcoming caution. The coach's door hung open. Roark peered into interior. It was empty. He jerked back. Only then did a semblance of reason overtake him—reason laced with confusion.

He walked slowly to the head of the coach, where the horses all stood quietly. The coachman still sat upon the box. With the reins in his hand, he stared straight ahead.

"Where did they go?" Roark asked the man. "Where did they go?"

The man turned his gaze down upon Roark. His features were coarse and hard—those of a cruel man. His expression, however, was dazed and humbled. "I saw a woman in the middle of the road. She glowed and you could see clean through her. The horses stopped. I whipped one, but he would not move."

"Where did Anna go?" Roark demanded, steeling himself. "Where did she go?"

"Hurry," a woman's voice commanded from behind.

Roark spun and saw a beautiful woman dressed in a magnificent wedding gown from another century standing before him. He could see through her.

"She escaped," the woman said. "But he chases her. He has the black soul to kill her. Follow me."

"Lead me," Roark said grimly.

The woman turned and moved swiftly through the woods. He followed just as swiftly. He no longer needed her guidance, for he could hear raised voices and thrashing ahead. As Anna shrieked, Roark crashed through the brush, coming upon Julian and Anna.

Roark did not slow, even as his mind recoiled from the sight. Julian had Anna shoved up against a tree, his hands gripping her throat. He shook her, the words he growled unintelligible. She clawed at him, struggling, though her movements were weak.

Springing forward, Roark gripped Julian from behind. "Let her go, Rothman."

"Seeton," Julian gasped. He did not release Anna, only shook her the more, applying all the pressure of his anger.

"Let her go, dammit!"

"Farewell darling, Anna." Julian released Anna. As she sagged slowly to the ground, appearing a limp, discarded doll, Julian actually laughed. "Another who couldn't live without me."

Shouting in rage and fear, Roark delivered a punishing blow. Julian stumbled back, but maintained his stance. His blue eyes glittered and he let out a maniacal laugh.

"Good! Now I can kill you as well."

"Try it," Roark growled, lowering into a fighter's crouch.

Julian charged at him and Roark met him with a heavy fist. Julian proved a stronger opponent than Roark had supposed, though Roark knew much of his strength came from crazed insanity. Yet Roark could only think of going to Anna. She could not be dead. She must not be dead.

Roark took each blow with that anguished thought, and he drove each punch with that prayer. His fists became slippery with blood, both his and Julian's. His lungs burst with pain. Still Julian came closing in, laughing. Exhaustion gripped Roark. Sweat blurred his sight. Darkness seemed to settle into his very soul.

"Roark!" Anna's voice, weak, but real, called out.

"Anna," Roark rasped. He only hesitated one moment to see Anna as well as to hear her.

That moment was a dreadful mistake. Julian charged at him, gaining a stranglehold upon his throat.

Roark stiffened, clamping onto Julian's arms. He stared directly into Julian's deranged eyes, even as he fought for breath. He smiled. "She's alive, Rothman!"

"No!" Julian howled. "Damn you to hell!"

"She's alive!"

Roark wrenched Julian's hands away from his throat. When Julian stumbled back, Roark followed. With a burst of energy that seemed to explode with light, Roark drew back and delivered a stunning blow. Julian, crying out, spun and fell heavily to the ground.

Drawing in a ragged breath, Roark stumbled over to stand above Rothman. Only then did he realize he truly was seeing everything through a glow of light. His heart stilled to a calmness as he looked down at Julian's sprawled body. The man's head was oddly twisted, with a large rock beneath it—a macabre pillow for his sleep of death.

Roark slowly looked up. The woman stood a distance away, resplendent in light. "Genevieve."

"Justice has been done," she said softly. "The story has been changed."

As she faded before his eyes, Roark felt a welling peace within himself. The story had been changed. *His* story had been changed and he had almost been too late to realize it.

He turned to gaze at Anna with fervent love and deep respect. She was slowly bringing herself to her feet.

"Who . . . what . . . ?" Anna whispered.

"Genevieve, I believe," Roark said, walking toward Anna. He slowly took her into his arms. "I love you."

"I love you too," Anna said, her voice a hoarse sob.

"Then let us go," Roark said, softly.

"But . . ." Anna said, drawing away. Her eyes were pools of fear.

"If you will give me your trust but one more time," Roark said, "I swear I shall never fail you again."

The fright drained from Anna's face. She nodded, and together they walked back through the woods. Love and pride swelled within Roark, for his brave Anna never once looked back. Nor did she say a word when they came to the road. The coach was still there, to Roark's surprise, and the driver still sat upon the box. Roark saw Comet standing a distance off.

He gently led Anna over to his horse. "Stay here."

"Yes," Anna said softly.

When Roark then slowly returned to the coach, the coachman only looked at him with dazed eyes. "She told me to wait."

"Your employer is dead. Find him and take him to the home of Lydia Talboth."

"Yes," the coachman said.

Roark walked back to Anna, who stood quietly. Then he mounted Comet and drew her up before him. After her body relaxed against him and she laid her head upon his shoulder, he turned Comet around and headed home.

"This is Henry's land, isn't it?" Anna asked.

"Yes," Roark said.

"In the daylight," Anna murmured, "you can see the most beautiful flowers in these woods."

Thirteen

Charles stood at the boundaries of Seeton land. He felt an energy he had never thought to possess since leaving his temporal body. It felt invigorating standing so very close to Anton lands. Strange, the living did not know that a ghost's heart could still beat fast, still wrench with pain and confusion and hope. They thought the heart but blood and muscle when the heart was so much more. It was as much of the spirit as the soul was.

Had he gone mad? Could a spirit go mad? He had always held madness peculiar to the living. Yet he had seen Genevieve. He had heard her as if it were yesterday. Even after all those decades of pain, of anger at betrayal, he chose to believe that she was there, and he yearned for her.

He waited. Then she was walking toward him, resplendent in a wedding gown. She was as beautiful as he had always remembered her spirit to be. "Genevieve, my Genevieve."

Genevieve came to stand at the boundaries of her land. "Charles, my love."

"You call me your love," Charles said, anguished. "How can you?"

"You have always been my love," Genevieve said softly, "though I was the cause of your death. My love for you was your destruction. I have prayed for your forgiveness, and I have grieved so very long."

"You were not the cause of my death, Genevieve," Charles said. "I vow to you I did not take my life that day. I vow it."

"No, William did," Genevieve whispered. "Just as he gratefully took mine, though he did not know the kindness it was. I would not have wished to live without you."

"What do you mean?" Charles asked.

"William came to me the morn of our wedding day. I was so wrapped in our joy I could not turn him away in his misery. He begged me to flee with him, for all was prepared. When I would not, he struck me unconscious. When I gained my senses, I found myself bound, gagged, and secreted away in the gazebo."

"My God," Charles cried.

"I tried to escape, and I prayed that someone would find me." She shook her head. "William was evil. You were always jealous of him, but I did not understand, for I could only see you. I did not see the wickedness in William, though he called it love. He secreted me in a place so very close that no one sought me. He returned hours later and told me how he had found and killed you. He was crazed. He thought that since you lived no more, I would go with him . . . that I could love him after he had taken my life when he took yours. I spoke the truth to him and he strangled me there, merely destroying my body after he had already slain my heart. He buried me there. This I know, for it has been my place of grieving throughout the centuries." Genevieve lifted her hand as if to reach out; then she lowered it. "Can you forgive me?"

"Nay. 'Tis I who must beg your forgiveness," Charles said, shaking his head slowly. "It was my jealousy that destroyed us both. You divined it on the eve of our wedding. If not for my jealousy, if not for my lack of faith in your love, I would have sought you that day. I would have found you. But I only thought of your betrayal," Charles whispered. "If I had believed in your love, I would have sought you even after death."

"If I had been stronger," Genevieve said. "If I had not chosen to remain lost and grieving, I would have risen from my resting place of blood and tears."

"But we remained," Charles said sadly.

Genevieve nodded. "We remained."

Charles reached out his hand. "I have felt you for so long. No matter how I've denied it, I have loved you."

Genevieve reached out her hand. "For centuries, I have grieved for what I was not strong enough to protect and what I destroyed, but I have always loved you."

Their hands touched and melded across the boundaries of nature. Time was forgotten.

Anna clung to Roark. She drew reassurance from the strength of his body and was comforted by the rise and fall of his chest beneath her cheek as he drew breath. She matched the rhythm of her breathing to his. It made her feel safe, bonded. The sound of the horse's hooves on the ground was another rhythm—a cadence demanding that Anna return to the reality of the night.

"Julian is dead, isn't he?" Anna finally said.

"Yes," Roark said softly.

"And Genevieve is here?"

"Yes." Roark's arms tightened around her. "She is the one who stopped your coach."

"Was she?" Anna shivered as she remembered Julian cursing when the coach had stopped. Remembered how she had prayed it was her moment to escape. Remembered running in the night. Remembered him catching her.

"And she led me to you," Roark said, his lips brush-

ing against her cheek, "for which I will always be grateful."

"Oh, yes," Anna said, sighing. "Oh, yes."

"As I will be to Charles," Roark said.

"Charles," Anna murmured. "I saw him just before
Julian abducted me."

"I saw him too," Roark said.

"You did?" Anna gasped, drawing back to stare at
him.

An actual chuckle escaped Roark. "Most definitely.
You have a strong protector in him. I would that I could
be as strong as protector."

"You are," Anna objected. "You saved me."

"Yes, but it was Charles who had to first convince me
that you were in danger, that you had not left with Julian
on your own free will. Can you ever forgive me?"

Anna thought of her fear and loathing of Julian and
how she felt utterly safe in Roark's arms. When she saw
the regret in his eyes, she smiled tremulously. "I can
forgive you readily."

"Genevieve said justice has been done," Roark said.
"She said the story has been changed. It *is* changed,
Anna, for me. I love and trust you. What I felt tonight
changed it all. I see now you were right. I wanted to
marry you even though I still held on to my bitterness.
I am sorry. It would have destroyed us both."

"But it didn't." Anna kissed him. "And it won't."

"It won't?" Roark asked, his eyes lighting. "Does that
mean you will marry me now?"

Anna snuggled close. "Well, not now . . . but in a few
more hours, I will."

Anna lay curled up in her bed. Her body was exhausted, but her mind fought sleep.

"Mistress," Charles said softly.

Anna smiled, opening her eyes. "I hoped you would come."

Charles grinned. "I must wish the bride well, must I not?"

"Yes, you must," Anna said, laughing. "Roark told me what you did. I thank you. And I must thank Genevieve."

"She thanks you," Charles said softly.

Anna frowned. "Why does she thank me?"

"It was you who drew her from her grieving," he said. "She said she was drawn to you whenever you came upon her land."

"Her grieving?" Anna asked.

"She did not betray me. Her love was true. She never ran off with William Thornton. He killed her, just as he killed me. She lies buried beneath the gazebo."

"The gazebo." Anna remembered the day she had seen it—and the sea of crimson about it. The roses should have been white for true love, but they had been red for tragedy. "My God."

Charles smiled slightly. "I believe there is one, though what He intends for my love and me I do not know. You thought I would be released if I discovered who my murderer was. I believe I have remained because she remained. Only my bitterness at what I thought was her betrayal kept me from seeking her. And she, my poor love, has rested all these years, refusing to leave, thinking she was unworthy because she could not stop William Thornton and because he killed me in hopes of stealing her love."

"I am so very sorry," Anna said.

"No. When one finds one's love again, it matters not the time that passed before. Tonight, Genevieve and I were able to change what we failed to change in the past. And it was because of you, my dear Anna. It was your belief in Genevieve that drew her, your seeking the truth."

"But it was her poetry that made me believe," Anna said. "It was her words of love."

"Perhaps. I only know that you have brought my love back to me."

"And it was you who gave me my love," Anna laughed, "no matter what your devious and outrageous methods."

"I am sure I will not appear at your wedding ceremony," Charles said before he began to fade. "Your love is true."

"But you will be there?" Anna asked the air. "Charles, I want you to be there! Do you hear me? I want you to be there!"

"Dear Anna, you are so beautiful," Aunt Deirdre said, smoothing the heavy folds of Anna's wedding dress into place. The rich brocade glowed in the sunlight streaming through the stately leaded glass doors open to the glorious June day. "I am so pleased you are attending your own wedding."

"So am I, Aunt Deirdre. So am I." Anna laughed, holding her bouquet of red roses close. She thought of Genevieve in deep gratitude.

The slightest summer breeze touched Anna, Beth, Aunt Deirdre, and Henry as they stood outside the entrance to the family chapel. The guests were already assembled within. Excitement filled her. It was to be her wedding day after all.

"Now you simply walk down the aisle," Aunt Deirdre instructed, her face marked with concern. "I know we did not rehearse this—"

"Do not fret. I believe I can manage walking. At least, I'll try not to run to Roark."

"Indeed not," Aunt Deirdre said in a serious tone. "There is no need for that. Roark will wait for you, I am sure."

"Just as all the guests are waiting," Henry said, finally stepping forward from his post at the door, which he had cracked open no less than three times. "Deirdre, the musicians have played the processional twice now. All will go well, but you really should take your place."

"Oh, yes," Aunt Deirdre said, flushing. "Of course."

"Besides, if you do not leave, I might lose all my control and take you down the aisle instead of Anna. But I assure you, I will not give you away."

"Henry, for shame," Aunt Deirdre scolded. "You know we weren't going to tell the children we are going to wed until after—" She gasped and glanced at Anna and Beth. "Oh, dear, he didn't really tell you, did he now? I did."

"Yes," Anna laughed. "But it certainly is no surprise. I think it marvelous."

"So do I." Beth giggled. "Everyone should be married. It is delightful."

"That is exactly what I told your aunt," Henry said, chuckling.

"Oh, the guests are waiting," Aunt Deirdre said quickly. "I am going to join them now."

"Ladies," Henry murmured, the most bemused expression upon his face. "Shall we start?"

"Yes." Anna turned to Beth, smiling gently. "It is right now, Beth—all of it."

"I am glad," Beth said, though a trace of concern passed through her eyes.

Anna knew what she was thinking, for Roark and she had told the family the necessary details. "Truly it is."

"Yes. Do you remember how displeased you were that I was going to have a June wedding in the wilds of Devonshire."

"Just so a ghost could give you the once-over," Anna murmured.

"Yes. And now it is you doing so instead of me."

"At least I know I have the ghost's approval," Anna said with a bittersweet smile.

"Anna," Henry said. "I do not mean to rush you, but they are playing your music the third time now."

"I am ready."

Anna took Henry's arm. She smiled slightly. She should have bridal nerves, yet she didn't. In truth, it was difficult to suffer from nerves when she felt so alive and could look forward to spending the rest of her days with the man she loved. She realized most brides generally considered those particular conditions to be the norm, yet Anna had learned that those two gifts alone should make a bride radiant upon her wedding day.

They entered into the chapel, with Beth following correctly behind. Anna halted a moment. It was not all the guests that stunned her. Indeed, the chapel was quite crowded with friends of the Seetons and all the invited villagers. Rather, it was the beauty of the bountiful roses and their arrangement that gave her pause.

"Henry, it is beautiful," Anna murmured.

"Thank you, my dear," Henry whispered. "I hoped you would be pleased."

Anna then saw Roark at the front of the chapel. He was perfectly attired, but there was no overlooking his bruised and cut face. He appeared more like a champion fighter worthy of Jackson's salon than a groom intent on his wedding day. Anna's heart flooded with love. He was all the more handsome to her for those bruises. He was her champion.

Anna walked down the aisle, her gaze steady upon Roark. His gaze was just as steady upon her. In truth, it was difficult to pay attention to the reverend as he spoke. Anna realized, however, when he requested her to take her first vow.

"I, Anna . . ."

"I, Genevieve . . ." a voice echoed.

Anna smiled, deeming it her own wishful imagination until the reverend jumped, peering about wildly. The stirrings and exclamations of the crowd from behind them made it clear they too had heard the voice. Anna turned her gaze to Roark in excitement and deep joy.

"They are both here."

"Yes." Roark smiled and looked to the clergyman. "Please proceed, Reverend Thomas."

"Er, yes," Reverend Thomas stammered.

Anna stifled a chuckle. It was fortunate Aunt Deirdre had not chosen Reverend Bertram to officiate, or else he would have been flinging Bibles and crucifixes about at that moment. Reverend Thomas prompted Anna and she spoke her next words. Genevieve's voice repeated them sweet and low: "To love and honor . . . in sickness and in health . . . for better or worse . . ."

The church had fallen silent. Reverend Thomas only choked and looked at Anna in awe when he delivered the last line of the vow: "For as long as I shall live."

Anna swallowed hard, the tears coming when she looked at Roark and spoke those words. Genevieve whispered, "For as long as I thee love," adding a poignancy that Anna could not, and would not, ever forget.

The reverend then looked up, his face totally confused and unsure. "Till death do us part?"

Anna's eyes widened. For Genevieve to say those words indeed would be impossible now.

"That death will not part," Genevieve said.

Reverend Thomas flushed. "That death will not part."

Anna gazed at Roark, all her love in her eyes. "That death will not part."

Reverend Thomas turned to Roark. "And do you, Roark . . ."

Anna's heart almost burst when she heard Roark respond before Charles echoed the vows. Reverend Thomas did not hesitate that time upon the last vow. "That death will not part."

Roark looked down at Anna, smiling warmly. "That death will not part."

"That death will not part," Charles said solemnly.

The reverend sighed in relief. "Roark and Anna"—he halted—"and—"

"Genevieve and Charles," Roark supplied.

"Ah, yes. Genevieve and Charles, I now pronounce you husband and wife. You may kiss the bride—or whatever."

"Fiend seize it!" Charles growled.

Roark let out a laugh. "Well, some things must be left to the living."

His eyes brimming with merriment, he drew Anna to him. Wonderment and joy filled Anna as she received her first kiss from her husband. Dimly, she heard gasps and exclamations from the guests. Roark finally released her. Dazed, Anna looked about, for the guests' clamor had not ceased.

Anna gasped because every red rose in the chapel had turned to white. Aunt Deirdre smiled, tears streaming down her face as she held Henry's hand. Beth stepped back and found Terrence's embrace.

Anna smiled, a deep peace filling her heart. The tears and blood were gone. The roses had bloomed white for true love. Charles and Genevieve were at rest and, Anna knew with a surety, eternally united.

"My love for thee is true," Anna murmured. She gazed at Roark, at last understanding Genevieve's words as only a woman completely in love could. "And only for thee, forever for thee, shall it bloom."

ABOUT THE AUTHOR

Cindy Holbrook lives with her family in Fort Walton Beach, Florida. She is the author of ten Zebra Regency romances. She is currently working on her eleventh, *On the First Day of Christmas,* which will be published in December, 1999. Cindy loves to hear from her readers and you may write to her c/o Zebra Books. Please include a self-addressed stamped envelope if you wish a response.